# OLIVIA FANE

God's Apology

ALSO BY OLIVIA FANE

Landing on Clouds

The Glorious Flight of Perdita Tree

OLIVIA FANE

# God's Apology

Published in 2006 by
The Maia Press Limited
82 Forest Road
London E8 3BH
www.maiapress.com

ISBN 10: 1 904559 20 4
ISBN 13: 978 1 904559 20 7

A CIP catalogue record for this book is available
from the British Library

Printed and bound in Great Britain by Cromwell Press
on paper from sustainable managed forests

The Maia Press is supported by Arts Council England

*For my five sons: Tom, William, Ben, Joe and Oscar*

All his happier dreams came true –
A small old house, wife, daughter, son,
Grounds where plum and cabbage grew,
Poets and Wits about him drew;
*'What then?' sang Plato's ghost. 'What then?'*

W. B. Yeats, 'What Then?'

# 1

WHEN I WAS A BOY I went to church. I went every Sunday with my mother; she went because she loved God, and I went because I loved her. It was our time, alone, together. 'Forgive us our trespasses,' we would say, and I'd try to catch her eye but she'd never meet it, not properly. Just a look which said, 'Concentrate.'

'Mother,' I asked her one day, as we walked home, 'you don't sin, so why do you ask God to forgive you?'

'Oh I sin,' she said, 'we all sin.'

'You don't,' I said, simply.

'We are all wrapped in sin.'

I didn't understand her then. A sin was something you did, I thought, like telling a lie or stealing. I didn't understand that sin is like skin, it's part of being human, it's what holds us down when we want to leap up. It's all the stuff we've accumulated, within us and without us, it's the stuff which stops us seeing the sky and smelling the earth. Forgive us our trespasses, our Father in heaven, redeem us, make us light.

Memory is a strange sifter. There is a fact out there, namely that I, Patrick German, deserted my wife, Kitty, and our eight-week old son, Joseph, on Boxing Day 1999. Apparently I did say a sort of goodbye, but my mind is a complete blank. The suitcase, however, its bulk, its colour of airforce blue, its nylon smoothness, its perplexing arrangement of zips, will leave its imprint for ever.

Of course, one doesn't just leave. I had my reasons, not least because there were moments when it crossed my mind that I wasn't worthy to share the bed of a good woman. I had neither the inclination nor the energy to make love to her, and it seemed a tactful thing to leave a space in the bed for someone who might. The matrimonial bed: make sure, they tell you, the springs are tight-packed so you won't feel the movements of your partner on the other side. How I would wish we were eighteen again, Kitty and I, sleeping together in a single bed, merged into one out of necessity. Choice is too complicated.

I want to write here for the record that Kitty is the only woman I have ever truly loved, and the reminder, constantly, that we were two entities rather than one has always been painful to me. Even when things were good between us, in the early hours of the morning, stray lines of thought would lead me to places of absolute separation from her, and I would grieve for the future.

It's so easy to belong as a child, to understand instinctively where the boundaries are and never question them. It's not that I had some sort of glorious *Swallows and Amazons* childhood, mucking about on boats with hugely wholesome friends. I simply had parents who loved me and a room of my own. I read, I made models, I did my homework. So, life went by.

My prizes were Kitty and Cambridge. And I worked and loved hard. Well done, the world said, you deserve it, a lovely wife, an enviable job with the most profitable publisher in London and a sunny first-floor flat in Balham. The world said, 'Take these goods, and be happy.' But did I suffer from ingratitude? Is this why you wished to wreak revenge on me? Or is it because I found you out, and saw you as the dud religion that you were? For the world is not a friendly mother earth, enveloping us in its bosom; the world is like a headmaster, writing 'SUCCESS' or 'FAILURE' on our foreheads in red biro as we walk on past.

I was branded with 'SUCCESS'. I entered the world of publishing and waited for its gods to tell me if I was performing well or badly; and whatever they told me I believed them and said I'd do better. I felt no qualms in rejecting manuscripts that weren't up to scratch. I remember taking one of my mid-list authors out to lunch, sipping fish soup from a mussel shell, and telling him that I wasn't sure of his latest offering, and what exactly was it that he wanted to say? Why did I let him babble on, humiliating himself? Why didn't he understand that we just didn't want his book? I never questioned my professionalism. I slept with an easy conscience.

Then, in October 1997, I made friends with a tramp, or at least, I became acquainted with him. On my way to work he would be sleeping, or sitting on a bench just near the Tube station. I'd call him 'Harry' because he wouldn't tell me his real name, he said it was none of my business. Sometimes I'd hand him a fiver; sometimes I'd buy two cups of tea and sit beside him to enjoy the early morning air. There was a sort of realness to the day, then; I can't exactly explain it, but somehow there was a feeling that we both had nothing to lose, sitting there together on the bench, sharing the weather.

But all this changed one particular Tuesday in March, when he casually remarked, *'Deus nobis haec otia fecit.'* I could just about recognise this was Latin, and looked at him, fairly startled.

'God gave us this peace,' he translated. 'It's a lovely morning.'

'How do you know Latin?' I asked him.

He just sighed, and pouted, in the way that Harry did, and I didn't see him again for three weeks.

Then one day he was waiting for me outside the Tube, and thrust something into my hand, like a discarded till-roll. 'You're a publisher, aren't you?' he said. 'I've been writing.'

He wouldn't let me talk to him about it, he just pushed me

away and told me to read it, he'd see me soon.

I was embarrassed at first. Friends had occasionally approached me with their half-baked first novels, imagining somehow that I single-handedly had the power to turn them into bestsellers overnight. Even if Harry knew Latin, it didn't mean he could write, and now our relationship would change for ever. Somehow I would have 'SUCCESS' written on my forehead and he would have 'FAILURE' written on his, and up till then we'd been equals in this life. But I took the till-roll home with me and began to read. It was a poem, about forty pages long, the story of an unhappy love affair, doubtless autobiographical, written absolutely from the heart, and brilliant.

I was shaking when I read it, and I showed it to Kitty, who agreed with me. I couldn't stop walking up and down the room in a state of pure excitement, I even rang a couple of colleagues that night and said, 'I've got something astonishing to show you.' The next morning I made them read it as soon as they came into work, and told them about Harry the tramp, and they all said, 'This is amazing, we'll certainly publish it.'

Every morning I would run up the Tube escalator ready to tell Harry the good news, but he didn't turn up again for about a month. I began to worry that something had happened to him, I even telephoned a couple of hospitals in the area. Then one day he was sitting on the bench again, and was looking, for Harry, for dear, impassive Harry, inordinately sad.

'You didn't like it, did you?' he said.

'Oh Harry,' I gushed, 'it was wonderful. And more than that, we all thought it was wonderful, and we're going to publish it.'

There's no doubt that Harry was happy at first. But over the next couple of months he changed: he changed from a man whose expectations were zero, and whose pleasures were simple (yes, I thought they were just in being alive, in having shunned the formula of the must-have society) to becoming – dare I say it – like any one of our authors, with an ego to be satisfied. The

10

crunch came when he understood our marketing strategy. It was obvious, even to me: he was a tramp who had presented us with forty pages of outstanding poetry, and wow, here they are. But according to him, he was no longer a tramp, he was a writer, in his soul he was a writer. And he wanted a deposit for a room he'd found in a house nearby, and when was he going to get his money? 'And stop calling me "Harry",' he said.

His real name was William Cartwright. He'd written a lot of poetry in his youth, he'd been to Leeds University for a while but the course hadn't been much good and he'd left. He'd never quite settled into a job, nor into a relationship. But he had had some poems published in *Poetry Review* while in his twenties – could we write that in his biography on the flyleaf?

I said to him, 'Harry, I mean William, you're a tramp, or how can I put that politely? You gave up everything, you were reduced to such straits that you gave it all up . . . It was a courageous thing to do. Most of us have spent a day or two wondering what it would be like to escape the shackles of life . . . Being a tramp, having been a tramp, is part of who you are, don't you see?'

He was furious with me. He strutted and fumed and said, 'It's all right for you, you smug arsehole. You won't let me have just one last shred of self-respect.'

The trouble was, I didn't know where I stood during those months, or more to the point, where I ought to stand. My boss's reaction to William Cartwright's insistence that there should be no reference to his being a tramp was swift and immediate: who buys forty-page poems written by no one you've heard of? Publishers had to make a living, too: they weren't charity workers.

When I finally told Harry they'd withdrawn their offer, he hit me full-square on the jaw and walked off. That was the last I ever saw of him.

I resigned in June 1998. This business of self-respect had

begun to get to me. I was in my early thirties, I was an 'achiever', and Harry the tramp taught me 'so what, we breathe the same air, we die the same death' but then William Cartwright the poet wanted to enter the world on his terms. Which of these two versions of the same man was the true one? And which of these two versions most reflected who I was?

Kitty thought I was crazy to resign. Publishing was as honest a profession, she argued, as any of them. It was self-deceiving, I said. 'What are you going to be, then, a priest? Even the Church hasn't exactly behaved itself over the centuries. What are you going to do, Patrick?'

We'd only had our own flat for a year, and we'd financially 'stretched ourselves', as they say. Kitty loved it, and had only just finished putting up the last strip of wallpaper, but her pay as a landscape gardener was sporadic, to say the least.

'Don't you trust me?' I asked her.

It was fairly wicked of me to ask her that when I didn't even know if I trusted myself.

'I love you,' she said, seriously. I shook my head and said, 'That's not the same thing.'

And so I decided to become a teacher. Kitty, was, on the whole, patient with me. When I first told her she told me not to be so ridiculous.

'You don't even like children,' she said. I said something pompous about knowledge being a good thing and imparting it to the young being an honorable activity.

'Imparting knowledge to the young?' she laughed, scornfully. 'Is that what you think teaching's about?'

I discovered a teacher training college off the Lambeth Road, and they quite believed my story of a 'lost vocation', so in September 1998 I enrolled and quite impressed them with some fine essays on child psychology and psycholinguistics. But when, in the following spring, I first entered a classroom, it felt like missing the turning on a motorway and driving fifty miles to get off it. I didn't even manage to get to the end of the register: fights broke out in corners of the classroom; a girl in the front row was applying lipstick; a small boy with eczema was banging his tin pencil case on the desk, and children were shouting at him to be quiet, and in the midst of it all you might just have heard a small voice saying, 'Please. Please.' That was my own.

Of course, Kitty could see by my face when I got home that things hadn't gone too well. I made myself a drink and slouched down into the sofa. The truth was that if Kitty had tried to comfort me I would have bitten her head off. She didn't, she knew me too well. She asked me questions like, 'How big was the class?' 'Did you have lunch with the children?' 'Did you like your placement supervisor?'

I said it was all fine, but that my 'supervisor' was too busy herself to do much supervising, which was probably for the best.

'Tell me about it,' she said.

But there was just the tiniest inflection in her voice which made me suspect her of disloyalty, of assuming that I hadn't managed it, of assuming that the day had been a bad one. So I didn't tell her about it. I just shrugged and asked her what we were having for supper.

Later that week my supervisor Kate, her hair cascading down her back in blonde dreadlocks and beads, came to sit in on a lesson I was giving. During the previous holidays I had more or less prepared every lesson I was going to give that term, so I could spend more time marking homework. What diligence! After day one I didn't even bother to consult my notes. But of course, I had to impress Kate, I had to prove that I was at least making some attempt to teach them, so I handed out a test on the parts of speech. A couple of the boys immediately turned their test papers into aeroplanes and flew them in my direction. Kate looked at me to see my reaction.

'That won't do,' I said firmly. Suddenly there were peals of laughter from the class. Kate smiled sympathetically and took charge. She picked up the aeroplanes and said, walking up and down between the desks, 'Whose are these?' When she found a desk without a test paper on it, she said to the boy, 'Missing something, are you?' She found two guilty pupils, and took them away with her, leaving me with a rather sobered fourth form. They never worked so quietly again.

I didn't mind telling Kitty about Kate. Kate with the hair and the sandals and the baggy clothes and huge authority over the children. I tried to make it sound like I was rather taken with her. I'd say things like, 'Now, here's a woman who knows where she's going.' Why does one do these things? What game was I playing? Power for the powerless, I say.

But that mode of conversation ended pretty sharply when Kitty told me she was pregnant. 'That's that then,' I said to her, and made some excuse to go for a walk. So there was to be no escape, ever. I wanted to hide in a cave somewhere, and live off berries and roots.

Kitty and I would lie in bed at night, with the absolute knowledge that the other was awake, and say nothing.

'I wish we could talk,' said Kitty.

'You sound like an American,' I said.

'I don't know where you've gone to. I've lost you.'

'Here I am,' I said, leaning over towards her, and stroking her thigh. Kitty didn't resist. Perhaps even the worst of me was better than nothing.

I somehow made it to the end of the course, and even managed in June to secure a teaching post at Aldover Comprehensive, Streatham, for the following September. But during the summer things went from bad to worse. We began to lose our friends. Friendship suddenly seemed to me to be such a flimsy, arbitrary arrangement. I would see familiar faces and wonder what it was that we'd ever had in common. So no, we couldn't make supper, or a film, or even a drink in a pub. Kitty's so tired,

I'd tell them, blaming it all on her – she refused to go without me.

I had a good friend, Stephen, we'd been at the same school, lived in the same street, played 'tennis' together every summer evening against the back wall of his house. He wanted to be an actor, and darn nearly made it, too. But he went into loss adjusting when he got married and found they were expecting twins. When I heard he'd given up I'd said to him, 'What a terrible waste,' but he smiled and said, 'You wait till you're expecting a child. All else is vanity, Patrick.'

Stephen came to supper with us one evening that summer, and he brought baby Dora with him, barely three months old.

Kitty was all over her. 'Do look at those tiny hands,' she cooed.

I said, 'God, she's just puked over your shoulder.'

'"Possetting" is the word,' smiled Stephen, enthusiastically.

'Puke's puke, as far as I'm concerned,' I mumbled.

'The trouble with you . . .' began Stephen.

'Yes?'

'You've lost your sense of fun.'

He could have said something much worse.

'"Fun"? Are we having fun yet?'

'I don't think he's in the right job,' suggested Kitty, safe in the threeness of us.

'Why d'you give up your publishing job anyway? Remind me.'

But baby Dora began to cry, and Stephen and Kitty took turns at trying to soothe her.

'I can't think in this din,' I said.

'I'll go home. Dora wants her mum. I'm sorry.'

'Didn't you bring a bottle with you? I've made a Thai curry.'

Kitty looked crestfallen. Stephen shrugged helplessly. Dora was inconsolable.

'I'd better go,' he said, and left.

We had a row that night. My dear, restrained, tactful, gentle wife told me what she thought of me. In a nutshell: not much. I didn't have the energy to resist her. What would I have told her, anyway? I couldn't remember what the matter was.

What was unsaid between us was: 'Would we be splitting up now if it wasn't for the child?' We lay in bed, on our multi-pocketed well-sprung bed which kept the great chasm between us, and Kitty said she was sorry she'd been so angry with me, and she turned towards me and kissed me. How I wanted her then. But when I stretched over and felt her extended stomach, my fingers might have touched a hotplate so immediately did they flee back to my side. Kitty jumped out of bed and locked herself in the bathroom, and I heard her sobbing there.

I began teaching at Aldover Comprehensive. Oh, but see me as a teacher now, see me striding up and down the classroom looking for any and every excuse to unleash my fury.

'Shut up, Finlay.'

'But I was only asking to borrow a sharpener.'

'Come up here and stand by the blackboard.'

'But sir!'

'You, Brown, where's your homework?'

'I didn't have the time to do it, my mother . . .'

'No excuses, detention after school.'

'I can't, not this afternoon. My mother's ill, sir.'

'Don't lie.'

I could see by his face that he wasn't lying, but it was as though I was being operated by a merciless clockwork which had nothing to do with me, but which was all I could rely on. And the boy did his detention.

Joseph was born during half-term: 28th October 1999. I think Kitty was hoping, even then, that I would magically be transformed into a Stephen, in spite of myself. I looked at Joseph in his crib in the hospital, and stroked his little head, but

I felt awe, rather than love. I couldn't touch him, not in the normal animal kind of way, when one holds one's own close to oneself.

'What d'you think?' asked Kitty.

'He's a lovely boy,' I said.

And then I couldn't help it, I wept there and then in the hospital, I wept for myself and for the loss of my wife and son.

I don't know why I should have been so surprised when the headmaster called me in to see him, why I was so self-righteous when he told me there had been complaints from many parents about my teaching methods. It was the parents' fault, I said. If they'd ever bothered to instil even a modicum of self-discipline in their children then some proper learning might get under way. But the headmaster would have none of it. I was only in my probationary year, he said, and it was within his rights to ask me to move on.

At moments like these it's very curious how all the tendons in one's body seem suddenly to relax, so that one is no longer a rigid body with an agenda but a flaccid body without one. If I'd had a banjo with me I might have strummed a few nonchalant chords. The headmaster told me that he'd spoken to the college where I'd received my training and suggested that I might be better off teaching at a primary school. I was to contact them if I was interested, but they were more than happy to take me back for a couple of terms and give me experience with a different age group.

But I didn't have a banjo with me and could only sit there like a benign tumour. It was a demotion from nothing. I looked at the photographs on the walls of his office – previous head-masters, rugger teams, though no rugger had been played at the school for a decade. There was one of the school in 1903: forty scrubbed children sitting in rows, the schoolmaster sternly surveying them over half-moon glasses, cane in hand.

'I didn't know the school was so old,' I said.

'They demolished the original building in the seventies.'

'A shame,' I said, lamely.

'Your future,' said the headmaster.

'Ah yes.'

'Tell me, Patrick, why did you join the teaching profession?'

'It seemed so straightforward at the time.'

The headmaster said to me, kindly, 'If I were you, Patrick, I'd look very carefully as to whether I was in the right job. If you're still committed to it in a week or so, will you do me a favour and contact the college?'

They'd even found a locum till the end of term.

'Think of it as paternity leave,' said the headmaster. 'You'll be paid until the end of the year.'

When I got home I couldn't tell Kitty. I didn't want anger, I didn't want sympathy, I didn't want to see her petty anxieties. She'd given up work to look after Joseph. What about the mortgage? What have you done to us, Patrick, what have you done to your family? I couldn't even look her in the eye. I just said, 'Don't bother to cook, I'll get a takeaway,' and went out again.

I knew even as I ran down the stairs that I didn't have my wallet with me, but all things considered, that wasn't too important. One thinks briefly of suicide on occasions like these, just a pleasant, flitting image of release, but it wasn't a noble sense of responsibility that stopped me. It was the very opposite. I wanted to drag Kitty down with me. At that moment, I wanted to destroy everything about her, the love she had for Joe, her attachment to our flat, every instinct in her which made her bother to wash her hair, iron her clothes, put fresh flowers in a vase in the kitchen. Three hours later, I barely apologised for no supper, or my unexplained absence. She was crying, and I watched her, I didn't even ask why.

The next morning, of course, I didn't go into work. I wanted to prolong her anguish as she came to understand the reason why. Then, when we were equal, I would relish her onslaught, be ready to counter-attack. But Kitty, my dearest, darling Kitty, hugged me and kissed me, her face wet with tears, and told me that it didn't matter at all, that it was a horrible job, and I was better off without it. She didn't see it as a failure at all, it was just one of those mistakes, one of those wrong turnings. I should have some time off, we could be together as a family, I'd get to know Joe – it was a real blessing.

In fact, it was me who said, 'What about the mortgage?' and it was Kitty who laughed and said, 'If we can't pay the mortgage, we'll sell the flat.'

What is it about self-destruction? Why does one pursue it in a heady, even wilful way, motoring breezily on down the road to nothingness?

I felt the hope in her. I lay in bed like an invalid, and she'd bring me cups of cocoa and read me poetry. I was the lucky recipient of Joseph's first smile, not least because Kitty brought him to see me whenever he was awake, and held him close to me so I could gurgle at him and pat his head.

It was Christmas which killed any prospect of recovery. Christmas lunch in my parents' house in Cheam. I hadn't told them about losing my job, and nor had Kitty – we were going to offer them a 'changing jobs' scenario when we knew what it was I was going to do.

My father made some remark – I could have put on a clean tie, something like that. And from then on it was as though everyone was speaking in echoes. My mind, which had been on hold ever since I lost my job, became as sharp as one of those guillotines which cut paper. Was it really necessary to fill the air with such rubbish, I kept thinking, is that what we really wanted to know about? Harmless remarks about cousins and neighbours, marriage plans, job prospects, hairstyles. Then I saw Kitty telling my mother the sad news *sotto voce*. Kitty, you traitor. You wrote 'FAILURE' on my forehead with your own pen, so my mother could read it. I watched my mother's face.

Suddenly I saw the span of my life as she might have seen it: this boy, so full of promise, who worked so hard and did so well, had failed us all, had failed his mother, wife and child.

So on the following day I left them. I had in my hand a large, airforce blue suitcase, and all I could do was follow where it led me.

# 2

UNHAPPINESS IS LIKE a low flat hum. Sometimes you can drown it out, you can turn the radio on loud, rev the engine of your car, shout at people. But when the night comes and all is still you can hear it in your head and in your heart, and you can't escape. Even in sleep you can't, the demons come to mock and taunt you, they crowd on round and tell you who's to blame.

I followed my blue suitcase to a hostel for single men. I had often passed this hostel on my way to the teacher training college. It used to be an asylum, and spiked railings twelve feet high surrounded it. I was drawn to it in the same way as I was to Harry, and while other pedestrians walked quickly past, I would pause and wonder. I came to recognise two or three faces, who would emerge from the building at half-past eight on the dot, dressed in pristine suits with briefcases. There was no camaraderie between them, no eye contact, every one of them self-contained and self-sufficient. If I tried to catch a man's eye, he would turn away immediately. Self-respect, I remembered. Hold on to that, boys. It's all you've got.

The suitcase was heavy and I carried it three miles to get there. It was only after a mile or so that I understood the direction I was going in: until then, anything was possible. I had no siblings to turn to; there was an uncle and aunt in their seventies but I hadn't seen them for years. My parents? I was angry with them. Stephen? He was angry with me. All my friends would take Kitty's side. Well, of course they'd take Kitty's side: Kitty was right, Kitty was good and pure and sensible, and now she was a mother and a deserted wife.

But I wasn't in total despair that day. When I knew where I was going part of me felt I was going home, my spiritual home. I understood then that Harry wasn't the genuine article, fussing about the deposit on a flat and whatnot. I was. I was ready to chuck it all in. On Battersea Bridge I almost threw my suitcase in the Thames. I thought of Christian ridding himself of his burden. I wanted to be light.

When I got there it was difficult to see who was in charge. I rang a bell by the outside gate, but no one came so I walked in and crossed the courtyard. Likewise I rang the bell by some large gothic wooden doors, but after a few seconds I realised they were off the latch and I just walked in.

I must have looked so strange there, this family man in jacket and brogues, clean yellow corduroy trousers. I stood for a minute or two in the hall, uncertain whether to call up the stairs or enter a door to my right. My hand was blistered from the suitcase, and I was sweating profusely. I sat down on a step to wait. Vaguely I wondered who I was waiting for. Perhaps I should accustom myself simply to waiting. Perhaps that was the next stage of my inner journey.

When no one came I knocked on the door, and when no one answered I walked in. The room was vast, and strewn with empty cans and crisp packets. Flimsy beige curtains hung at the Victorian windows, which were at least ten feet high. A tiny TV stood in the corner, and in front of it were three men slouched in low-backed chairs, smoking.

'Hello,' I cast out into the air. What a hollow, tinny sound it made. One of the hunched figures looked behind him and the others didn't seem to hear.

'*Dr Doolittle*!' I exclaimed, 'I haven't seen this since I was a boy.'

I carried over a chair and joined them. Suddenly a man with red hair and a goatee beard got up and I thought for a moment he was going to introduce himself, but he walked out of the room and a while later came back with a new packet of cigarettes. He turned over the channel and no one even murmured in protest, though I was quite getting into Rex Harrison's rendition of *Talk to the Animals*. Two minutes of horse-racing later we were back again.

'You seem to have had quite a party here,' I said.

They looked at me now, all three my accusers, and I gestured towards the half-hearted Christmas decorations hanging in loops over the walls.

The man with the goatee beard said something dismissive in a thick Scottish accent. I could only gather that they hadn't had a party.

'Perhaps you'll have better luck at Hogmanay,' I suggested. The man lifted his eyes to heaven and began to turn away again.

'I was wondering if there was a free room here, is there someone who could tell me?'

The man shrugged and said something in which the only two words I could distinguish were 'wait' and 'dawn'. It was getting dark now – was it possible he was telling me to wait until the dawn? It crossed my mind that these men, silent as they were, might be acutely aware of the rhythms of the day. For to everything there is a season, and a time to every purpose under heaven.

'Shall I come back at dawn, then?' I asked.

'Dawn's comin' Monday,' volunteered the back of a head, whose face had realigned itself with Rex's, setting out now on his quest for the pink sea snail.

'Monday,' I said. 'Good.'

My suitcase. Where was my suitcase?

'Where's my suitcase?' I said to the three. I was standing in front of them now. 'Someone's just come in here and taken it.

Who was it? You must have seen who it was!'

One of them got up and told me to get out of the way.

'Who was it?' I said, meeting the challenge of his stare.

'Yer 'ad no fuckin' suitcase, mate.'

I saw a glimpse of blue in the hall. I couldn't apologise. I walked out of the room and took my suitcase away from that place, far down the road, my face flushed, my blisters unheeded. I set off down the New Kent Road, and walked towards Bermondsey, relishing the anonymity of everything I saw, and the tawdriness of it: the bright lights of the video stores and takeaways, the all-night supermarkets; and I relished my own anonymity, my own irrelevance: a single unknown cell in this urban place.

I found a bench in Southwark Park and sat down. I sat there for perhaps twenty minutes, just breathing in the damp air. I wondered whether this was what mediation was like: the gathering together of oneself, and pure detachment. Nothing mattered; my mind was numb, but not in an unpleasant way. Ah, the uncluttering of life, the lights blinking on and off in the houses off the bowling green, the purring of engines starting, the chattering of the human beings walking by, which seemed strangely equivalent to the animals in *Dr Doolittle*, making neither more nor less sense; even the sound of a car door slamming was real and healthy and good. Nothing could infringe my sense of peace.

Except the cold. I unzipped my suitcase and found two more jumpers to put on, and covered my legs with a white fluffy bath towel. I laughed inwardly at the sight of it. What a long way I'd come since this morning. Then someone came by who was eating a shish kebab. Godammit, food. Godammit, I hadn't even eaten breakfast. So I put the towel back in my suitcase and went to the shish kebab shop, but when I came to pay I was fifty pence short and he wouldn't accept a cheque. I asked him where the nearest cashpoint machine was and when he said half a mile on up the road I said, 'Shit,' and sat down, suddenly weary.

My shish kebab was sitting on the counter getting cold. I thought, if the proprietor sees me suffer like this he'll give in. So after a minute or two of sighing and shuffling I caught his eye, but he just shrugged and served another customer. Then I noticed a sign: 'Cheques: £10 minimum' and the night was saved. I bought three shish kebabs and a tin of lemonade, and went back to my park bench to eat them.

Two shish kebabs on and I was restored to my previous good temper. Only now it lasted about ten minutes, rather than twenty. My gut had been spurred into action again, and I needed to find a gentlemen's lavatory, and quickly. I was directed across the other side of the park, only to find them 'locked over the holiday'. I looked desperately about me for a pub or a café; briefly I attempted hiding myself in the middle of a bush, but a giggling couple noticed me and I had to emerge again. There was nothing for it: I entered the gates of a modern residential development, and found a house with a wreath of holly and mistletoe on the door knocker. They would help a man in trouble, surely.

An Indian woman dressed in a red silk sari answered the door. I had evidently interrupted a Boxing Day party, and there were laughing children darting across the corridor behind her.

'Can I help you?' she asked sweetly.

'Yes,' I said, 'I need . . .'

'Yes?'

'A taxi,' was the first thing I could think of. Or of course it was the second thing.

'Are there none about? I could call one, there's quite a reliable company near here . . . one moment . . .'

'No, no, no, don't worry, it's all right, I'll find one.'

I ran back out on to the main road and within a moment a taxi was all mine. I turned back to wave at the Indian woman but she was gone.

The driver asked me where I was going.

'A good question,' I said, as I settled myself back into the leather seat to consider it.

'A gentlemen's lavatory' sounded pompous and peculiar; 'a toilet' sounded crude.

'A hotel,' I hit upon, 'a good hotel. One with my own bathroom.'

'Local?'

'Yes, very local.'

We reached it within a matter of minutes, a four-star tower block, and I said, 'You couldn't have done better.'

I dragged my suitcase into the foyer, as well as the taxi driver, because I hadn't the money to pay my fare – fifty pence short again. I slipped into the gents of the hotel without saying a word to anyone, and the relief of feeling myself again should have taken me onwards to a place more fitting to my new station in life. But the taxi driver was waiting for his fare; and the woman at the reception was waiting for me to register. There was no alternative but to befriend them both, which I was in no mood to do, while I cashed a cheque with the one and gave a large tip to the other. I saw my face in the tacky mirrors behind the reception desk, and I thought, so that's what an in-between face looks like, one that's already gone from its ordinary life but hasn't yet fully entered its flip side. For aren't there Harrys within all of us?

All the measured voices about me, the 'Please sir, just sign here, sir,' the 'Would you like any help with your luggage, sir?' were like echoes from some former existence, and I barely knew how I answered them, though civilly enough to be above suspicion, I think. But I was loyal to my suitcase at least, and insisted on carrying it up five flights of stairs to our new home, declining even the use of a lift. Room 505: the air was warm and stultifying, the mattress too soft. It was perfect. I fell asleep in my clothes.

My mother asked me a couple of years ago how I could have done it, just like that, left Kitty and Joe without so much as a murmur as to where I was going, or how they could contact me. I tried to explain to her how it feels when you fall apart, when the parts of you that think become divorced from the parts of you that love, the layers grating in opposite directions, and the self too tired to continue to hold them together. If my mother had pointed her finger at me at the time, there in room 505, she wouldn't have found anyone much to argue with; Patrick German had been gone a long while. I think I would have lowered my brow in a gesture of non-understanding – indeed, even to use the word 'I' is misleading, there was no I, there was no one in charge, collating and sifting, reasoning this, justifying that. And how could I have sent Kitty my address? The Queen's Moathouse Hotel cost £150 a night, and we had about £300 between us. Kitty would have called it irresponsible, but it was obvious to me there was no alternative.

I stayed there for a fortnight. I even saw in the new century in my comfortable enclave, snug as a bug with a bottle of champagne on my bedside table and the TV on all night. 'Cherie Blair is blooming,' said the commentator at the Millennium Dome. So much celebration. But I took it all quite airily, I suppose. I watched Stephen Fry pretending to talk to his mother on his mobile phone. Didn't he try to kill himself once? That was a cheery thought. But what's the point of doing anything so drastic till you've used all the credit on your Barclaycard? So I worked out my very upper limit, and informed the hotel of my date of departure: 8th January 2000. I would leave the hotel a free man. I would say, 'Fate, I am yours.'

Pull yourself together, Patrick. That's my mother, accusing me again. But mother, don't you see that 8th January will never come? Can't you see that I'm safe here?

Oh, I'm sure there's masses about Time's winged chariot in

the poetry books. But for me clutching my pillow, phoning room service, eating steak and chips in bed and flicking through the TV channels, Time was like a cocoon, gentle and enveloping, holding me within itself. It soothed me, it told me to forget and be calm, have a bath (another? three in a day? Yes, said Time, I exist for you, I won't desert you. Watch a midnight movie, if you like, watch another . . .) and I trusted that the days would continue, and that I could lie and watch the evenings draw in for ever.

But when the day came to hand myself over to Fate and pay my two thousand three hundred and twenty-three pound bill, Fate laughed at me. 'Let me not exist,' I pleaded, but Fate laughed. She sent me back to that same bench in Southwark Park, and made me rip up that Barclaycard, and put it in the bin beside it.

This time I spent the night there. I wasn't hungry enough to forget what I was doing, and what I had done. Kitty would open the bill and wonder who I'd been with. All anxiety, all sympathy gone in an instant. Did I really expect her to feel sympathy? The extraordinary truth is that I later found out that she did, even then.

I remember shivering violently for hours, but that was all right by me. I wanted to catch a fever. I wanted to hallucinate. But for the four nights that I made that bench my home I remained quite healthy; and nor did my staunch companion of a blue suitcase get stolen, though I left it once for half an hour to get cash (and the ten pounds the machine delivered me I gave to a busker with a dog). I also got through my dry clothes at quite a rate – despite changing only when the wet and the cold became unendurable. It both alarmed and amused me to see the speed of my decline. A lesson for our times: this grand effort we all make, day by day; don't pause, any of you, not even an hour.

Then there was a pivotal moment. I was rummaging around in my suitcase for something dry, and I came across a Bic razor.

Now, I hadn't shaved for days, and in the mirror of the gentlemen's lavatory could barely recognise myself. But it seemed that I held in my hand, at that moment, a possible future. The wet clothes had now made the dry clothes damp; and I understood suddenly there were two paths. If I became ill, if I went to hospital, I would be confronted, sooner or later, by Kitty's pity and contempt. But if I shaved I might once again be presented with the gleaming badge of personhood, and who better to present it to than the principal of my old teacher training college? After all, it was barely six months since I'd graduated, and I'd once written a fine essay for him on the subject of 'Why Children Fail' which had made me seem positively human. He would surely restore me, if no one else could.

So I walked the three miles back to the college off the Lambeth Road, and even the damp clothes I was wearing dried in the sun. And when the principal saw me, all polished and gleaming in the frame of his office door, he leapt up from his chair and invited me in straightaway, a prodigal son, all sins forgiven. The only way I had failed him, he said, was not to let him know what a miserable time I'd been having at Aldover: several of his other graduates had come a cropper there, too. Why hadn't I let him know sooner?

For the previous fortnight, I realised, I had barely addressed a word to anyone, and it's shocking how easy it is to get out of practice. I was slow to follow all the cues; I enthused almost too late. I kept trying to associate this teacher person he was speaking of with myself; it somehow seemed a mistake that any description could be predicated of me at all. But finally I was able to tell him I had been thinking, and it had occurred to me that I would be better suited to teaching at a primary school. 'I want to be given another chance,' I managed. That, said the principal, he would most assuredly give me. I would requalify by July; the new term's lectures had yet to begin; I couldn't have presented myself at a better moment. And before I left, he shook

me warmly by the hand and told me how very, very pleased he
was to have me back.

I've never been a controller. It wasn't ambition and driving
against the grain which made me an early achiever, got me to
Cambridge and the like. These things just happened to me. I
'succeeded' in 'life' with no struggle and, it seems in retrospect,
no real input either. I was a teenager who preferred books and
solitude to parties and sports, that was all.

Likewise, this label of 'teacher' seemed to fall on me from
nowhere. I tried to remember where it had come from. I walked
down the corridor of the college and looked for clues on the
walls. There were prospectuses of local schools, a course on
'play therapy' to be held in the lecture room on Thursday morn-
ings at 10 a.m. and 'thoroughly recommended for those
intending to teach in primary schools'; there was a list of place-
ments available for the summer term. One of the lecturers
passed by and seemed genuinely happy to see me. How was I
getting on? he asked. I gave him a description of myself I didn't
know, of a man who'd weighed things up and decided (all things
considered) that I would find the younger age group more
rewarding to teach. (Our paths didn't happen to cross in Southwark Park this morning, did they? Did you see me with a razor
in the toilets?)

So you see, things came together again. There was a card-
board cutout of a life out there and I simply manoeuvred myself
within it. I went back to college, and shared a house with three
other students in their early twenties. There was some business
about whether I was able to get a grant – I had supposedly graduated from the college the previous summer. But the principal
didn't like to think of anyone 'failing' so he made a special effort
on my behalf and persuaded the powers that be that not only
should I be given another chance but that I should be paid for it.
And then there was the question of Kitty.

At the end of January I wrote my wife a letter. I told her where I was living, that I wasn't happy, but that it was a manageable sort of existence. I apologised about the credit card bill, and told her, which was true, that I was working at a fish and chip shop, and would soon be sending her regular cheques, as much as I could manage. I'd told Barclaycard that I'd moved and to send my bills to my new address. I also told her that I couldn't bear to see her, nor our son. I tried to think of a justification but I couldn't, and so I left it at that.

Once Kitty had an address she wrote me letter upon letter, but I couldn't bear those either, and after the first I didn't even open them. From the few lines that I had the strength to read I gathered that she loved me and missed me, and she'd gone over everything a hundred times and still she couldn't understand how things had come to this. And nor did I.

In the middle of February Kitty came to visit me. She was so thin I hardly recognised her. I was lying on my bed when one of my fellow lodgers knocked on my door and said I had a visitor. I said, 'I'll come down,' but I went to the window first to see if it was her. It was nine at night, and had begun to rain. The street lights cast grey shadows on her face. She looked like a ghost.

I didn't feel sad so much as sick. I came downstairs and tried to sound normal, because at college I was doing just fine, I was saying the right things, writing essays, getting on with life. But I couldn't even say her name.

She put out her arms to embrace me, but mine stayed locked to my sides, not because of a conscious decision to resist her – no, indeed, she looked so awful and so tragic that had she been anyone else in the world I would have taken her up in my arms and kissed and kissed her. But my body refused to listen to the instructions I was urgently giving it, be natural, just hug her, do the right thing.

She wanted to be somewhere private, so of course I took her upstairs. My bedroom was small, uncomfortably small for two, but it didn't seem to bother her. She began talking almost as soon as the door was shut, but I only heard the first few things she said, about Joe mostly, and then for some reason I just switched off. I watched her mouth opening and closing for a long time, I saw how dry her lips were and wondered if she might be getting a cold sore. I opened the window for air. Then suddenly she said, in quite a different tone, 'Patrick.' She'd spotted her unopened letters on the chest of drawers, a dozen of them, at least.

'I couldn't,' I said, shrugging.

'D'you know what?' she said. 'You're weak. You're pathetic. You don't see things when they're right in front of your nose. If Joe grew up to be like you I'd be ashamed of him.' And then she left. I heard her running down the stairs, and the front door closing behind her. I shouted 'Kitty' after her, but she didn't hear me, which was probably for the best, because if I'd even begun my confession I would have broken down.

As it was, I didn't. It would have been too much to ask for a good night's sleep, but on the following day I was back at college, sorting out my placement for the following term, and even sharing a joke or two with my colleagues.

Kitty didn't bother to write any more, but when Joe was six months old she sent me a photograph of him. May 2000: Joe was laughing in a swing. Now if he'd been crying I would have taken more notice. But I thought to myself, Joe's fine, so am I, and left it at that.

When I acknowledged any guilt at all for my behaviour, images of my mother fretting made me write and explain all, or at least, give her an explanation she could understand. That phrase she used to bandy around, 'nervous breakdown' – that's what happened to one of her neighbours and a cousin, and there was a sort of mystery about it, a sort of awe which made one not ask too many questions. So I told her that things had spiralled downwards after losing my job and I'd had a 'nervous breakdown' but was back on my feet again, retraining at the college, and though as yet I couldn't predict any future, was confident that all would be well. My mother didn't write back. Or at least, of course she did, a hundred times, but she would have shown each letter to my father, and he would have said to her, 'Don't send it, he doesn't deserve it.'

By June I was able to send Kitty cheques in almost the same spirit as I would pay any bill. I would write her name and address on the envelope, stick a stamp on it and put it through the letterbox with absolute detachment. I even spent a night or two in the pub with the lads I shared the house with; they invited me to go clubbing with them on Saturday nights, but that was when I was doing my fish and chip shop stint, and anyway I was ten years older than they were. They asked me questions about why I'd decided to go into teaching so late, whether I'd ever been married, things like that, and by then I had the answers off pat. I could even look sad about the demise of my marriage, and one of them would put a reassuring hand on my should and say, 'These things can happen to anyone, mate.'

I had to apply for a job for the beginning of the next academic year. Another probationary year, explained the Principal. That was all right by me, I said. He said I'd picked myself up remarkably well. Reports from my placement at a local primary school said I was becoming a true professional; he could foresee no problems in getting a position.

'Do you want to stay in London?' he asked me.

'Not particularly,' I said, 'I don't mind.'

But then I would be leaving them, I thought, I would be leaving Kitty and Joe for ever. That night, as if from nowhere, the tears came and I sunk my head in my pillow to stifle the sobbing. I felt sick and dizzy and powerless; but by the morning I knew I would resist nothing.

In my pigeonhole that day I found fifteen job descriptions with a note from the principal, 'Take your pick.' I barely looked at the geographical location, or the head's statement describing the ethos of the school; nothing seemed relevant, all seemed chance. I applied to the lot of them: ten of the schools were in parts of London, the others in Totnes, Chippenham, Lymington, Rugby and Cromer. Whatever may be may be. I was sinking back into a low, safe place.

# 3

I'M SITTING AT A RED formica table in a small kitchen, marking homework. On the top of the dresser to my right are four long brown envelopes; they're from Kitty's solicitor, and she wishes to divorce me. I haven't opened them yet. Thank God there's no phone here. I was offered one when I moved in and I said no thank you, I liked the peace.

Outside my open window I can hear the tractors harvesting the sugar beet. Three-quarters of the fields around here are already ploughed over, ready for winter. Sometimes the seagulls come, though I'm four miles inland. I wonder if they're lost, or whether in their sweeping aerial views they manage to keep just a sliver of sea to orientate them.

I'm teaching at a primary school in the nearby village of Gresham, on the North Norfolk coast. It's a four-hour drive from London and I get lost on the lanes, but I don't mind. It's not like I'm heading anywhere, much. To the supermarket on the outskirts of Cromer, perhaps. I've discovered a good range of frozen ready-made meals for one. I'm having chicken dinner tonight, in a foil tray, with its own portion of bread sauce, and a sausage, too. It's on top of the oven, thawing.

I don't even mind the children. There are twenty-eight in the class, and half of them are in their final year. I like teaching two year groups in one. There's less of a gang mentality, and the older girls, in particular, seem to take care of the newcomers. And I'm enjoying the illusion that I'm actually teaching them something. (It occurs to me that the opposite of illusion is dis-

35

illusion – how, in this world, can you win? One is either being tricked or disappointed.)

I don't much care for the headmaster, Mr Birch, but he's friendly and, on the face of it, unobjectionable. Perhaps it's his hair I don't like: there's too much of it, and it's white and thick and makes him look like an ageing Hollywood star, though I don't even have anything against ageing Hollywood stars. Jocelyn Fairbrother is thin and tweedy, and Marion Hardy keeps inviting me and my wife (I wrote 'married' on my application form because it was true) to supper, and I keep having to make excuses. 'Ah, sorry, Kitty has yoga on Tuesdays,' that's what I said last time, and Marion exclaimed that she does yoga too, and where was Kitty's class? So I keep trying to keep my distance from her, but she seeks me out all the same.

Last week Marion told me about Mr Birch's passion for model railways, and now I know what to look for I keep noticing magazines with titles like *Model Railway News* in amongst various financial statements and textbook price lists. But if Mr Birch's commitment is somewhat lacking, the same can't be said of Jocelyn Fairbrother. The school is her pride and joy, and the most remarkable thing about her is that she has taken on all the cleaning side of things. The school saves about three thousand pounds a year thanks to her industry, and she insists that every pound of it is spent on books. At seven-thirty every morning you will find Jocelyn pouring bleach down the children's toilets and cleaning out the sinks; at break times she's wiping up crumbs and milk; and at lunch times she's masterminding a system of 'rubbish in the bin, children, clear away, wipe down', with almost military zeal; and she has on hand several warm, wet J-cloths which the children dutifully take, use and return.

'Jocelyn's quite magnificent, isn't she?' said Marion to me last week. We were sipping tea in the staff-room at the end of the school day when we heard the hoover beginning to whirr.

'Where does she get her energy from?' I said, because the implication was that Jocelyn wasn't magnificent at all, but faintly ridiculous.

'Funny you should ask,' said Marion, and I had to think twice to remember what it was that I had asked. 'Her husband left her about seven years ago. I've always thought it was displacement activity. She's not getting any sex.'

'Could I suggest another motive?' I said, popping her smug little balloon, 'I think Jocelyn does it for the school, because she's a good woman and the budget is tight.' I said this in such a way that it was impossible to disagree. Marion was embarrassed. I think she felt she'd misjudged me.

'You're probably right,' she said, rather more demurely. 'I tried helping her once, but she wouldn't have it. She was so adamant that I don't even feel guilty, just sitting here, drinking tea.'

When I just looked at her fairly coldly she said, 'I should, of course.'

She was pleading with me to let her off the hook. But I didn't. I just gathered my things together and left her there.

I've been living here a couple of months now. It's the end cottage of a terrace of four, and the other three are occupied by farm labourers. Two live alone, like me, and the fourth – my neighbour – has a girlfriend, or perhaps they're even married, but the way she flirts, even with me, makes me think they're not. I say 'flirt' but perhaps that's not quite right. Perhaps she's just being friendly. She says things like, 'Come on, sunshine, things can't be as bad as all that.' When I helped her carry a bed upstairs the first day I moved into the village, she said, 'I hope you don't mind, Rod's hurt his back, and my son's coming to stay tomorrow.' Her name's Linda and she wears short skirts and doesn't look a day older than twenty. I like Linda. I watch her from my bedroom window, carrying bags of shopping up the garden path to her front door; setting out again to God knows where, car keys in hand, slipping into the seat of her battered old Ford Cortina with real style. Linda's the upside of nature's creation, I think to myself.

Our landlord owns all the land around here for miles, and in fact it was a school governor who suggested I got in contact with him after they gave me the job. He said he'd heard a cottage was vacant in Beeston, a hamlet about a mile's walk from the school. Or rents were quite reasonable in Cromer. It depended what I was looking for. I said I was longing for the country, I could hardly wait, and a smile was locked on my face like a gargoyle's.

Linda and Rod drove off early this morning. Linda saw me at the window and waved, as if she knew I'd be there, and Rod looked up and was angry. I imagine he said to her, 'Bloody peeping Tom, he can't keep his eyes off you.' They might have had an argument in the car about it. The trouble is there's nothing to look at here in the country, no general hubbub of human activity. Everything gets too personal too fast.

Today is Saturday, 23rd September. This morning I lay on the hill behind the church and ate an apple. It's strange, I endure the anger of all those I love, and suddenly the glower of a farm labourer who doesn't know me from Adam made me feel unfathomably sad. I said, 'Lovely morning,' because isn't that the kind of thing one says in the country?

I feel trapped in a self-made construction of myself, which allows no ordinariness, or allows only ordinariness. I can't speak. I've turned myself into one of those people I've always despised, who speak from the skin rather than the heart. We bear our histories and devise the means of hiding them. I felt such shame, there on the hill. I'd come to Norfolk to hide, and a farm labourer, in one swift, contemptuous gesture, had found me out.

When you're unhappy it seems there's no alternative, neither for you, nor for anyone. All those who sing, lie. Melancholy is the natural human condition, and those who attempt to jog themselves out of it are denying their humanity. We work, we play, we sleep, we hide. Stand alone; stand naked; hold your faces in your hands for shame.

And I was doing that, I had my hands covering my face, when some walkers came up to me.

'Excuse us,' said the woman, who was the outdoor type, fit and wholesome, 'We don't want to wake you from your reverie, but we can't find the path to the medieval fort. You couldn't put us on the right track, could you?' The man put his arm about her waist. What a *we*, what an *us*, they were!

'You're so lucky living here,' she went on, handing me an Ordnance Survey map; and I read their map for them and pointed out exactly where they should go. In fact, I sounded quite like a schoolmaster. And when they thanked me and waved goodbye I could even pretend I was living on the same planet as they were, and I thought of them setting out on their journey and envied them a destination.

Then, of course, I am a schoolmaster. I returned, in role, to my cottage, and made myself a cup of tea. I sat down at the kitchen table, on which lay a neat pile of twenty-eight exercise books. I gave the children a poem to write for homework: 'The Sky at Night'. When I'm in teacher mode I use a red biro and write comments and give grades and put ticks in the margins. I'm getting to know the children by now, I'm getting to learn what I can expect of them. But this is the first poem I've got them to write and there was some protest. By the end of the lesson I said, 'It doesn't matter if you only write two lines, I want you to have a crack at it.'

In the first few books I open, I see they've taken me at my word. But I'm not angry. I only wish 'night' didn't rhyme with 'bright' as it's tending to be a little repetitive. Here's an example of what they've been writing for me:

> 'When I look at the sky at night,
> I see the stars, so very bright'

or here's an even shorter version:

> 'The moon is bright
> In the sky at night.'

or here's one that even managed to make me smile:

> 'When I look at the sky at night,
> I think I see Uranus
> You like to moon
> So come back soon,
> And let's see it againus.'

That's by Ralph, and I write 'terrific' at the bottom, and I congratulate myself for not writing some tight little instruction to stay behind at the end of school.

Then I read Joanna's poem. I don't mark the others. I stop here.

> 'When the night comes,
> And the spirits descend,
> They hold out a mirror in the darkness,
> We flit and flee, unnerved by our reflection,
> Seeking refuge.
> But let us look closer
> Let us stand and be firm
> And in amongst the mire
> We shall find shards of the divine.'

I can't look in mirrors. I use them to shave, but I don't see. I have brown eyes, but I don't see them. I don't look at myself like there was a human being there. There is the 'I' and there is the 'me' and they don't meet.

Joanna was ten then. There were a few moments when I couldn't even put a face to her. Then I remembered a slight girl, pale and fair, sitting at the back of the classroom. She never put her hand up to answer questions; her other work, as far as I remembered it, was unexceptional. It occurred to me that perhaps she had simply copied out the poem from a book at home, and the thought comforted me. One other thing came to mind – she only ever used her Christian name on the front of her exercise books. Joanna. Joanna who?

I never knew who you were, Joanna. I was the innocent one. But I was keen, wasn't I? You made me restless, you made me want to know. When I went into school early on the Monday morning, I was looking for evidence. I rummaged through your desk with an urgency which was pathetic. There was nothing there, of course. Textbooks, exercise books, neat handwriting, but mistakes, like all children. What was I looking for? Signs of genius? An Oxford career beginning at thirteen? No, Joanna, I was actually looking for you.

Kitty used to say that she loved me because I wasn't a cynic, but I don't think I ever managed to persuade her quite how sincere I was in my desire to teach. No, it wasn't through any love of children that I gave up my former life; it was because I hated the quality of worldliness, and teaching is fundamentally unworldly. Its lack of relevance to everyday life is precisely its virtue: it can stand back and judge. I had this idea that I could somehow make my pupils, yes, every one, my protégés, and we would all be unworldly together, untainted by mundanity, fresh and open and new. But if ever I tried to explain myself to Kitty, she would laugh, and say, 'Just you wait.'

Then to my dismay I discovered that by the time I got to these children I was too late. They already belonged to the world: each and every one of them on a precise and inevitable journey. If I wrote on a report card, 'Could try harder,' what I meant was, 'Will never try harder.' If I wrote, 'Is disruptive in class,' I might just as well have written, 'His family hate him and so will his subsequent wife and children.'

On my first day at Gresham I made the children come up to me one by one to introduce themselves and shake me by the hand. Their attitude to the whole procedure, as far as I was concerned, cast them in a role which they would bear their entire lives. If they were shy, they would always be shy, however much they tried to hide it. If they laughed, they would be loved and sought out for ever. These children came ready-made; their destinies complete.

I also used my little scheme as a way of remembering their names, something I'm usually quite good at. A boy with closely cropped hair and a pale face introduced himself as Mark and I remembered 'Stark Mark'; a pretty girl with orange hair and freckles told me she was Nicola, and she became 'Freckola Nicola'. But when Joanna shook me by the hand she seemed so good and pure, so like an angel, that she became 'Hosanna Joanna', an aide-memoire so perfect that I had forgotten the aide and could only remember the memoire. But when I saw her arrive at the side-gate at half-past eight that Monday morning, I could have sung 'Hosanna' there and then, and all that morning I couldn't look away, so rapt was I by every tiny movement that she made.

Our first lesson was maths. How schoolchildren fidget, how they fiddle with their fingers and their pens and stray wisps of hair, how they rock on their chairs. But Joanna was so still, so poised, so graceful. I watched her write out an exercise in algebra with as much fascination as if she had been dancing for me. How was I ever not enchanted with her? Her blonde hair was tied tightly back away her face, which gave it a sculpted and perfect quality. But she was too thin and pale, too humble. If I discovered she had simply copied the poem, I might even forget her again.

During break I hurried to her exercise book to see if she'd got the sums right, and felt an absurd pleasure that she had. In geography I told the class about rivers, erosion and valleys; or, the truth was, I told Joanna about them, and sent any children out of the class who interrupted us. Then in English I gave out the books and told them there had been a few good poems but they hadn't been long enough. There was a whine in unison: 'You said it didn't matter how long they were, sir.' Three or four of the children told me I hadn't marked theirs. I told them to bring them up to me, and then, because I couldn't rouse any interest in them at all, I told them to read them out to the class. There were murmurs of protest; I can't tell you what the poems were like because I wasn't listening.

After they had finished I asked the class, 'What is poetry? Why do we write it?' It wasn't even a question I had asked myself. 'Joanna, you wrote a good poem. Why did you write it?' We were suddenly all quiet, waiting for her reply.

'Sometimes the things you know . . .' she began.

'Yes?' I said, encouragingly.

'The things I know . . .'

'Yes?'

'Sometimes one needs a place for them, and a poem is like a room.'

'So how do you know what you know, Joanna?'

'I think everybody knows what I know.'

'If everyone knows it already, why do you bother to write it down?'

'To remind people of what they know,' said Joanna. She looked at me and I sank back.

'Does anyone else have any ideas why we write poetry?'

Freckola Nicola put up her hand.

'Nicola,' I said.

'Because it's fun,' said Nicola.

'Absolutely,' I said, 'because it's fun.'

I was reprieved.

Waking up is not always a pleasurable activity. Babies cry when they wake; the rediscovery of consciousness is a difficult thing even for the happiest amongst us. The texture of my life was quite apparent to me; it was an ugly thing, where the threads were synthetic and the weave not my own. Within the boundaries of such a life, the colours are mute, the sky is uniform, and the music dies. One is left with the lowest common denominator, reason, a sort of universal computer language by which we humans communicate. And reason had been telling me these things for months: that life is a cheat, it has no value besides that which we humans say it ought to have, we are all duping ourselves if we believe anything more than that. We speedily sign our names as paid-up members of a civilised society, we adopt its values, and then for ever wonder what it is that we've actually signed up to and, more to the point, what we've signed away.

It occurred to me the other day that human beings are the only species that can defy their biology. For the laws of evolution would suggest that our primary function on this earth is to reproduce fine examples of our race; and I, as a human representative, have produced a son. So why am I here, away from him? Why am I not fending off predators and protecting him? Where are my instincts now? Why have they deserted me?

Or perhaps they haven't. Perhaps they're insisting, rather, that I should love another woman, I should be giving my genes indefinitely to the world. I'd like to ask a little about efficiency here. Why does every cell in my body demand that Kitty be with me now, to have and to hold, and yet I've instructed my solicitors to keep my address from her? If Nature is so wondrous why did Nature make me?

That week I hovered in the school playground, hungry for a private moment with Joanna, but Marion was on guard to thwart me. She would sidle up and ask, 'Are Fridays a good evening for you to come and have supper with us?' or, 'We're having a dinner party at half-term, we'd love it if you could join us.' I'd had to explain that Kitty and I didn't go to dinner parties. And then she'd tried again, godammit, on the Wednesday: 'You know, I'm quite determined to pin you down for a date,' and I snapped at her, 'Kitty and I just don't like going out.' So on Thursday she let me be, and I sought out Joanna, expecting to find her on a bench, reading, or standing alone somewhere.

I found her holding on to one end of a skipping-rope, right at the centre of some childish activity. The other girls were arguing about whose turn it was to go next, and when the present skipper stumbled, the two redheads in the class, Nicola and Caroline, both ran into the rope at full speed and began spitting at each other. But Joanna seemed oblivious to the scene, so intent was she on the rhythm of the swinging rope. Each time the rope hit the ground, her head would nod and her arm lift upwards with the movement of a conductor of an orchestra. I went up to this little ensemble and asked the redheads why they were spitting. Nicola looked up at me and tripped; she then burst into tears and ran into the cloakroom. The rope stopped swinging.

'Joanna, what's been going on?' I asked her.

'You know already, you were watching,' she said.

Then she hung her head as though she'd spoken out of turn, and walked back into the school.

The bell went, and for the rest of the day Joanna avoided me, and wouldn't catch my eye.

When I came in to the staffroom to collect a book, I had the distinct feeling that Marion and Jocelyn had spent that lunchtime discussing me. Neither made their customary attempt at conversation, and when I left them alone again I overheard the words 'his wife'. But I had no interest in their guessing games. My mood had risen from a thick nothingness to a thick sadness; the young poetess was unsettling me.

On the Friday morning Joanna was waiting for me at the school gate, smiling, more open than I'd ever seen her. 'I've written you this,' she said. She handed me a brown envelope with 'Mr German' on it. 'Read it when you get home.'

How could I wait till I got home? I locked myself in the staff cloakroom and opened it then and there. It was only a few lines, written in turquoise ink, and round it she had drawn childish stars and moons:

> 'In the beginning was the One
> And the One created Other
> And Other sprang onward and outward
> Searching.
> Only when he fell
> Did he find a kinder orbit,
> Only when he let the heavens carry him
> Did he glimpse his journey's end.'

For a brief moment my reaction to the poem was sincere. I felt tender, overwhelmed. But moments are sometimes dialectical, and react to the moments preceding it in whimsical, antithetical fashion. So suddenly I heard myself laugh the stupid laugh of a man who doesn't cotton on to a joke but laughs anyway, and I saw myself as this ridiculous figure locking himself in the lavatory to read a pupil's poem as though it were an item of pornography.

Things sank further when I found Mr Birch waiting outside. I was about to explain, let him in on the joke, but there was too much, of course, far and away too much, so I plunged the poem deep into my pocket with my clenched hand, and felt the paper tear as I did so. I expected him to say, because this was the look on his face, 'What's that you've been reading there, German, hand it over,' and then I remembered we were grown men and I'd probably get away with it. But I didn't. He summoned me to his office like a retrograde pupil.

As Mr Birch quivered furiously up and down his study, I was so filled with a sense of the ridiculous that for the first time in months, even years, I felt positively light. His railway magazines, which he'd tended to keep hidden away from us prying staff, suddenly appeared in great piles in every corner of the room. 'Down the track with the new Hornby 108,' I read, 'Does your countryside look a bit plastic?'

'I have never,' spluttered Mr Birch, 'in all my time . . . what were you thinking of? What were you thinking of?'

He tossed me Ralph Harris's exercise book. 'Mrs Harris has been on the phone to me this morning. She's threatening to go to the Governors unless steps are taken to . . . What were you thinking of?'

So I read the whole of Ralph's poem out with due expression.

> 'When I look at the sky at night
> I think I see Uranus
> You like to moon
> So come back soon
> And let's see it againus.'

'I suppose that's the kind of thing they wrote for you in London.'

'It's actually rather more talented.'

'Mr German . . .'

'Call me Patrick, why don't you?'

'This is North Norfolk. There are still standards in North Norfolk. What Ralph wrote was filth, and you know it was. The boy's eleven, you should have sent him to me, for God's sake. And what do you do? What do you do? You write "terrific" at the bottom of the page. What kind of message is that sending out? We don't go in for sarcasm here. It's not our style.'

'I wasn't being sarcastic. The rhythm, the rhyming, it's very good. The rhyming of "Uranus" with "againus" was superb.'

'What do you mean, it was superb? It's not even a real rhyme. "Againus" isn't a real word.'

'Ralph made it one.'

'I don't understand what your game is.'

'I'm not playing a game.'

We looked at each other across the abyss and I said,

'What can you tell me about Joanna?'

'Joanna who?'

'Joanna, Joanna . . . I can't remember her surname. She's thin, her hair's rather fiercely scraped back, she doesn't talk much. You might have taught her for a couple of years. I don't think she's new.'

'Joanna Wells. Ah yes.'

'What do you know about her?'

'She's never caused any trouble.'

He saw by my face that this wasn't a good enough description of her, and he made an effort to be more perceptive.

'She's a bright young thing.'

'Did she ever write poetry for you?'

'I don't think children of eight and nine can write what you call poetry. We read a little, of course, we did some rhyming games – more to help them read phonetically, I think, than to spur their muse.'

'Joanna seems very gifted.'

'Oh yes, we even get gifted children out here in the sticks.'

'But you never noticed that Joanna was in any way exceptional?'

'Her family's rather exceptional,' evaded Mr Birch, 'She's the youngest of nine children.'

'Have you met her parents?'

'Yes, of course, we meet all the parents, there are parents' evenings all the time.'

'What are they like?'

'I have to confess the most memorable thing about them is all those children. They seem quite ordinary. Dark. In fact they look rather like gypsies, I remember Mrs Wells saying they had gypsy blood in them.'

'But Joanna is pale and fair.'

Mr Birch emitted a strangulated laugh and said, 'Perhaps her father isn't her father, then. It has been known to happen.'

'You're probably right,' I said, 'I bet her mother's been fucking around.'

'Mr German,' managed Mr Birch.

'Patrick, please!' I insisted.

'We are colleagues, and may it long remain so.'

'God save the Queen,' I said, and I left the room, happy and glorious, and wildly victorious.

Marion was standing just outside Mr Birch's door, doubtless eavesdropping. But even she had the benefit of my unquenchable good humour.

'Do you know what?' I said to her, 'I would love to come to supper. Name a day.' And she did.

# 4

MARION SOON GOT the upper hand, of course. These women can't resist the power they wield simply by being jollier than their prey. The moment she detected the merest smidgin of melancholy she condoled, 'Kitty won't be coming, will she? It's my business to cheer you up.'

Marion explained it would be 'just the three of us', and the third person in this instance was her husband, Dominic. Though Dominic didn't feature very much; he was sitting at the kitchen table doing *The Times* crossword, oblivious even of his two ten-year-old sons, identical twins, called Georgie and Joey. They seemed to be making random, circuitous movements round the kitchen, rather like a war dance, though I subsequently learnt they were looking for the Marmite.

'Let's leave them to it, shall we?' said Marion, closing the kitchen door and taking me into the sitting-room. 'I'm afraid nothing will make those lads go to bed before ten. We've tried threats, bribery, everything, but that's just the way they are.'

Marion shrugged apologetically and offered me a drink. 'You'll have to have whisky,' she said, 'that's all there is. Ice is optional.'

'I'm sorry, I should have brought a bottle . . .'

'No, no, no, I've put a bottle of something aside to drink with our meal – you're not a vegetarian?'

'No,' I said, as I accepted the proffered glass of Jack Daniels.

'I didn't think so. You don't give off vegetarian vibes. Do I?'

'I don't . . .'

'I'm so rude, sit down,' said Marion, 'if you can find anywhere which doesn't have hair all over it. We've got this wonderful wolfhound. He really ought to have been put down. He bit the postman rather badly and he threatened to take us to court, so then we had to persuade him that we had had him put down, and every morning we have to shut him up in the bathroom when we see him coming up the path.

'But he's such a darling, really, we couldn't possibly murder him like he was a common criminal. Anyway he's called Larry and he does have a tendency to moult. Here, sit here, I don't think you'll catch anything off this chair, Larry can't squeeze himself on to the seat.'

'I hope you haven't put him in the bathroom on my account,' I said.

'Oh no, he's fast asleep on our bed upstairs. Terrible habit, I know, not too good for marital relations.' Marion laughed and immediately looked rather ashamed. 'I'm so sorry,' she said, 'I invited you here to talk about you. '

'There's not much to tell you, I'm afraid.'

'I think you'll find I'm a friendly ear, Patrick. Separation is such a sad fact of modern life.'

'I never told you I was separated,' I said.

'But you are, aren't you? You see, I have a sixth sense about such matters.' Marion lifted her eyebrows and turned her head a little to the side, as if to show me what a very fine, friendly ear she had. But I didn't so much as blow into it.

'Ah, but I see you're not ready to talk. Don't worry, I won't press you. I'm not a bulldozer.'

Another pause. I smiled politely.

'Do you know, Patrick, I used to be a vegetarian. For twenty years I didn't even eat fish, but it was the pretence I couldn't bear, the going to a supermarket and buying great slabs of pork wrapped in polyurethane, and being unaware of the awful condition in which the pig had lived its pitiful life. Now we breed pigs ourselves. I watch them grow from little piglets, the sweet little noises they make, and I make them delicious meals, and when they're grown I slit their throats, in the kindest possible way. If you do it in the correct way they feel no pain at all. And I've learned how to gut them too, how to prepare each part of the meat, and I've even learned how to make simply delicious sausages, and tonight we're having pork casserole with butter-beans. His name was Robin.'

'I think you're right, Marion,' I said, 'I think that's the right way of going about things.'

At supper-time Georgie and Joey were lured away into the sitting-room by a Batman video, and the three of us, Dominic, Marion and myself, drank a toast to Robin's life before we ate him.

'You're driving so I'll just give you half a glass,' said Dominic. His tie dipped in the casserole while he leant over to pour my allowance of red wine.

I said, 'I'm a risk-taker, Dominic, fill me up.'

'Dominic, for heaven's sake,' said Marion.

'Okay, okay,' said Dominic. 'I just didn't want him to lose his licence, that's all.'

'Do you know,' said Marion, 'when I first met Dominic he played the bass guitar in a band, and he never wore ties. For God's sake, Dominic, can't you even take your tie off when you're home? Look at it, it's disgusting, take it off. I never imagined in those heady days that I'd end up married to an estate agent.'

'I am a land surveyor, Marion.'

'So you keep insisting. But why couldn't you have been a spy or a stripper, or a code-breaker?'

'I do a job, and I work for my family, do you think I'd choose to work?'

'I used to be a singer, Patrick. Dom and I were in a band together at Nottingham Uni. "Thieves like us" it was called.

Dom played, I sang. That's how we met.'

'For God's sake, Marion,' said her husband.

'Well, we did fall in love. We did all the right things.'

'The beans aren't cooked, they're still hard.'

'Then it was you who forgot to soak them. Anyway, they're fine. They just aren't mushy, that's all. Are they all right, Patrick? You're not gobbling them down too quickly, are they horrid?'

'They're delicious,' I said, 'and Robin's life was well worth it.' We paused a while to eat, and heard our cutlery rasping against the plates, and a few 'pows' emitting from the sitting-room. We had a pudding of baked apples, picked from the garden only that morning.

'I think I hear the credit music. What about putting the boys to bed, Dominic?'

'It's your turn. It's Friday.'

'Our guest, Dominic.'

'All right, then,' said Dominic, and he got up and left us.

'There, that's better,' purred Marion, the moment we were alone. 'Sometimes I think I have three sons, I honestly do.'

Marion filled our glasses again and leant back, seemingly restored. 'Tell me about Kitty, then.'

'I'd rather not talk about her, if you don't mind,' I said.

'Was it very awful? Poor love. Did she find someone else? Marriage nowadays doesn't seem to be worth the paper it's printed on.'

I didn't know quite what to say. Then Marion put her hand on my knee and squeezed it.

'I really did invite you here to give you a chance to talk, get things off your chest. There's nothing worse than keeping things all bottled up. Was there another man, Patrick?'

'Yes,' I said, 'I discovered I was homosexual.'

'Homosexual or bisexual?' she pursued, indefatigably, her pupils dilating.

Then I got up and said, 'Kitty, how do you expect me to tell you anything, I hardly know you.'

Marion took my hand as I tried to leave. 'I'm not Kitty, love. Is it Kitty you want to talk to?'

So I just ran out of that place. Who wouldn't?


Is the pursuit of purity:

a) a waste of time

b) nostalgic

c) written into the evolutionary design of man in an attempt to ensure consumption of germ-free food?

Why do we so long for what is light and clear and true? Why do we have tongues when we speak only in bite-sized chunks of nothingness, illuminating nothing, communicating nothing, holding up to the light no more than our own emptiness? Perhaps it's ambitious to expect more, perhaps it's beyond our template, perhaps we should just eat, drink and be merry. Perhaps we should seek beauty and have sex and eat clean food.

Melancholy is an old disease. It reassures me sometimes to think these moods of mine can't be blamed on the traffic, or high crime levels, or over-population, or alienation from the land. There's too much black bile coursing through my veins, I need leeches on my liver. And melancholy is also pure in its way, in the blank grey of it, in its uniformity and stillness. It's a quiet place, unpersuaded by bright lights and extraneous noises. It's a human place, where honesty and sorrow mingle; and it's the place where I retreated and found solace when I left Marion's house.

I lay on my bed in the dark with the curtains open, and the moon and the stars made me remember the largeness of things. I tried to pray, though I knew no God and no prayer, just this thirst for the pure.

I sought out words, but words seemed too narrow, too defining; so I imagined myself on a great journey flying in orbit around the earth, and an angel was there beside me as I flew. I felt the comfort of his large wing, I heard the music of the heavens. It was like a dream, but the air was cold on my cheeks and the harmony was too perfect, in combinations unknown to me. I flew over the mountains and the seas and turquoise lagoons; and when I was more courageous I flew lower, and lower still, so that I could mark out shanty towns in Africa, and herds of wildebeest. But a corner of the plain had become a dumping ground for old tyres, and I said, no, no, not here, and I flew down to touch them, to make sure I was seeings things properly. The angel brought me up again, scooped me up in his wing and told me not to worry about the tyres, he was going to show me heaven, he was going to show me his world. I saw two bright pathways, one slightly narrower than the other. I asked him why there were two. 'For the angels descending and ascending,' he said.

On the Monday Marion was friendlier than ever. She seemed to think her soirée had been a huge success, only regretting that I had needed to leave so early.

'I can't tell you how terrific it is to find a real soul-mate at work,' she said in the staff-room at break, as we watched Jocelyn sorting out some playground squabble from the window. 'Your predecessor was terribly dull.'

'What do you think a soul-mate is?' I asked her.

'Someone you feel you can talk to. Properly. Someone on the same wavelength.'

'But you don't know the first thing about me, Marion.'

'There's something about you I like,' she said, and for want of eye-contact she touched my hand. I shivered, but I couldn't even bring myself to look up and glare.

I spent the day watching the class as I sometimes do, as utter strangers to me, a species to wonder at. After hundreds of thousands of years of evolving from an amorphic living jelly, we had arrived at Form Three, Gresham Primary School, North Norfolk, Planet Earth. Evolution is the thesis that we have the best of all possible worlds. So Freckola Nicola over there, picking her pretty little freckled nose, was bound to exist as surely as any strapping great Brontosaurus a hundred million years ago. That desire to live and thrive throbs in us, doesn't it? What about Susan here, ah, the sorrow that is Susan, already a plump little thing, and heavy in the head, too, what hope have you? A necklace factory? Too clumsy for necklaces. Perhaps sausages. Sixty per cent rusk, ten per cent water, and in sorrow you'll fuck your way round the factory and you'll get caught in the toilets with your white net hat off and the hygiene manager will terminate your contract and in sorrow you'll have a child. Perhaps I'll be her teacher here, too, in this best of all possible worlds.

I wonder, sometimes, why life was so eager to get going. Why it seemed so obvious at the beginning that the life of a gastropod was better than no life. Why did DNA get so excited by the prospect of its own invention? Why did it replicate, replicate, replicate? I might have been a boiling sea, or a mountain, I might have existed forever, but instead I shall end up in a grave with Susan and her daughter, the three of us with sorrow spreading through our bodies like maggots, and Freckola Nicola and the rest of Form Three will gaze on and sing hymns.

I remembered David's name because he was small and puny and as unlike King David of Goliath fame as was conceivable. His hair was mousy, his face pallid, and his invisibility such that no one had really noticed that he was just crying out to be bullied. He was an industrious boy, though. He'd never been any trouble, and I'd noticed his school reports were always glowing.

On this particular morning he came up to tell me he had a tummy-ache.

'Is this serious, David?' I said. 'Couldn't you just sit on the toilet a while?'

I'm sorry, David, you were so discreet you almost whispered, and I let your mates laugh at you.

So I had to take David out of the classroom, and suddenly I saw my opportunity to escape. We went to Mr Birch's office and phoned David's mum, but his mum didn't have a car so I offered to drive him home. I told the class I'd be back in half an hour and I said, 'I want you to write a poem for me.'

'What about, sir?' moaned the class.

'Evolution,' I told them.

'What's evolution, sir?'

'The best of all possible worlds,' I said, and because they still looked blank I told them to write about our beautiful world, and they seemed quite happy with that.

I settled David down in the front of my car, I even made sure his seat-belt was done up, and when I set off I noticed Marion smiling at me, and waving.

I said, 'Where to, David?' in a jolly sort of a way, and he told me he lived on the further edge of the next village. So we drove on, and we didn't say much, and I turned on the radio to distract myself. I heard the words 'German' and 'industrial' and for some reason I found them soothing, and in my mind's eye I was in a German car factory, and quite happy there, in my blue worksuit, light streaming in through high windows, and my headphones on to drown out the noise.

'This is my house,' said David.

It was a new house, built in the seventies, perhaps, and his mum came out to greet us. Her lipstick was fuschia pink, and I noticed she'd just applied it. She invited me in, and for some reason I said, ' Just for a moment, then,' because she had a friendly, ordinary face, and her lipstick had somehow arrested me, like a colour on a poster that makes you give it a second glance.

But no sooner had I crossed the threshold of her germ-free house, than I realised I had made a terrible mistake. She offered me tea. 'The pot's already made,' she said. 'I want to know about David's progress, do you think he'll get level 5 in all his SATs? He gets such good school reports.' She smiled; the fuschia pink had carried over to her teeth.

She took me into her sitting-room, and I admired the immaculate cream carpet, and noticed to my astonishment there wasn't one item out of place, not one magazine lying askew on the gleaming glass coffee table, not one dead insect on the window sill, not one well-thumbed book on the bookshelf, which she used instead to display a selection of ornaments and holiday souvenirs from Tenerife. I looked at David's mother and suddenly I couldn't see beyond her lips, which opened and closed like a fish's – in her case, like the lips of a bright pink tropical fish – but as to the words spewing out of them I remained perfectly oblivious. It took all my natural wit to guess that what she was wanting from me was confirmation of her son's genius, which I was too much of a professional to give her without the props of a desk and a few exercise books. So I looked very serious and thought a while, scratching under my chin with my forefinger.

'Call me Kay,' she said.

Then suddenly I heard a retching sound. David had been sick all over the immaculate cream carpet, and the sick was an orangey colour, and call me compassionate if you will, but I was as anxious as David's mother that it wasn't going to leave a stain on the carpet. She rushed out and filled a plastic bowl with water and 1001 carpet cleaner. I followed her and suggested fetching some loo paper.

'Thank you, thank you,' she gushed, 'the toilet's upstairs.' While I was upstairs I had a quick look round the house, and I touched the pink satin coverlet on her bed.

'Mr German, Mr German, are you coming?'

'Ah yes,' I called down. 'Yes, I've got the loo paper.'

I ran downstairs as fast as I could, but it turned out she'd got beyond that stage and was already scrubbing furiously with a brush.

'This won't do much good for the pile.'

I looked at her blankly. David took some of the loo paper from my hand and wiped his mouth.

'Look, Kay,' I said, 'I've got to hit the road. Come and see me after school one day and we'll talk about David's progress.' I found myself yearning for my bright blue German overalls and the privacy of my car.

'Don't go,' she said. 'Oh bother.'

'Come and see me after school one day and we'll talk about David's progress.'

'Is Thursday good for you?' asked Kay.

'All days are equally good,' I told her.

'But Thursday. This Thursday.'

'Can I let you know?'

'Yes, thank you, Mr German.'

I patted David on the head and told him to get better soon.

Kay waved from the door, and I was free.

For a brief moment I thought it might be a good opportunity to go to the sea. I hadn't been to the coast yet, despite living only four miles away from it. It was mid-October, and for the first time that year there was a chill in the air, and quite a wind brewing up. I wanted the wind to blow cold, cold to my bones, and to stand all alone on a beach and watch the white horses winging their way over the sea. But I missed the turning to the sea and drove on back to school.

When I got back to the classroom I found Jocelyn telling them to be quiet, 'and it's not the first time I've had to cross the corridor this last hour,' she said, looking at me. 'David was sick,' I explained. The class laughed merrily, 'Ugh, you mean, really sick, on your shoes, yuk.' Jocelyn left me to it and I said, 'Come on, you lot. Show me your poems, then.' There was giggling and, of course, only one or two had written anything at all. But

I saw something on Ralph's desk, and I ambled over and read it out to the class.

> 'The flowers are blowing in the breeze,
> But oh, good gracious, how I sneeze,
> Sometimes in spring I even wheeze
> And envy all the birds and bees.'

'Excellent, Ralph,' I said, 'you have a real knack.' 'Doesn't seem a very wonderful world to me,' said Freckola Nicola, so I said to her, 'Tell us about your world, Nicola.' But she hid the couple of lines she'd written under a book, and I didn't humiliate her, because I was already walking up to the back of the class to find Joanna. 'Let me read yours,' I said to her.

It was two weeks since I'd spoken to her. The poem she'd written for me lay creased and torn in two on the chest of drawers in my bedroom. I'd never even mentioned it to her for shame. Anyway, was she asking me to comment on it as a piece of poetry, to congratulate her on its metre? Or had she given it to me as a patronising way of getting a man three times her age to set out on his journey to self-knowledge? The thought had made me angry with her. But I wasn't angry now. She was looking too vulnerable. Her arms were by her sides and she didn't even flinch when I took the poem from her desk. I read it out loud to the class:

> 'Fish have fins to swim with,
> Birds have wings to fly with,
> Snakes have skins to slither with,
> And men have hearts to love with.'

I looked at her and I said, 'Surely, Joanna, you mean, "Men have brains to think with."' But Joanna was adamant. 'No Mr German,' she said, looking at me, gently, 'Men have hearts to love with.' And we left it at that.

On Thursday morning David's mum brought him back into school. She wasn't wearing her lipstick and I didn't recognise her.

'That's still all right for this afternoon?' she said.

I wondered what she was talking about.

'I'm sorry?'

'Just a quick word about David's work, now he's in the top form. I know there's a parents' evening coming up, but there's never much time in those, is there?'

'Of course, Mrs Motley. It always gives me pleasure to discuss a good pupil's work.'

'Oh, do call me Kay.'

'I'll see you later, then, Kay.'

'Thank you so much, Mr German, you are so kind.'

We waved goodbye to each other like firm friends.

I never could bear talking to these parents. I'd gone to one parents' evening during my training and more often than not I didn't know where to begin. How could I have explained to them that their mediocre children would grow up into mediocre adults, and that an A here or a B there wouldn't make the blindest bit of difference? Their expectant faces waited for me to give the verdict on their offspring, and I'd say something like, 'Frankly, your daughter's not terribly good at maths,' and the mum would giggle and say she'd never been able to string two sums together herself, and the father would glare at me and say, 'Well, what are you going to do about it then?' A hundred wicked solutions simultaneously presented themselves. 'Have you tried camomile tea?' I'd say.

So after school that afternoon I cleared a space on my desk and brought up another chair and breathed in a few assertive breaths; and when Mrs Motley came in, reeking of perfume (alas, my breathing had to become rather shallower) we sent off David to help Jocelyn tidy up class one where they'd been doing art. Mrs Motley had brought in with her a small pile of David's school reports for me to peruse and enjoy, and indeed I did enjoy them. Mr Birch himself had effused, 'David is a model pupil and a pleasure to teach. He will go far.'

Mrs Motley straightened her back and assumed an air of grandeur when she asked, 'Are you of the same opinion, Mr German?'

'Am I of the same opinion?' I repeated. I rocked back in my chair irreverently and chewed the rubber on the end of my pencil; and while I was perched rather precariously on one leg it seemed that to tell her 'yes' or 'no' was as delicately balanced as I was: one way or another a word would come out of my mouth and I was as curious as she to see which one it would be.

'Maybe,' was the word. But that long pause during which we were both on tenterhooks only seemed to add a certain gravitas to that considered opinion of mine, and 'maybe' immediately translated itself into barely restrainable beams of delight on the part of Mrs Motley, as though I'd more or less promised a job in the Cabinet on his coming of age. Of course, I didn't want to disillusion her, or deprive her of the pleasure of mulling over to herself for months to come the full potential of that little word, so the rest of our interview consisted of little smiles and unspoken admiration for each other.

So we bade each other farewell, and Mrs Motley went off to reclaim her son, and I saw her kissing him and putting a proud arm about his shoulders, and I felt that genuine glow that only comes when you've done someone a good turn. Then while I was leaning back in my chair, still enjoying that warm aftermath in solitude, Marion came in.

'Oh Patrick,' she said, I'm so pleased you're still here. I need to talk to you.'

Where was the self-contained Marion now? Where was the self-righteousness? She was altogether different, anguished, even, and her hand sought my own, and what could I do but let her hold it?

'I know,' she said, 'that what I'm going to tell you is ridiculous.'

So obtuse was I, that even then I didn't anticipate what she wanted to tell me.

'Patrick, I'm in love with you.'

I didn't tell her that I didn't love her. In fact, I barely liked her, but it was those stray, stranded emotions in both of us that did not know their right home, and which, at that time, demanded our attention. I hadn't thought about sex for months, I hadn't thought about Woman with a capital W, I hadn't even fantasised about my pretty neighbour Linda, but when I understood that it might be my prerogative to actually slip my hand into Marion's bra, I was immediately sent back into that ethereal place where a 'yes' or a 'no' are equally valid, and secretly, furtively, is born a 'why not?'

So we had sex, Marion and I, and the lights were off in the classroom, and a street lamp shone through the arched Victorian window. It was good, it was sexy, it was extreme. The right number of shadows, the right smell, but the best part of the whole business was that I managed to avoid Marion for the whole of Friday. I didn't even acknowledge her half-smile in assembly, and I escaped at the end of the school day, as it seemed, unscathed, to begin a week's half-term. In fact, I was even quite jolly as I locked up the car and made my way up the garden path. Guilt is a strange thing; it doesn't catch up with you until you're caught, and then it overwhelms you, like a thick, grey curd.

A policewoman was waiting outside the house.

'I'm afraid I've got bad news for you,' she said. 'Mr German, I think I'd better come inside.'

# 5

WHEN I WAS A BOY my father would occasionally buy my mother a box of violet creams in black chocolate. It seems obvious now that the gift referred back to an earlier time, before I was born, perhaps during their courtship, even; because my mother's careworn face would suddenly give way to a smile as sweet and innocent as the girl she had once been. My mother kept these chocolates in the bottom drawer of her dressing table, and I never in all my childhood saw her actually eat one. But I myself kept a close eye on the only confectionery that ever entered our house. I would creep upstairs while she was doing the washing, or baking a pudding, and count these chocolates. If the box was nearly full, who would ever notice the loss of just one of them, popped into my mouth before you could say Jack Robinson, and allowed to melt slowly and deliciously in the privacy of my own bedroom?

My mother never found out, and to this day I have never confessed. It's as though I never did anything wrong. Of course, the first time I stole – because that's what I was doing, I was stealing – I was awake all night for fear she was opening the box at that very moment, exclaiming to my father that there had been the most terrible theft. But when I realised that my mother was not only oblivious to the difference between thirteen and twelve chocolates, but also between eight and seven, I could sleep quite soundly. My guilt was in an exact ratio to my fear of getting caught.

Was I a villain, or a normal child? If I had been caught, if I had known guilt, if I had had memories of my mother telling me I would rot in hell for less, would I have so happily deserted wife and child, so happily enjoyed those momentary pleasures with Marion? Sometimes people argue that the very existence of a conscience is proof somehow there is a God; it is the internal yardstick of morality. But the things I felt at that time were not as clear as having a conscience. If they were, I would have done something about them. But I was living a life so tight and frozen that any natural feeling I might have had was long gone.

I'm not making excuses for myself so much as trying to understand what was going on at that time. I left Kitty because I felt hemmed in by the duties of living, by the necessity of having to act, and be, something which I wasn't. I was, simply, pathologically perhaps, irresponsible. I was feeling everything in my head, when – oh Joanna, men have hearts to love with, and our hearts are free and good.

We are all of us living in a given structure, and that structure either tends towards the good or the bad, and it brings out the best, or the worst in us. At every level this is the case: from the macro-political right down to the smallest case of toothache. Now Marion caught me for a moment in a quiet, darkening classroom; and 'opportunity' is a long and cumbersome word for what was light and easy and pleasurable for both of us. The circumstances of the moment were right, even perfect; the piece of the mosaic deep red and well-polished. It was only the larger picture which was ugly, with the colours mis-matching. I didn't notice the mis-match till I saw the policewoman at my door.

She can't have been more than twenty-one. But she invited herself into my house and I immediately wondered which of my family was dead. Was it my mother, my father, my wife or my son? Perhaps, if I could somehow jolly things along a little, manage to convince this harbinger of doom that things were actually quite fun, and merry, and that there were still jokes to be had, then her news might sit quite happily in the new medium, with a drink in her hand, and a bowl of KP nuts between us on the table. But she turned down the whisky, and didn't take to my light-heartedness at all. In fact she seemed quite puzzled by it. It gave her the strength, and perhaps even the anger, to give me the bare facts of the case: my son Joseph had fallen out of a first floor window, and was in intensive care at St George's Hospital. She spoke; but my head was floundering and I hardly heard what she was saying. I was only aware of her face, which was contorted not with pity, but with fury, as though Joseph might have been toddling up and down this little kitchen if I had only taken care.

'Is that what you've come to tell me?' I said to the woman. 'You understand my dilemma, don't you?'

'No, I don't understand it,' said the policewoman. And she left me alone, to peer into the crevasse which was my life.

I didn't have a phone. I might have rung the hospital first, to put me in the picture, but driving is so simple. I got in the car and I drove four hours, in the dark, in the rain, the bright lights of oncoming cars distracting me. At a garage on the outskirts of London I bought an A to Z. Even so, I hoped I'd get lost. I hoped I could just drive round here and there, in a hopeful vacuum, stopping at street corners, buying a local newspaper, finding out what films were on at the weekend. But the traffic, at 9.30 on a Friday night, moved quickly and it was the hospital which seemed to find me. I parked the car; I locked it; I paused a while to study an old tube ticket in my pocket; every action I wished would take an eternity. Then I followed the signs which directed me to the reception and told the lady behind the desk the name of my son.

Ah, sweet professionalism. The receptionist had been drinking tea, and laughing with another woman about a wedding – either one that had just happened or one about to happen, I didn't quite hear; but when I asked her about Joseph she put on her glasses, and said, 'One minute, please.'

While she was keying his name into the computer, I wondered about this person with a name, who had a history now, who was logged in to the Great Database, Joseph Alfred German, now a year old almost to a day, whose father had abandoned him, and had returned ten months later to watch him die.

'He's on ward B2. That's down the corridor to your right, take the lift up to the second floor, and the ward's to your left. He is your son, you said?'

'Yes,' I said. 'I thought he was in intensive care.'

'No, it seems he's in a ward. Now, you are his father? We don't like visitors so late in the wards unless they're parents.'

'I have some ID,' I said, defensively.

'No, that's fine. It's the second floor, on the left.'

After all of that the only thing I understood was that my son was on the second floor, so I wandered down a corridor or two, oppressive with the glow of neon light, looking for the stairs. He was so close to me now, this boy, this part of me.

I pushed through heavy doors to find the stairwell. I heard a woman crying somewhere above me, her sadness cascading downwards. I remember thinking, as her sobs became louder, and our inevitable meeting on the stairs was on the verge of happening, that here were two wretched lives which would cross at this one juncture, at this one moment in time, and then each of us would go past the other, onwards, to privacy.

It was Kitty. We met on the stairs and stopped. She looked down on me, her eyes red and swollen with weeping, her face gaunt, her hair in knots. My Kitty. I waited meekly for the tears to turn to venom. I was ready, even hungry, for my punishment. But instead she whispered, 'I'm so sorry,' and as she looked at me the tears came thick and fast and silently.

Suddenly I heard the noise of someone opening a door above us and running down the stairs.

'Kitty, Kitty,' a man's voice was calling, 'Wait.' When he arrived he didn't see me. He said, 'Kitty, darling, she didn't know what she was saying. Let's go home for an hour or two.'

'I don't want to go home,' Kitty sobbed.

All the while she was watching me, but the man, who had red hair, didn't notice her distraction, and he put his arm around her shoulders and led her away. As she turned the corner of the stairs she looked back at me.

How did I find the strength even to climb the twenty steps to the second floor? I found a ward full of cots, and in each one might have lain my Joe, this one here with a dummy in its mouth, or the baby with the moon-face who was starting to cry, and I thought that somehow I would recognise him, because he was my own flesh and blood, and I didn't want to read the names in the slots at the end, because what father needs to do that?

A nurse came up and told me that no visitors were allowed after eight o'clock. I told her I was looking for Joseph German.

'Well, you'll have to come back tomorrow,' she said.

'I'm his father.'

'Wait a minute.' It was obvious she didn't believe me, and she was going to ask the sister what the security procedure was.

'I thought I recognised your voice,' said a woman in the doorway. 'Your son's in here, Patrick.' It was Kitty's mother.

There was nothing left in me either to ask questions or to offer explanations, and Margaret, to do her credit, understood that, and she let me cry even before I saw his little figure in the cot.

His hair was still matted with blood, and there were bandages around half his head and across his nose, but he opened his eyes briefly when I touched his chin, and I could see he was a serious boy. There was a cheek, too, which he let me stroke with the back of my forefinger, soft and warm and yielding, and his eyes closed again and he slept.

'His fall, thank God, was broken. He fell into his own sandpit, but his ear hit a Tonka toy, and they're doing plastic surgery on that in the morning. He might be a bit deaf in that ear, they say. He broke his nose and a leg. But his brain is fine. The boy is still himself, Patrick. You can read to him, if you like, and talk to him, and know him, and love him, if you like.'

When the sister came in she found us both in tears, and I think she understood that even if I hadn't been a father a few minutes ago I had suddenly become one. She offered to bring us cups of tea, but Margaret said sternly that it wasn't the time to sip tea, and both the good nurse and I realised there was still no end to this night.

Neither of us spoke for some minutes after the sister left us. I was sitting by Joseph's cot and watching him breathe, but suddenly all I could think of was Kitty.

'You did a foolish thing,' said Margaret. 'You've lost a good woman.'

Of course I was ready for every conceivable kind of recrimination; I deserved every insult she could throw at me, and in fact, over those many months of separation I had plated my soul in lead for just such an eventuality as this. 'There's a man who wants to marry her. But it's too soon.'

I wrapped a blond matted ringlet round my finger. 'Tell me about Joe,' I said.

'He took his first step a week ago today, he took it at my house, but don't tell Kitty. She's working now. She's just got a good commission, an acre plot in Richmond. The accident happened yesterday. I don't know what they were doing, what they were playing at, why they didn't see . . .'

Then my mother-in-law broke down herself, and began shaking and weeping. 'I love that child so much,' she said. 'You should have been there.'

You can't escape, can you? It wouldn't matter if you went to the ends of the earth, it wouldn't matter even if you killed yourself, there's a role in which you're cast and you're cast for ever, and I was there with Kitty, and I was there with Joe, and there was a place for me at their table, and there was a place for me in Kitty's bed, and even now my shadow's there, lurking, and I'm saying, look at me, Kitty, remember.

I went to stay with Margaret. It's strange, I never really got to know her. She's a thin, noble woman, deserted by her own husband well before I met her. I don't understand women and their daughters.

Kitty always said she was mean and pinched and solemn. She said she wasn't surprised when her father left her for his buxom red-lipped secretary. Why had her mother never bothered to make herself attractive for him? She never wore make-up, and her glasses hung on a chain around her neck. Why did she wear them round her neck, for God's sake? Other people's mothers wore glass beads and amber, and coloured skirts and trendy boots. How sweet and free the life at school, after their dour and monosyllabic coexistence at home. Kitty's father, meanwhile, worked his way through the full range of secretarial staff, and a couple of young waitresses at the cafeteria, too, but Kitty would giggle and say, 'Too typical. Well, it's their own fault.'

I drove Margaret back to her home in Crouch End. I knew, even as we sat silently in the traffic, that she'd ask me to stay, and that I'd be happy to acquiesce. It wouldn't have even crossed my mind to ask her either to understand or to forgive what I did to her daughter. We stood awkwardly together by the fireplace in her prim sitting-room. She asked me if I wanted something to eat, but neither of us could have swallowed a morsel of bread, nor enjoyed the comfort of a cup of tea.

'I'll just put a clean sheet on your bed,' she said, at last.

'Really, Margaret, don't bother,' I said.

'The sheets tend to get rather damp when they're not used.

Would you like a glass of . . . whisky?'

There was a brass tray of five or six gleaming bottles on a table in the corner of the room; and I suddenly had this vision of Margaret actually polishing them.

'Thank you. That would be really nice.'

So she poured me out a glass and gave it to me, and then went upstairs to bed. I heard her cleaning the sink, or so I imagined, or perhaps she was doing her teeth, something familiar, something alone.

On Margaret's mantelpiece, in that harshly lit room, was our wedding photograph, and her duster would have slid over it even this morning, even this morning before setting off back to the hospital. But the happy couple could have been any happy couple; that man in his morning-suit kissing his bride had neither history nor future, and the bride herself smiled the smile of brides.

'Patrick,' said Margaret, gently.

I was waiting for her to tell me what a lovely couple we made; I was still waiting for the great speech of recrimination, that I'd been waiting for even in the hospital. I was waiting for her to tell me that everyone's lives had been tainted because of what I'd done, that the finger could be pointed at me again and again and again. But she didn't, she told me she'd switched on the fan heater in my room and could I remember to switch it off before going to sleep.

Of course I was grateful to her. Though in a way I wasn't. Sometimes the need to be punished is greater than the need to punish. I wanted her to be angry and to take that anger on, somehow, to help me find a person long since lost. I wanted some part of me to react to her, but she never summoned it. What we had in common was a woman we both loved, but she never mentioned her.

The sheets were cold, and the heater whirred in vain. I shivered, naked, in the single bed, watching a daddy-longlegs climbing over the pink lampshade above me, and suddenly I remembered Christmas '88, and I was shivering then, too, waiting for the house to be still and Kitty to creep into bed with me. And I missed with all my heart not the woman but the moment, when everything was so simple and so light.

The following morning I watched Margaret with her Hoover and washed up our tea-cups and we set off together back to see our Joe. He was sleeping when we arrived, but we were told he'd spent a good night, and had drunk a bottle of milk that morning.

'But he's a little disorientated,' said the nurse. 'It might be better if his mum or dad spends the night. Quite a few parents do, you know. Hospital's a strange place for these little mites, and it's such a comfort to be with someone they really know.'

I turned away and Margaret spoke to her.

'His mum spent the first night with him, of course. He was in intensive care, you know. But last night was so . . . difficult.'

'Don't feel I'm pressing you,' said the nurse. 'The little man just didn't know where he was this morning.'

'Oh Joe,' sighed Margaret, but my own sighing was so deep that no one would have heard it.

When the nurse was gone we sat there, Margaret and I, just watching him. His mouth began twitching and his arm kept jerking upwards towards his damaged cheek and ear, and Margaret suddenly stood up, alarmed.

'He's having a nightmare,' she said. 'Do you think we should wake him up?'

'Perhaps he's in pain,' I said.

'But he's sleeping, you don't feel pain when you're sleeping.'

'We'd better leave him, then.'

We must have been there forty minutes or so, during which time there was no strand of hair on his dear head that I had not come to know and love, no sudden shudder that I did not empathise with, heart and soul. Other fathers might know this feeling at birth: but Joseph was mine that morning; we were one, he and I.

'It wouldn't surprise me if Kitty didn't come,' said Margaret, suddenly.

'Surely . . .' I began.

'It's my fault.'

Then I remembered Kitty crying on the stairs.

'I said terrible things,' said Margaret, mournfully.

'She'll understand,' I said.

'None of us can understand anything at the moment.'

'Joe's waking up,' I said, 'Look.'

Joe opened his eyes and looked around him, before trying to sit himself up in the cot. He looked at me, as though trying to gauge whether I was part of his dream or the real world, and I gave him my finger to hold and said, 'Hello Joe.' For a few moments he gave me the benefit of the doubt and was still, his hand lying limply on mine.

'This is your dad, Joe,' said Margaret, close to tears; but Joe didn't know 'dad'. 'Dad' might have been 'gorilla' or 'bad cad' for all Joe knew of the word. He began to cry, not a whiny, babyish grizzle, but a heart-rending, pitiful cry from his very being, and I wanted to cry with him, but my mouth was dry and no sound came.

'Oh Joe, oh Joe,' murmured Margaret, lifting him from the cot and holding him close to her. But whenever Joe's breathless sobs began to abate, he would look over his shoulder and see me standing there, and they began again with renewed vigour.

'I'd better go.'

'Don't go, Patrick, he'll get used to you, it just takes time, that's all.'

'But it's not a good time right now.'

'He probably thinks you're one of the doctors. He had some

stitches in his cheek and they only gave him local anaesthetic. He's just a bit sensitive, that's all, and who can blame him?'

'I'll come back another day. When he's out of hospital.'

'Don't desert him now, not when you've just found him.'

But Joe chose that moment to redouble his opinion on the matter, and made such a noise that a nurse came into the room to see what was wrong.

'I'm just going,' I said. 'Thanks for having me to stay, Margaret.'

'What did you say? Hush for a moment, Joe.'

'Thank you,' I mouthed. Margaret shrugged and looked sad, but she let me leave.

I found Kitty in the hospital car park, though she looked so blotchy and red-eyed, her hair so unkempt, that I hardly recognised her.

'Kitty,' I called after her, and when she didn't look back I understood that she had probably seen me first and wanted to avoid me. I ran up and put my hand on her shoulder, and she didn't start, so she must have heard me.

'Kitty, I want to write to you. I want to be a father.'

'Being a father is not something you choose to be. You are, and you have been.'

'Your mother tells me . . . there's a man.'

'Oh yes, and what else does she tell you? She has no right to tell you anything.'

'He's moved in with you, hasn't he?'

'You can tell my mother he's moved out again.'

'Oh Kitty, will you write to me, Kitty? Perhaps you could send me a lock of hair, a photograph, you could tell me how he's getting on. It's such a relief, isn't it, that he's going to be all right?'

Kitty smiled strangely and said, 'Do you know, just for a moment, I thought you were asking for a lock of my hair.'

She looked at me as though for the first time, but I couldn't tell you what she was thinking. Then she suddenly turned her back on me and walked away.

I'm back in Norfolk. A typical Saturday afternoon in Beeston. It's sunny, but cold, a chill wind threatening the few stalwart leaves still resisting autumn. Three cars are parked up the muddy lane that runs up alongside my cottage, and as I'm walking up the path to my door I watch a family wiping their muddy boots on the grass verge, three or four children and a mummy and a daddy. Daddy's concerned they don't get mud all over the car, and Mummy says, 'I think we deserve a mug of hot chocolate after that, we must have walked at least four miles,' and Daddy says, 'Four miles? Don't be silly, I should think two and a half at the most.' 'You always underestimate,' insists Mummy. And one of the older children says, 'Anyway, we did five. I've got the map.' 'But you can't read maps,' says another child. 'I can!' 'You can't!' 'I can!' 'Shut up, you two!' And the family drive away.

For us outsiders the family seems an organic being in its own right, a conspiracy with its own rules and ridges, and bridges and breaches, a matrix so self-contained that no one is allowed to enter. We envy it. Or I envy it now, with an acuteness that surprises me, and when I notice there's a kid's bike in Linda's garden next door it becomes invested with a poignancy which is absurd.

I let myself into the cottage and it's as if I've never been there before. I notice how narrow the stairs are, how surprisingly steep, and how the wood is worn on the treads. I wonder for a moment about all the children who might have lived here, who might have shared one of the two small bedrooms, I think I can feel them about me, I think I hear their shoes clattering up and down. They're eager to get outside into the woods to play. Their ghosts are more real than my own.

At my feet there's a bag of schoolbooks. It never got as far as the sitting-room. This is where the policewoman stood, in another era. I go into the kitchen and put the kettle on, believing, somehow, that the familiarity of that ritual will remind me of who I am. But I don't want to sit and sip tea. I don't want to put on the radio, or take out the exercise books for marking. I don't know what I want.

I decide to write a letter to Margaret. It's a cold letter: it's polite, of course, grateful for her hospitality at no notice. It asks her to pass on my address to Kitty. It asks for news of Joe. I don't expect a reply.

I spend that half-term sitting at my bedroom window watching Linda's six-year-old son playing in the garden. His name's Jimmy, but he's obviously been told to steer clear of me, because he runs inside when he catches my eye. Even his mother doesn't look at me now. Perhaps her boyfriend's finally persuaded her I'm some sort of pervert.

But if they could see through me they would see so much love as would feed a hundred hungry souls. I am filled so full I cannot breathe, I cannot think, I cannot go about the ordinary business of life. Dear God, I pray, make me a gateway. These are the words that come into my head, and I don't even know what they mean.

# 6

I STOOD UP AT THE FRONT of my class on Monday the 30th of October and said, 'Welcome back, everyone.' I think they were as surprised as I was. Joanna smiled at me. But I was still too ashamed to smile back; rather I wanted to take her to one side and say, 'It's not what you think. I'm a hopeless case, Joanna. Worse, I'm a hopeless father. Don't think things are any better because I'm greeting you this morning. No, they're worse. They're far, far worse.'

So we went on with the day, my class and I, and I asked them what they would do and where they would go if they had a time machine. Would they like to meet a character in history, I suggested, enjoy a grand banquet with Elizabeth the First, or breakfast with Napoleon? Or would they choose to go into the future, and meet their great, great grandchildren? And then I asked them if they had any regrets, if they'd like to go back in time just a few days, take back things they said, and say things they hadn't said?

'That would be boring,' said Ralph.

'Haven't you said anything you wish you hadn't?'

Ralph thought for a few moments and bit the end of his pencil. 'Not really,' he said.

'But sir,' said Freckola Nicola, 'I don't understand the other bit.'

'The other bit?'

'When you want to say something, you just say it, don't you? The words just pop out.'

I wanted to say, 'Tell us your secret, Nicola.' But I was more prosaic. 'Sometimes people don't say what they want to say. Sometimes they forget. Sometimes you might forget to say thank you to your mum.'

Ralph laughed. 'You don't have to say thank you to your mum. She's your mum, isn't she?'

The other boys in the class evidently agreed.

'Joanna,' I said – I felt brave and thought I could ask her – 'Do you have any regrets? Should you ever have spoken out when it was simply easier to be quiet?'

Somehow I never thought I had the power, if that's the right word, to make Joanna blush, but she did, and she said, 'Oh yes, all the time.'

'Then we have that in common,' I said, oblivious to our audience.

She looked up at me from her desk, from her schoolgirl, inky, graffiti-ed desk, with the compassion of someone five times her age, as if she knew already, as if she knew in every cell of her body, that I'd forgotten to tell Kitty I loved her.

At the end of school I went after Joanna. She was one of the first to leave the classroom, and I watched her from the window walking purposefully across the playground. I needed to speak to her, so I quickly packed my bag and hurried the other children into the playground to be picked up by their mothers. I'd long lost sight of Joanna by now; but I knew the direction she walked in, I knew her route alongside the beech woods and across the fields to the village of Holywell, where she lived. The sky was overcast, and it was already growing dark, but I needed to see her, and it couldn't wait.

As I began to walk, I wasn't sure whether to call out. I walk quite quickly, but I didn't want to seem to creep up from behind and alarm her. On the other hand, if I called out, my voice would sound too desperate, too unlike a schoolmaster's. I was already three or four hundred yards along the way, and beginning to feel like some ignominious stalker. I walked on beside the forest, which as I set out seemed rather dark and forbidding, but the moon was now giving it a silvery hue. Then all I once I saw her.

She was kneeling under a tree, swaying as though a breeze had caught her, and singing, but a song which was more a part of nature than a fanciful addition to it, each note separate and still, all in a minor key and painfully beautiful.

When she saw me, or I suppose it was my silhouette she saw, she said, 'Is that you, Mr German?' Her voice sounded calm and happy.

'I was worried that you didn't have a torch, it gets dark so early nowadays,' was my excuse. 'It's a long way you have to walk.'

'It's not dark. It's twilight.'

'Then I mustn't keep you. You've got to get home.'

Suddenly Joanna walked up to me and burrowed her small, silky hand into mine. 'Is that why you followed me? To offer me a torch?'

Before I could say a word, she resumed her journey, with a self-possession that I'd never seen in a child, and after fifty yards or so she turned back to wave at me. 'Good night, Mr German,' she shouted, 'Good night.'

I stood there for some minutes, though I don't know why, and I couldn't tell you what I was thinking of. But I was conscious of the wind, and of the clouds moving fast across the sky, sometimes shrouding the moon, and sometimes revealing it, in the way that a backcloth of velvet sets off a precious stone. I meandered back beside the wood, aware that animals were beginning to scuffle in the leaves, making ready for their night forage. But what struck me most was the sound of my own feet: I was moving swiftly, almost gliding along, with a lightness in my tread that I hadn't experienced for years. I was too happy to analyse it at the time, but in retrospect I wondered what it was that I'd needed to say to Joanna, and why it had seemed so urgent, when of course I'd told her nothing. And yet I'd rid myself of a huge weight, as though I'd spoken to her well into the night, and she'd said, 'Yes, I understand everything, Mr German, have hope.' Because, as I walked towards the school, I was abundant with hope.

When I got back to the school I noticed that a light had been left on. Jocelyn was a stickler for never wasting electricity; sometimes she would come into my classroom and turn the light off even before I'd packed up my bag (apparently once I had let her down and actually forgotten, and she'd never quite trusted me since) and so it surprised me and made me wonder whether all was well. Then I saw that the lit classroom was Marion's; and worse, that she was now approaching fast.

'Where have you been?' she asked me, brusquely.

I shrugged. 'I'd forgotten to tell Joanna . . .'

'Yes?'

'Something or other. I had to catch her up. That was all.'

'You've been gone almost an hour, Patrick.'

'Well? Is it against the rules?'

'And what was so important that it couldn't wait until tomorrow?'

'She'd forgotten her homework. It's not like her. I thought something might be wrong.'

'And was something wrong?' Marion inquired sarcastically.

'Oh no,' I insisted, 'just your average sort of forgetting.'

'I don't understand you. You're lying.'

'For God's sake, Marion, is there a problem? I run after her, I find her almost immediately, and I decide to have a solitary amble in the wood. Is there something so incredibly strange about the desire to be alone sometimes?'

'You're alone all the time.'

'Then I envy you, Marion, as a married woman.'

'As a married woman, perhaps,' she sighed, 'but happily married?'

'Marion, I can't help you, you know I can't.'

'So tell me where you were walking just now. It's such a lovely evening, isn't it, I can see why you wanted to walk. Where did you go? Into the woods? How deep did you go? Will you show me? Will you take me there?' Her voice had suddenly become all soupy. I was more comfortable with her anger.

Marion took my arm and more or less dragged me in the direction I had just come, and blindly led me down deep into the wood away from the path. Oh, of course I should have resisted her, but she was so determined to lead me onwards it would have required brute force. And then, when we were some half a mile further, clambering over fallen branches and negotiating some kind of path through thick undergrowth, we found ourselves in a mossy hollow, and Marion said, 'We'll wait here a while.'

So we did. There were no forest noises, no rustling leaves or creaking branches, no owls, just the sound of ourselves breathing, and the smell of rotten, fungal wood.

'What exactly are we waiting for? A bus?' I asked her.

'You know what we're waiting for,' said Marion. 'What we've both been waiting for, a while now.'

Marion moved closer to me; I could feel the heat of her well before her hand had found mine. Then she leant up against me and tried to kiss me. I pushed her away.

'No, Marion,' I said, 'This isn't right.'

But even then, Marion was undeterred. 'How can you say it's not right? We're part of nature, Patrick! Look where we've found ourselves! We're the night life of the undergrowth! Just feel this moss, it's softer than a mattress, and it's barely damp.'

'It is damp, though, Marion. And it's so dark I might as well be blind.'

'You don't have to see! Patrick, just feel me! I've taken off my clothes.'

'You're crazy,' I said.

'Come to where my voice is, then.'

'Where have you gone?'

'I'm six feet to your left.'

Six feet to my left. Of course, I should have gone to my right. I know it. But these were extreme circumstances, and in the mood I was in I could have thrown myself down a crevice and hoped to find heaven. I found Marion naked and shivering, and I suppose I was suddenly touched that she should expose herself like this for me. I didn't kiss her, though, but lay on her with my full weight, explaining that I had to keep her warm. What more was there to say? Deep in the black wood on the mossy bed she was Marion no more, she was Woman, and Other, what Man could have held himself back? Her flesh was generous, full and yielding; though even to say 'her' is a misrepresentation: the flesh was yielding, inviting me in. Why is sex so sexy when there's no love? Perhaps it's a trap to catch us spiritual vagrants: we have such a frantic need to feel and sex is the most profound and fundamental place we can go to.

There are other feelings, though, in the aftermath, much less satisfactory. It took over two hours to find our way back to the school. If we'd been married, we'd have bickered, we'd have said, 'Whose fault is this?' and blamed the other. But Marion and I didn't have what you might call a 'relationship'; we had no ground rules. Of course, if I'd gone six feet to the right I would have had things to tell her. How she should be getting her marriage sorted out and leaving me alone, and all such self-righteous twiddle-twaddle. But as it was, I didn't have a leg to stand on, did I? A part of the structure of the decent one-night stand is to be able to leave soon after the execution of the sexual act; to be able to enjoy a glass of whisky in privacy, or a cigarette, or even some mellow Billie Holliday song. But Marion and I continued to fumble in the dark, well after our time was up, and there were empty spaces in our conversation, where we tripped and found no touchstone.

At eight o'clock we found ourselves in the car park of the school saying goodbye. We were so awkward with each other we might have been fifteen years old. But I knew, even then, that l could have made everything all right: I could have kissed her. That would have meant thank you, that was amazing, and I want more of the same. In which case the sighing and the floundering would have been forgotten, and our mossy bed remembered.

Marion looked at me with pleading eyes, but I wouldn't give in.

'Dominic will be wondering where you are,' I said to her.

'Do you know something?' said Marion. 'You're cruel.'

'I know,' I said.

'I'm not surprised your wife left you.'

'I left her.'

'Well, that proves you're a bastard.'

'I am,' I said.

And then the poor hopeless woman flung her arms about me and cried, 'Oh, but you're not a bastard.'

I remained as stalwart as a soldier. 'I'm sorry,' I said, 'I can't do anything for you.' Finally I patted the back of her head, as you might a strange dog that for some reason you felt obliged to acknowledge. None the less Marion found warmth in the gesture when there was none, and murmured, 'Thank you, thank you.' At last, she got into her car and drove away, waving.

Tonight I need to go somewhere. No, not somewhere, not simply away, but to a fixed point. Because there is nothing in me that is simple and singular, and that is what I crave.

Tonight I'm seeking truth, I'll make no bones about it. I need to disentangle myself from the quagmire. Every rational part of me rebels at what I'm doing, walking up the hill to the church, feeling my way beside a high bank. I laugh at myself. If there was a God He'd blow the clouds away and give me a little moonlight to see by. After all, He must know a potential devotee when He sees one. He must know I'm ready to hand myself over to Him, sin and all. What if I give up on my pilgrimage just because I don't happen to have a torch on me? What would you think about that, God? A missed opportunity, to say the least.

I'm here, I'm at the portal; I have my hand in the round iron handle and I'm turning it. I'm walking on flagstones, and the breeze has given way to a stillness, and already I feel I'm in the church's shelter, and part of me thanks God for bringing me here, and part of me scoffs at this other part. My mood is shifting every moment, now; there's a dam waiting to be opened in my very gut and then there's me, guarding against foolishness. I call out, 'God, are you there?' in the black echoing church and then I laugh at myself. I envy those simple believers of the past and I feel my way to a pew to sit, and then I think perhaps I should kneel, perhaps God will hear me better if I'm kneeling. But I can't pray. Does one pray in paragraphs? There is an address, a middle and a conclusion. I whisper, 'Our Father who art in heaven,' and think for a moment of my mother, who taught those words to me, and I remember the six-year-old boy who believed her, who saw a sky of heaven-blue filled with angels. How many of us in how many generations have yearned to hear Your trumpets? It would have been a lie to have continued with the prayer. So I get up, and in more sombre mood feel my way to the light switches on the wall.

When I see where I am I'm restored again. The height and the shape of this place uplift me. I look up at the carved faces of cherubs supporting the rafters, and feel the polished old wood of the pews. Even if God is not with me, I think to myself, every man, woman and child who has stood where I stand now is somehow joined with me tonight, joined to me at least in hope if not in faith. I suddenly notice that I'm walking on grave-stones, and I crouch down to read the worn epitaphs; there's a baby buried here, too, and a child, but the stone is too worn to make out the dates. Is this a sixteen, or an eighteen? Did a baby die in this village four hundred years ago? Why did they bury him here, to be walked over? I have an image of hundreds of feet walking down this aisle, some to be married, some bearing a coffin, some to receive the sacrament, and the feet have shoes on them, leather open sandals, or white silk on dainty heels, or black velvet with diamond buckles, or tough hobnail boots. And when I look upwards at their figures and their clothes, I envy them. Because every one of them, rich or poor, in rough worsted or fine satin, would have known how to pray.

I'm reading a plaque on the wall, and another, and another, these honourable lives, committed to our memory by marble. But I wonder whether even marble has saved them, whether anyone hereabouts much thinks of Harold and his wife Agnes Phipps, or even of their seven children, three of whom are buried with them, a baby, William, only a month old, and two others who died in the same sad week in February 1769, Alfred, aged two, and Elizabeth, four. For a moment I see Elizabeth in her pink dancing shoes and her pink frock, holding her mother's hand at the altar, and then I see the polished black shoes of the pall-bearers, bearing two small coffins. And I watch the congregation weeping and praying, and I envy them.

Then here is a man who, 'in reward for leading an amiable and exemplary life was spared the knowledge that he had survived his only son'. For some reason anger begins to stir now, I can't understand this way of thinking, it's too easy. What about the woman who loses husband and son in the same week? Was she a sinner, did God think it about time He punished her? And the man who lives sixty-five years, he's devout, he's good to his neighbours, he's faithful, in every sense of that word. So God is good to him. And He blesses him with

Ignorance, the ignorance of his son's death, and someone proclaims, What a Good Thing.

When I decide to go I'm in a worse state than when I arrived. I'm crying now, but no, its not a good cry, not a simple cry of grief or sorrow, but an angry, spluttering useless cry, that can't channel itself, that feels itself wanting to destroy. So when the vicar comes in, explaining that a villager had rung him to say there were lights on in the church, and owing to a number of burglaries recently . . .

I don't let him finish his sentence. I say, a little aggressively, 'No, vicar, I've not come here to steal anything.' He immediately apologises, and in any other circumstances I think I would like him. He's dressed in an old hand-knitted jumper and worn corduroy trousers that are too big for him. I should think he's about fifty, and though he speaks gently I have a feeling he doesn't quite trust me.

'I don't think we've met,' he says.

'No, I don't come to church.'

'Do you live locally?'

'Two hundred yards down the lane.'

'Ah, you live at Number One Manor Cottages, yes indeed, in fact I've knocked on your door a couple of times. I'm so pleased to meet you.'

I'm conscious that I don't tell the man my name, but for some reason I need the awkward silence which ensues. I want the opportunity of recasting ourselves, I want us to be angry with one another, I want to say, 'Why are you in this job, for God's sake?' Then I hear myself actually saying this. He laughs.

When he sees my face he's suddenly apologetic. 'It's nothing,' he says, 'just that you said the reason yourself. "For God's sake". I'm in this job for God.'

'And how does God reward you for your good works? With a wife who doesn't snore, with a child who isn't ill? With a parish so cosy the chances are you won't get mugged in your own church?'

'Not even God's Son had special privileges. I doubt I have.'

'Then why do you bother to pray? What are you praying for?'

'Have you ever prayed?'

'I don't even know what a prayer is. Father, I beg you this, I beg you that. Father, do this for me, and I shall adore you. Or don't bother, but I shall adore you anyway. I could never worship. It requires a certain mentality. I don't possess it.'

'The Latin root of adoration is *adore* – I embrace. The point is that one is very close to God. To adore him, to embrace him, if you like, is simply to acknowledge that closeness.'

'What do you embrace, vicar, when you embrace your God?'

'What do you love when you love your God? That was Augustine, he didn't know either. How can any of us know?'

'So what is the point of praying into the stratosphere, when we don't even know if there's a consciousness understanding them?'

'We pray that God should receive our prayers, not understand them. A prayer is not a verbal address, it is an attitude. You won't like it if I tell you it is an attitude of humility; though some find strength in that. A prayer is the attitude that you don't have control over your life. You are handing it over to God. But it's a happy, not a fearful, surrender. That is what faith is.'

'Then I don't have it,' I say, sadly.

'The first step is to repent.' For the first time I feel him putting on his priest's mantle.

'What sort of word is "repent"?' I spit it out.

'It means "be sorry",' mutters the vicar, not a little repentant himself.

'Then I repent that I've bothered you.'

'I'm pleased you did,' says the vicar patiently.

'Stop behaving like a bloody vicar.'

Those are my last words to him. For the time, at least.

OLIVIA FANE

The following morning there was a typewritten brown envelope on my classroom desk. I thought it was something official, some tedious offering from Mr Birch. But it was worse. It was Marion, telling me she was going to stay behind at the end of the parents' meeting that Thursday, the 16th of November. I told her in break that I wouldn't, but Marion smiled, and said she admired my resolve and wished she shared it.

My strategy was to ignore Marion and seek out that fine broom-wielder Jocelyn in the staff-room, the only one of us four who drank in the school air as though it were a veritable eau de vie. I began to ask her questions about her life before Gresham. It was quite difficult to get her to talk, at first. I imagined, as had been my experience of ladies of a certain age who live by themselves, that once I let Jocelyn talk there'd be no stopping her. But she seemed to be rather admirably self-sufficient, and I noticed (unlike her three colleagues) that she always had a novel or a history book in her handbag. She told me she'd been at Gresham twenty years, preceding Mr Birch by fifteen. I asked her what the school had been like before, whether she thought it had improved. I thought she'd want to tell me about it, but she suddenly said, 'I don't like the way you look at Marion. It's unprofessional.'

'What do you mean?' I said, defensively. 'How do I look at her?'

'Thou shalt not covet.'

'Oh for God's sake,' I said.

'You're married, and she's married. It's not right.'

'What sanctimonious rubbish.'

'Mark my words, you'll regret it,' insisted Jocelyn.

Then Marion came in and smiled at me; I turned my head and fumbled for words, and Jocelyn looked towards heaven and left the room. Marion took my hand and placed it on her bosom, and I slipped my fingers through the buttons of her shirt. 'Thursday,' she whispered. Desire is such an easy rule to follow.

It was my first parents' evening at Gresham. On the whole being a teacher is rather a secret activity. When I was at Aldover I rather admired a colleague who taught religious studies in rap. 'Kids, hey, get your textbooks out / let's see what God is all about.' The kids loved him. In fact, it was a hard act for the rest of us to follow. That's the one good thing about being a teacher, there's usually no other adult in the room to witness you at work. Then suddenly, every so often, you are accountable again. These parents want to know if you're viable, and you have to persuade them that you are. You dress the part, you comb your hair, you make sure that the chair you give yourself to sit on is rather higher that the kids' chairs you normally give the parents. Yes, it's all about authority.

So when I saw Kay Motley waving at me through the door (the wonderful woman had been waiting half an hour to make sure she was first in the queue) I was rather pleased. I knew I was in charge.

She walked up to my desk like a queen, pink lips glowing. I exclaimed, 'Kay!'

'So how's my lad getting on?' she inquired, with fake nonchalance.

'Marvellously,' I enthused. The occasion demanded it.

'Oh Mr German, is that really so? And I thought you'd tell me his work's going a little downhill. I mean the grades you've been giving him . . .'

'When a child is truly talented, Kay, I mark them very toughly. If he gets a C now, it stands for Could Do Even Better.'

'Do you mark any of the other children so toughly?' Kay gushed.

'Oh no, it wouldn't be good for their morale.'

'So you think he'll get into Felston?'

'The world is David's oyster, but I don't need to tell you that. The chances are he could get a full scholarship to Winchester.'

'Winchester?' inquired Kay, blankly.

'Or Eton, if you prefer.'

'Eton? Not the Eton? You mean, the school Prince William and Harry go to?'

'The very same. Yes, your son will be mixing with royalty.'

'Oh Mr German, I don't know what to say. I do wish David's dad were here to speak to you. He's so narrow-minded. He doesn't believe our David's exceptional at all, he says he's like any other lad. But I always knew he was. Do you know, the midwife told me the moment he was born, "You've got a special boy here," she said. And there was some test she did on him, to see if he had fast reactions and the like, and he scored ten out of ten. His first test, and he got full marks. And I thought, "You're going to do us proud, David."'

There was a small queue, meanwhile, gathering impatiently behind the proud mother, and I confess to beginning to drift again, so I said goodbye to Kay and shook her firmly by the hand. But no sooner had she vacated her seat, than an altogether trickier customer sat down, a woman as thin as a pin in a tight beige suit and a parrot-brooch on her lapel. My God, this was Ralph's mother, Ralph's own darling mother, I would have recognised her anywhere. For the desire to write poetry springs from a need, and already within my own very unpoetic breast I was feeling something stir. Hello Mrs Pin, let's go for a spin, let's take down that skirt, and I'll give you a squirt. But I restrained myself, of course. Instead I told her that I was encouraging her son to become a troubadour.

'A troubadour?' she quivered.

'He is a rare and fine poet, your son, you should be proud of him. He should be encouraged to seek out exotic women and sing love songs to them.'

Mrs Harris's shoulders began shuddering, and it occurred to me that she moved like a hungry bitch devouring raw meat.

'Of course,' I continued, 'the career structure is rather difficult in this line of work. Sometimes it seems as though one is promoted and demoted at whim. But Ralph really has what it takes. Sometimes he shows signs of real genius.'

She turned her heels on me, and I waved and smiled sweetly after her. The other parents in the queue were very sympathetic. Freckola Nicola's mum in particular was a dear, and said, consolingly, 'Sometimes mums expect the world from their children.' I told her she was the spitting image of her splendid daughter, and I'd mistake them for sisters.

So I got through the queue of parents quickly enough, and in fact I rather enjoyed matching them with their offspring, like dogs with their owners; and from time to time I would think of Marion, and the pleasures to come, because I was long past resisting them.

Then a large woman with a mole on her chin and a mass of dishevelled grey and black hair suddenly pulled up a chair before me, and her skinny moustachioed husband sat down beside her.

'Mr and Mrs Wells,' said the man. 'We're Joanna's parents.'

'Joanna Wells's parents,' added his wife.

'He might be able to put two and two together, my dear,' said Mr Wells. But I couldn't put two and two together at all, and looked at them quite blankly.

'You know, Joanna, the pale one,' explained Mr Wells, patiently.

'She's quiet as a mouse, perhaps you've not noticed her yet,' offered his wife.

'She ties her hair tightly back,' continued Mr Wells.

'Too tightly, I think. She tends to sit at the back of the class,' said his wife.

'She's . . . she's . . .' I began. I was nervous. Godammit I was nervous!

'I remember Mr Birch didn't have much to say last year,' laughed Mr Wells. 'She's not a striking girl.'

'But she's helpful in the house,' said his wife.

'She's a very good poet,' I ventured.

'Poet, is she? Hear that, Maureen? Joanna's a poet.'

'Well, I never,' said Maureen.

'Does she read much?' I asked.

'You ever seen her read, Maur?'

'No, Fred.'

'Nah, I wouldn't call the mite a reader. But books are expensive nowadays. It's not a priority in a large household like ours to go buying books. She's the last of nine. In fact, God knows how she even got here, Maur was sterilised the year before she had her.'

'I was,' laughed Maur.

'We tried to sue the hospital, but I dunno, so many forms and rubbish they send you, we couldn't be bothered with the whole business. But she wasn't one of those crying babies. I couldn't have stood one of them criers, we had a few of them earlier on, didn't we, Maur? But Joanna, she's always been a good girl, never any trouble at all.'

'She's still a good girl,' I ventured, and for want of anything better to say I asked them whether they were from Norfolk.

Joanna's father lolled back in his chair and laughed.

'You're not from Norfolk, are you?'

'Nah, we're a little bit of this, and a little bit of that, aren't we, Maur? Well, I am. Maur's true Romany. She's the genuine article. In fact, she's a bit of a dab hand at the old fortune telling.'

'Oh Fred,' sighed Maur.

'That's how I met you, dammit. Great Yarmouth. '68. If you play your cards right, Maur might just read your palm.'

'Oh Fred.'

'You must drop by some time. We're just a couple of miles up the road. Holywell. There's three council houses on the left as you come in. We're the middle one. Just pop in, Mr German. It'll only cost you a tenner.'

Mrs Wells began scratching her mole and smiled anxiously, revealing broken, blackening teeth.

'Well, you never know. I might be knocking at your door.'

'It was a pleasure to meet you, Mr German,' said Fred.

'And you too,' I said. 'A pleasure.'

Maureen Wells just took me by the hand and gave me a meaningful look, as if to say she knew something that I didn't, and one of these days she might just tell me about it. It occurred to me to mention that they might like to see Joanna's grade card, a list of straight As of course, but somehow it seemed refreshingly irrelevant.

So the last parents left, and it became the business of us four, Marion, Jocelyn, Mr Birch and myself, to clear away the plastic cups and restore some kind of scholarly order to our school. Jocelyn was naturally busier than the rest of us; she put the chairs on the desks and began wielding her broom. Mr Birch was huffing and puffing about nothing; he emptied the urn of water and polished it with his handkerchief. Marion pushed the metal lid back on the large can of Co-op coffee and claimed the rest of the milk for her twins; I poured the sugar back into the bag and tried to catch Marion's eye, but she resisted me.

Mr Birch said, 'These evenings are always rather a nuisance. We have too many of them, but thanks, folks.' For some reason Jocelyn shot him an angry look, and the truth was she was angry with all of us. She insisted on being the last to leave because she wanted to make quite sure the lights were turned off. Then Marion said she needed to get home to her boys, and Mr Birch followed her on her heels. When they were gone Jocelyn asked me what I'd said to Mrs Harris.

'Mrs Harris?' I asked, innocently.

'Ralph Harris's mother.'

I laughed. 'I told her her son was hugely gifted. And for once I could tell the truth.'

'Mrs Harris is a polite, decent woman, Patrick. She goes to the same church as I do.'

'Mrs Harris doesn't approve of modern teaching methods. I hope I look for talent in each and every individual.'

'I don't know why you went into teaching.'

'Jocelyn, why are you so angry with me?'

'Go on, off you go, on your way. I want to lock this place up.'

I did as I was told. I watched Mr Birch drive off; Marion's car had already gone. I have to confess, that instead of relief my one overpowering emotion was one of thwarted sexual desire. I looked vaguely in the direction of the woods – perhaps Marion was waiting for me there – but everything was still and dead and dark. Then Jocelyn drove off and I was alone.

I was unlocking the door of my car when quite suddenly I felt two arms about my waist.

'I parked my car round the back,' whispered Marion. 'God, it's like having your parents watching you.' I turned round and kissed her, a real snog from the heart, and Marion said, 'The next thirty minutes are yours, Patrick.'

Sometimes thirty minutes is a very perfect length of time. I was as happy to greet her as I was to say goodbye.

# 7

THERE IS MEMORY, and there is forgetting. I'd no strength to remember, my only solace was to forget.

You wonder why I don't sleep. Or perhaps you don't wonder, perhaps you're wiser than I am. My dreams are taken over by devils tonight. They come up to my waist, and they're ugly creatures with pale faces and black hair slicked back with brilliantine, and rosebud lips painted red. They're taking me round an Egyptian palace, and I look up and see ceilings made of mother-of-pearl inlaid with turquoise. They're laughing at me and prodding me, but I'm too curious to fear them. We're walking down the centre of an enormous hall, lit by sunlight pouring in through high windows. I feel my back straighten with the sense of occasion. From behind the pillars to the left and right of us emerge pretty young girls who dance with snakes, and one of them is smiling at me. But my consorts push me on, and at the end of the hall there's a platform with a large throne embossed with jewels and I suddenly understand that that throne is mine. I wonder for a moment whether I'm already king or whether this is my own coronation, but I'm confident everything will be made clear. My consorts are laughing and I think, why not, this is a happy occasion. Then one of them, with the gesture of a subservient waiter, takes the seat from the throne to reveal a porcelain basin of water, and I think, how wonderful these Egyptians are not to forget water in their great artefacts. It all seems to make such sense.

But then I look up and notice a long gold chain hanging down from above me, with a handle at the end of it; and my consorts go on laughing and they're telling me to pull it. And when I resist, just a little, they start pouting and flirting with me, touching my clothes and slipping their long fingers between the buttons of my shirt. But when I pull the chain, the throne begins to fill up with shit, and it doesn't stop, it's coming up from the ground beneath it. Everyone in the hall is laughing and jeering, and the pretty girl who smiled at me is waving at me in a friendly way, as though this is all quite normal, and she manages to make me think that it is. So I leave the throne that is frothing shit, and I push past the tugs of my consorts, and I go out into the crowd to find her. She's waving and her face is friendly, but as I get closer I see that it's covered with a bloom of fine blond hair, and then I notice hair on her chest, but she smiles so sweetly, and above her belly button her hair is coarser, like a man's, and she takes my hand suddenly and puts it down her skirt, and everywhere is hair, not like a man's but like an animal's, and suddenly my hand is wet with mucus and I pull it away in disgust and where oh where in this Godforsaken place can I clean it?

She looks at me quizzically, and she seems hurt. I wake up. Even to wake up and leave her is a betrayal.

That Friday I decided to walk to school. It was only a mile's walk across a few fields, and I couldn't think why I'd never done it before. It's true there was a biting wind, but sometimes you need to be bitten by cold winds, sometimes that's what they're there for. So who came into my head while I walked, that quiet time? Was it Kitty? Was it my Joe? Was it Marion, or Joanna? No one did, because that's who I was, I was no one, and I concentrated on keeping the cold away from my neck, pulling up the collar of my jacket and holding it tightly about me.

But it was Marion I thought of first as I peered through the window of my classroom. There was another brown envelope on my desk, and I feared the worst, another rendezvous, another hint at some conspiracy between us. I instinctively washed my hands before entering and reading my fate, but this envelope was addressed to a 'Mr Jermond'. I was both relieved and curious, but when I turned it over there was a poem written in pencil on the back of it.

It was Joanna's handwriting, and I flinched.

> 'The music waits for those who hear,
> Remember who you are,
> You'll never know a love so dear,
> Remember who you are.
> The angels wait for those who see,
> Remember who you are,
> A naked heart will set you free,
> Remember who you are.'

I ripped the envelope open so that 'A naked heart' was torn in two and the angels were simply waiting. The letter inside was from Joanna's mother. I thought, 'How interesting. These two are in it together. They're conniving.'

The letter read:

'Dear Mr Jermond, I need to talk about your future.
Cost: only £10.
Yours sincerely,
Maureen Wells.
P.S. Tuesday afternoons are best. Send note back with Joanna.'

I wrote a note and said I'd be there on Tuesday.

We walked together, Joanna and I, the same route down which I had found her swaying under the tree. We passed the same tree and were silent. She lightly touched its bark as a mark of affection, and I briefly remembered my exalted mood when I had found her there. But the memory of an emotion is always mixed with the painful recognition of its present absence. The sky was already rapidly darkening; I felt sad, and heavy, which surprised me as I'd eaten breakfast that morning in a mood of ironic curiosity: which was exactly what my 'good' moods comprised in those days.

'Do you get on with your mother?' I asked Joanna.

'I love her,' she said, simply, 'but then I love you.'

'When you reduce love like that it becomes meaningless.'

'Love creates meaning. Love is the first,' mumbled Joanna, 'but I'm mumbling, and I should sing, shouldn't I, Mr German?' And for a brief moment my Joanna looked like a pupil needing reassurance.

'Of course you should sing.'

'Music comes just after Love, Mr German. And Number, and Order. Music is Ordered Love, it's Love reined in and understood. Does your heart sing sometimes, Mr German?'

'No,' I answered, solemnly, 'I can't say it does. It's a staid old heart, my heart.'

'Tell me, Mr German, when did human beings begin to call the soul the heart? It's always struck me as very strange.'

Joanna began to fidget with the ends of her hair; she looked anxious, and frowned.

'Men have hearts to love with.' Didn't you write that once?' I asked her.

'But you know as well as I do that hearts are rather slimy organs that pump blood round the body. You know as well as I do that you love with your soul. The two are completely separate, Mr German. I was just using a manner of speech.'

'Do you really think they're separate, Joanna?'

'It's not a question of what I think. It's a question of what you know, already.'

'There'd be some who'd challenge you.'

'And there'd be some that tell you that you don't hear what you hear, and don't see what you see.'

'I think you should sing, Joanna.'

'No you don't. You think I should shut up.'

She was right, of course. She was always right. And indeed we both did shut up, until we arrived at the stile which took us into the village of Holywell. It was dark now, and I told her that she really must take a torch with her, remembering at the same time that I hadn't brought one of my own, and that the walk back along the road would be a few miles.

Joanna lived in a 1950s detached council house. It was made of dull yellow brick, and it was large, thanks to a rather ungracious extension made of painted concrete blocks which surrounded it on two sides like an L. I vaguely remembered the village as one I'd driven through on the way to Cromer, but the houses in it were too scattered to give Holywell a sense of identity, and I'd never noticed a church (though, as we all now know, Joanna's Chapel, the only surviving remnant of a medieval house that had long since burnt down, was hidden in a small copse a couple of fields' walk away from her house). It seemed strange that the Victorians had never fallen upon this village and decided it should have a proper church, but the signboards announcing 'Holywell' were a mile and a half apart, and with barely more than thirty households in between them, loving your neighbour was never the natural consequence of being hugger-mugger, but required keeping appointments, and breaking them even, when the wind from the North Sea blew too cold and too fierce.

I don't even suppose if you'd asked a villager at that time where the well was from which the village took its name he would know. Why should he? If he liked maps and was curious about where he lived he might have sought it out. But there were no signs of it in those days, and the old metal grid which covered it was submerged in couch-grass. It was, of course, the well which had provided the old house with water. Why it was considered 'holy' no one could say, not even Joanna. She had no doubt, she told me, that the water was blessed, and would be blessed in perpetuity, but she wouldn't have thought much of these miracle stories that have so proliferated recently. She always sought the simplest explanation for things.

'A good priest must have consecrated it,' she said once.

'But is that good enough to name a whole village?'

'You underestimate what people know in their bones. People would have just known this water was holy. They didn't need to find the date and the moment and speak to five independent witnesses. They would have just known.'

Mrs Wells was on the doorstep to greet us. Mr Wells was 'on business' and it occurred to me that however Mr Wells occupied his Tuesday afternoons, this was the very reason a Tuesday would suit his wife so well. Again I was wary of connivance between mother and daughter; I was alert to how she would greet Joanna, but in fact she didn't greet her at all, she more or less pushed her into the kitchen and told her to put on the kettle for 'our guest'. She took my hands in hers for longer than I would have wanted. Hers were faintly wet and smelt of root vegetables.

When my hands were free at last, and when she had taken me into her sitting-room, and sat me down in an armchair covered in old patched rugs, she offered me a cigarette and began to smoke one herself. I noticed she was trembling, and was looking at me very hard. I soon learned that in order to endure our meeting I would have to breathe through my mouth. I even wondered, for a moment, if there was a dead body under the floorboards. It was as though no air had left or entered that room for years, and when I subsequently asked Joanna about it she said that no air had, the heat had to be kept in, that was the first rule of the house. I asked Mrs Wells whether she kept cats, and she said that she knew I'd have a nose for such things, and I didn't know whether this was a joke, or whether she was referring in all seriousness to some deep and mysterious power of perception I might be gifted with. But yes, she did have cats, I counted about four of them, and they wandered in and out at will and clawed at the carpet, and climbed up on to my knees and tore at my trousers with their claws. Out of her eight other children I managed to distinguish about four lumpen creatures, all dark and overweight like their mother – or perhaps they weren't overweight, perhaps it was just the impression they gave, as they heaved their schoolbags about the house, and shoved past each other like some sort of blind, primitive mammal.

'I am bound to say,' Maureen Wells began, ponderously, and then didn't say anything at all, but lit herself a second cigarette and muttered, 'Where is that girl?'

'Do you mind if you pay me a tenner up front?' she said, suddenly. 'That's not to say I don't trust you, but we don't have all the time in the world, and while we're waiting for the tea, and I don't know why that girl's taking so long with whatever she's doing . . .'

'Of course, Mrs Wells,' I said. I'd completely forgotten that our interview was going to cost me, and I could only hope that I had the money on me. Counting out my change became more embarrassing than doing it at the front of a long queue in a supermarket. I was eighteen pence short, and I feared for a moment that she was going to send me away as a fraudulent customer.

'I can trust you,' she said finally, as though that were a conclusion she'd reached only after a careful weighing-up.

'I'll give the rest to Joanna tomorrow,' I promised. There was another painful pause before she said, 'I'm sure you will, Mr Jermond, I'm sure you will.'

'Actually my name's "German",' I said.

'Then why did Joanna call you Jermond? What a silly mistake. And where is she?'

Finally Joanna came in to relieve us of each other. She came in carrying a little tray with a pot and china cups on it, all sparkling clean – in fact, her delicate, gleaming figure seemed a veritable island of cleanliness in this dingy room.

'You took your time, Madam,' said Mrs Wells to her daughter. 'I'm sorry, mother, I couldn't find the china.' In fact, as Joanna told me later, she couldn't find any china. She'd eventually found the stuff in a box out in the shed, left over from a car-boot sale. Surely, I had said, fortune tellers always have a stock of good china, it's as necessary as a crystal ball, it's a tax-deductible item. She hasn't told fortunes for years, Joanna told me. It was her father who wanted her to start up again. He said it could be a valuable source of income.

So Joanna left the room and Mrs Wells and I drank our tea without addressing a word to each other. Clatter-clatter went her cup on its saucer, miaow-miaow went a couple of cats, their claws scratching and dragging on the curtains.

'You know, fortune-telling's all a con,' said Mrs Wells, suddenly. 'It's all a gimmick. The stones, the crystal ball, the tarot cards, the palm-reading. I don't need to see your hands, Mr Jermond. I can tell you straight. I don't know what you're going to do on this earth but you're the most important man I'll ever meet.'

I laughed outright and said, 'I like your style.' But she became so abashed after her outburst, so uncertain whether she should look me in the eye or show me the door, that I was forced into making some sort of speech about how grateful I was she should have such faith in me. 'Unfounded I'm sure but none the less true,' was the compromise I hit upon. 'I must go. Before it's dark. Or perhaps I should say, before it's light again.'

At the front door Mrs Wells took me by the hand as though she were seeing off a young prince, and Joanna asked if I could come again. 'Oh yes,' she spluttered, 'Mr Jermond's welcome any time.'

I was appalled. I needed the cold and the black and the three-mile walk lit only by the headlights of occasional cars to give me any sense of perspective at all. That they were in this together was clear. That they had some outlandish designs on me was equally clear.

I didn't meet Joanna's eye on the Wednesday at all. I was brusque and impatient with the class; I shouted at Ralph and I made Freckola Nicola cry. Then that night it was my turn to cry: I got a letter from London. Memory is cursed, unless the lines are straight and good and true.

For a moment, when I saw the London postmark on the envelope, I thought it was Kitty's writing or, at least, I longed for it to be hers, and then almost immediately I dreaded that it might be, and wondered what it was that she might have brought herself to tell me. But it was Margaret who wrote, briefly, to tell me that Joe had made a full recovery, and that Kitty's boyfriend had moved out of the flat, and perhaps it was a good moment to write to Kitty, who was feeling not quite herself at the moment, who was feeling rather at a loss.

She had also enclosed three photographs of Joe. At first I barely glanced at them, and threw them back on to the mat with a couple of unopened bills and warmed my hands under the tap. It was December now, and there was no heating in the cottage, just a coal fire that I could never be bothered to light. But later I took them and laid them on the end of my bed, and scanned them for clues as to who this little boy might be. In one he was on a toy mobile phone. But he wasn't ringing me, no one was saying to him, 'Are you talking to your daddy, Joe?' The terrible truth was that without his bandages around half his face I was unable to recognise him.

It may have been the shock of this not-knowing; it may have been that my mind, as it then was, was unable to understand even the first few basic rules of being able to connect, but it didn't even occur to me to write to Kitty, it didn't even occur to me that Joe would or could ever be restored to me. It was as though Margaret had sent me evidence of other lives that barely infringed upon my own, like reportage from a newspaper. I sobbed the night through, but if someone had confronted me and asked me why, I could only have presumed it was something I ate, or a strange heaviness in the weather.

The next day I forgot that Joanna was scheming with her mother, and told her that I wanted to go for a walk with her at the weekend. Her smile was angelic. 'Come early,' she said. So we walked eight miles, Joanna and I, along the coast of North Norfolk, starting soon after breakfast on the Sunday. Mrs Wells sent us out with two pink apples with wrinkly skins, and I told her that I'd bring her daughter back by lunchtime. 'I trust you, Mr German,' she beamed, her hair hanging limply over her broad shoulders, and Mr Wells waved at us from the back garden, where he was splitting logs with an axe.

The fact that Mrs Wells had finally got my name right made me wonder about the kind of conversations Joanna and her mother might have had about me over those last five days. ('That schoolteacher of yours is quite an exceptional man.' 'Mother, I know. Why else do you think I wanted you to invite him here?')

I remained wary, as we walked, thinking that Joanna was far from the innocent she seemed, and that she might be on the point of making some enormous demand of me, possibly on her mother's behalf. We didn't say much for a mile or two, but it didn't feel awkward. In fact, to have understood the place where Joanna came from, incongruous though it was, made her seem less mysterious. Why shouldn't the girl write poetry, after all? It was a reaction to, rather than a consequence of her background. She was a nice, dear girl, and it was good to be out with her on a day like this. A surprisingly warm wind was blowing in from the dark grey sea, a wind to embrace rather than shy from; the sky was a translucent pearly white, and the land was ploughed and black. Joanna's hair was tied back, as usual, but less harshly than at school, and she wore a blue jumper and an old wool skirt that almost reached her ankles, and no coat, just a scarf around her neck.

'Can you sing, Mr German?' she asked me suddenly.

For a brief moment I wondered whether the Wells family were a wannabe von Trapp family band and needed promotion.

'Well, everyone can sing, I suppose,' I confessed, reluctantly.

'You're right,' smiled Joanna, 'people should sing more, shouldn't they?'

'That's not exactly what I said.'

'But it's true, isn't it, Mr German?'

'I didn't say people could sing well. It'd be a nightmare if people started singing in supermarkets or railway stations.'

'They need practice, that's all,' considered Joanna. 'If they sang in tune, if they sang songs to music, others might even want to join them.'

'I'm afraid, Joanna, people would turn their backs on it. Then they'd go home and write letters to their MP and call it a gross invasion of privacy.'

'What is this thing called privacy? Why do people grow their hedges so high?' sighed my companion.

'People need it,' I said. 'Privacy protects them from the world. It's a good thing.'

'Privacy makes people hide from the world. It doesn't protect them. It makes people think that they're different.'

'But people are different, Joanna. And they need that sense of difference.'

'You're wrong, Mr German. What they need is the sense of being the same.'

'People don't want to be the same at all. Look at communism.'

'But what about compassion? You know what it is to suffer. You're not alone in that suffering.'

'I know what it is like to suffer . . .' I began, fumbling rather, a little less like a schoolmaster.

'And so you must sing, Mr German. The best songs stem from suffering. And then others might join you.'

'I have this image, suddenly, of a group of shoppers breaking into a solemn dirge down an aisle in Asda.'

'And why shouldn't they? Have you ever noticed what it feels like to sing? Have you ever noticed the part of you that sings?'

'No, I can't say I have,' I said, 'My mouth, I suppose.'

The sun made a brief and powerful appearance from behind the veil of cloud, but it was too bright and hurt my eyes, and I preferred the sight of the rotting leaves at my feet. I watched the hem of Joanna's skirt, just a few inches above her walking shoes, her feet so small for this girl of ten, who made me feel about six.

'But is it worth it?' I said. 'Is it worth the suffering for a few good songs? But you're too young, I suppose, to know.'

'I can't defend it,' Joanna said, quietly, so quietly, in fact, that I had to ask her to repeat what she said. 'Children don't know what suffering is,' I said, 'I wouldn't expect you to make a defence of it. Why would you wish to defend it, anyway?'

'Children know everything about suffering. Their souls are so near the surface of their being that the merest murmur makes an imprint. It's you lot that don't know about suffering. It takes quite a lot to make you wake up and feel again.'

'How do you know, Joanna?'

'I'm alive, aren't I? I watch. I listen.'

'Tell me about your parents. Have you seen them suffer?'

'No.'

'Your brothers and sisters?'

'One of my brothers, John. In fact you might have seen him when you came last time. He found a wounded blackbird once and smuggled it into our bedroom, and even fed it worms that he'd collected in the garden. He kept the bird in a shoebox under his bed, and it really seemed to be getting better. I remember, he used to feed it milk from a pipette he'd taken from school. But then one day the bird and its little home were just gone, my mother had found it, and she was angry, I suppose. She didn't kill the bird, but the cats got it. Its feathers were scattered round the garden for days. John should have gathered them and buried them, but he didn't. John suffered.'

'Why should he have buried them?

'He should have buried them and he should have sung. And I would have sung with him.'

'Why didn't you tell him what to do?'

'I did, but he didn't listen. It's quite easy not to listen. Anyway, I was just his little sister.'

'Have you suffered, Joanna?'

'I would say I have, Mr German. I would say that I do. I'm a child, remember. And you?'

'"Suffering" is too big a word. Very few people really suffer. You suffer if your child dies, or your wife. Or if you witnessed the Holocaust. But that hasn't happened to me. I don't think my small parcel of suffering really counts.'

'Even so,' said Joanna earnestly, 'your small parcel of suffering, as you call it, shouldn't set you apart from the world, but join you to it. That's why you should sing, Mr German, to make you part of the world again.'

I laughed. 'What song would you have me sing? Will you teach it to me?'

'The song is yours, Mr German. You know your song. You sing it.'

Suddenly she took my hands in hers and looked at me very hard. Then she began to sing herself, one note at a time, crystal clear, and it was the saddest song I'd ever heard, and I wondered what its secret was, what notes they were, what order they came in, and I wondered how so much suffering and so much beauty dare meet like this, like lovers. And then for a moment I stopped wondering, because there was no 'I' to wonder, I left behind the particular history of Patrick German, I hardly knew what country I was in, and the tears streaming down my face belonged to the heavens, they weren't mine. Because for one moment I saw the truth, and it's not a truth that comes in sentences, it's a truth you apprehend with your heart or, as Joanna would say, with your soul. For that one moment I knew God.

Sometimes it's possible to forget moments like this. You can't record them, you can't discuss them. In other moods you explain them away as some peculiar psychological reaction, 'unsurprising in the circumstances'.

But a few minutes later something happened which made forgetting impossible. I was reeling away from this moment, trying to orientate myself, retrieving the horizon between sky and sea. I was busy returning to myself, returning to logic and words and descriptions. And I was climbing over a barbed wire fence when I cut my hand.

It was a curious accident. There was no pain, but the blood spurted out like a small jet, and I thought I'd snagged an artery. Joanna was quite calm. She took my hand and covered it with her own, and I remember that she smiled coyly, as if she was doing something she shouldn't, but could hardly resist. Then, when she took her hand away, the blood had stopped. And when I looked closely I saw that the wound had totally healed, as if it were a month old.

# 8

THE VICARAGE WAS built in about 1960. It was a bungalow made of factory red brick with large PVC windows. I thought to myself, as I held my finger down on the white plastic buzzer, 'How can they build something so ugly for a man of God? Shouldn't Beauty and Godliness walk hand in hand?'

The vicar seemed genuinely delighted to see me. I suppose vicars don't get many opportunities to save souls nowadays, and he saw in me a *bona fide* customer. And I thought again, as I had in the church when we first met, that here was a good man, even a wise man. I felt ashamed at the way things had gone that night. I wanted to put things right. But even more pressing was my need to tell him about Joanna and the miracle.

He held out his hand and introduced himself as Roger Halliday, and I told him my own name, and immediately began to apologise for my behaviour. He brushed it aside and offered me a cup of tea. He said I'd come at a good moment because his wife Deirdre was out Christmas shopping. We had the house to ourselves, no interruptions, no deadlines. 'A rare treat,' he laughed, 'in this business.'

I was so longing to tell him what had happened to me, and hear his take on it, that it was almost more than I could bear to watch him fill the kettle, and wait for it to boil, and choose two mugs, and find the tea and the sugar. Finally, we sat down in his sitting-room, which was cosy and brown and lined with books, and in a leisurely mood entirely incompatible with mine, he asked me why I had come to live in Norfolk.

'Does it matter?' I quipped. I wasn't in confessional mood at all. 'Would God think it mattered?'

'I think God would say it did matter,' said Roger, calmly.

'So,' I said, 'You think he's fretting on my behalf. If he is, I imagine he's got rather a lot on his plate. But I haven't come here to talk about me. I want to talk about God.'

'I don't believe you can talk about one without the other. Our experience of God is within us, after all.'

'But how do you recognise it? How do you know that it's God you feel within you? Is it like, "Bingo!"?'

The vicar laughed, 'Yes, sometimes I think it is rather like "Bingo!" as you so eloquently put it. Union with God lasts barely a moment, it's a flash, a dart, a moment of absolute knowledge. But it doesn't happen often. Sometimes I can be on my knees for half an hour, and feel, at most, rather uncomfortable.'

'Reverend,' I said, 'I have absolute knowledge. God exists!'

'Yes, yes, he does,' said the Reverend Halliday uneasily. 'So could you tell me why I never see you in church? That isn't an accusation, incidentally. I'm curious.'

'What, and be part of a congregation? Part of a worshipping community?'

'Is that so abhorrent to you?'

'Do you believe in miracles?'

'I do, after a fashion,' said Roger nervously.

'But only after a fashion?'

'I'm not sure whether interpretations have to be literal.'

'Do you believe in the Virgin Birth? Do you believe in the Resurrection?'

'I do, I think.'

'Then what are you doing here? Why are you living in a bungalow in Beeston? How are you pretending that ordinary life is even possible?'

'What do you suggest I be doing, Mr German?'

'Why aren't you living on the top of a mountain? Or in a desert? Or in a chapel in the Western Isles of Scotland?'

'Where have these strong feelings come from, all of a sudden?'

'Surely, if God exists, then feelings should be strong. You ask why I don't wish to become part of a congregation. When I was a child I used to sit in church and wonder, if these people really did believe with all their hearts that a man had died on their behalf in order to save them, to take them to heaven with him, why do they all look so glum?'

'Are you a happy man, Mr German?'

'My personal life has nothing to do with this,' I snapped.

But the Reverend Halliday was gentle with me. He sipped at his coffee and considered. 'We are all human and therefore earthbound, I'm afraid. Church is about making a deliberate space in our lives to remember, if we cannot feel, that there is a realm beyond us. And for some of us, even if we had access to that feeling which I think you're referring to, it's glorious, yes, but also frightening. Sometimes awe has to be broken down into manageable segments.'

'No,' I said, 'I don't think awe should be manageable at all.'

We looked at each other like rivals. 'I should know,' we said to each other with our eyes.

'I'm sorry,' said the Reverend Roger Halliday. 'I've not been very inspirational, have I?'

I mumbled something and got up to leave, stroking the mark on my hand, now five days old.

If there was such a thing as a scale, on one end of which was joy and on the other naked wretchedness, I could not have told you even into which half my own mood fell. In the classroom, I found it difficult to concentrate. I became taut, restless. I decided it was my duty to take the children out on a nature walk every morning to admire God's creation. Mr Birch raised his eyebrows but said nothing; Marion surveyed me anxiously, as I hurried the children into their coats.

My class, on the other hand, thoroughly caught on. Ralph was a real star, and wrote lyrics for us all week about the ant, the robin and the earwig. If you'd been walking your dog near the village of Gresham some day during the last week of November 1999, you might have come across a very merry band of troupers indeed. To the tune of, 'We all like to be beside the seaside,' you might have heard us all sing:

> 'We all like to be on a nature walk,
> We would all like to thank our God for this.
> The robin on the tree
> Who sings in perfect key,
> Yes, nothing's gone amiss.'

But something had gone amiss, and that something was me. My voice alone sounded strained, though only Joanna noticed it, of course. I yearned for the occasional smile she used to give me, but she kept her distance. I hoped we might go on another walk that weekend, but on Friday afternoon she had slunk away home in the drizzle before I could ask her.

Then, as I was packing up some exercise books to mark over the weekend, Jocelyn came into the classroom with a basket of dusters and a Windolene spray.

'That was a long sigh,' she said to me.

'If I had more breath in me it would be longer still,' I said to her.

'I don't wish to intrude,' began Jocelyn, 'but if there's anything I can do . . .'

'There's nothing anyone can do.' That was all I'd intended to say. But the dear woman looked so sympathetic that I suddenly found myself confiding in her. I told her that I knew, I had absolute proof, that God existed, but far from being comforting

114

it was rather disorientating. I didn't know what to do with that knowledge, I simply didn't know where to put it.

'It's quite clear to me,' said Jocelyn, 'that you need to go to church!'

I was about to tell her that I didn't want anything to do with churches, but she'd already insisted that I come with her that Sunday. I didn't have the energy to resist her.

'All right, Jocelyn,' I said, 'I'd like to do that.' She looked so happy. It was obviously the right answer.

We agreed to meet at her church ten minutes before the service began at eleven. It was a large red-brick Victorian church, on the edge of Sheringham, one of those churches which makes you wonder who makes up the congregation when they could go to a far lovelier church a few yards up the road. But in this case it was quite clear how the Reverend Barry Chuck – 'Call me Barry' – had managed to lure the forty fine ladies and a few gentleman into his church. When Jocelyn introduced us in the porch (it was drizzling, and a number of us were taking shelter there) I thought at first he was a second-hand car salesman, dressed in his immaculate crease-free navy blue suit, with such perfect teeth I wondered whether they were false.

'We don't believe in formality here. We are all equals in the sight of God,' he told me, shaking my hand as though we had clinched a deal.

Perhaps I should have had more time for Barry Chuck. After all, I witnessed forty stiff matrons relax the lines on their faces and positively glow. Jocelyn sat next to me and occasionally clutched my elbow in pleasure; even Ralph's mother waved at me from another pew, all sweetness and light.

'Holy, holy, holy,' chanted our Barry, 'What do these words mean to you? They mean Our Lord Jesus Christ.'

'Not necessarily,' I said, a lone voice in the audience.

OLIVIA FANE

Nor was I particularly surprised to hear myself speak: it wasn't the first time that week that Mrs Wells's prophecy sprang to mind – I was the most important person she would ever meet, and perhaps she was right, perhaps I would be God's very own spokesman. The Reverend Barry Chuck was no match for me, I presumed.

'Are you suggesting that Jesus Christ wasn't a holy man?' I relished the quiver in Barry's voice, and paused for poetic effect as I considered my reply.

'No, I'm just saying he might not be the only holy man. And actually, as soon as you said "holy", or after you'd said it three times, I immediately thought of someone else.'

The shocked murmur in the audience was palpable, even delightful. I felt like blowing a kiss to Ralph's mother who was suddenly far less sweet and positively dark. But Jocelyn, to do her credit, was curious, and wanted to hear what I had to say.

I would have stood up anyway, I hardly needed to wait for Barry's pseudo-invitation to replace him on the podium, and even in my own moment of glorious self-promotion I noticed that Barry's main concern was to keep his loyal congregation in the right humour, whatever that might be in the circumstances, cheering, hissing, or simply directing forty cold shoulders towards the Great Blasphemer.

A week on, I still hadn't told a soul about Joanna, about the miracle. Here at least, I thought, I would be preaching to the converted, I would summon a few gasps and 'Praise the Lords'. Perhaps I don't have the knack of telling a story, but almost as soon as I began I understood the benefit of a crease-free suit and a perfect smile. I wanted to tell these women and the few gentleman about my Joanna, this pupil of mine, this ten-year-old who writes damn good poetry and seems so much older than ten. I told them she had blonde hair tied back like so and her clothes were too big for her because her parents were gypsies and couldn't afford much else. Even by then, I could tell at least half

116

of them were thinking I was a paedophile. But I needed to tell
the story, and how she sang to me in a voice so pure that even
the heavens shuddered in anticipation of every note. Then I
showed the congregation my hand and told them that Joanna
had healed it, and a few women from the front row came up and
asked to see it, and one said she could still see a mark and the
others agreed.

Then the Reverend Barry Chuck stood back a few feet to
make room for me to step down from the podium and, as he
smiled condescendingly, I felt my cheeks burn red.

'Thank you . . . What was your name? Patrick? Thank you
Patrick for sharing that with us. Has anyone else had an experience they'd like to tell us about?'

An overweight woman stood up with some difficulty to tell
us how she'd had a sore throat and the doctor had told her it
might be sore for a week but it had gone after only two days, and
Barry Chuck said 'Praise the Lord'; then a thin stick of a woman
wearing almond-shaped glasses stood up to tell us – and it was
by no means an easy thing to get off her chest – that her pregnant daughter who'd been considering an abortion was now
going to marry her boyfriend. 'Praise the Lord,' intoned Barry
Chuck.

'We love you Jesus,' shouted someone in the audience; and
suddenly there were five hands up, five happy stories to tell, but
the wise Barry thought it was time to sing a hymn of praise and
the organist began to play a heavily syncopated version of 'At the
name of Jesus, every knee shall bow', which might have been at
home in a jazz bar. 'Next time,' said Barry, 'I want you to bring
in your tambourines.' The ladies giggled excitedly. 'No excuses
this time, ladies. Music is the way to Jesus' heart. Let's make
Him hear us!'

Throughout this little scene I was sitting next to Jocelyn
with my head hung low. I couldn't even acknowledge her. My
shame swiftly turned to hatred of this idiotic man. But when he

declaimed, in that sing-song voice of his, that 'music is the way' he made me wonder whether somewhere deep under his mask he did know something, whether he had once had in his days of innocence an experience like mine. Then why didn't he recognise me as his fellow? Why did he humiliate me?

When the service was over Barry didn't even acknowledge me. One by one his congregation crept up for his blessing in the porch; he accepted Lily's invitation to a pre-Christmas drink; he castigated Josephine for not being able to get to church the previous Sunday; he asked Mary whether she was practising her clarinet. Jocelyn kept her distance and stuck by me, and afterwards said she'd been surprised by his rudeness.

'But I hope it won't put you off coming again,' she said. I shrugged, but hadn't the spirit even to answer her.

'See you at school,' was all I managed, as I drove away.

It was four in the afternoon and already completely dark. I was sitting at my desk in the classroom and Jocelyn was standing in front of me with her broom, like a queen with her sceptre.

It was now two weeks before the end of term, and it would have been difficult to have judged who was more consumed by melancholy, Joanna or myself. Marion was slightly relieved, I think, to find me more like my old self, and mentioned a weekend in the holidays when Dominic and the twins would be away in Ireland staying with his mother. But in fact it was Jocelyn who was my real friend, who asked me what I'd be doing at Christmas, who suggested we pray together one evening, who told me that she knew I was telling the truth, and had even wondered about Joanna herself when she'd taught her in the first form.

'Such a clever girl,' she said, 'even at six. And she wrote wonderful poems, even then.'

'Do you believe there's something . . . supernatural about

118

her? Did she ever do anything odd? Have you ever noticed anything . . . peculiar?'

'She's always been aloof,' said Jocelyn, 'I suppose some children are. But there's more than that. I know there is. A few years ago, Joanna . . . I might have imagined the whole thing, Patrick.'

'Go on,' I said, 'What did she do?'

'There was a boy hiding in a tree throwing stones at some girls who were skipping. One of the girls got hurt, not badly, just a graze on her cheek, but she ran off crying to find her brother, and the brother was furious. He climbed up the tree and pushed the boy off, and he fell so violently on his knees that he screamed out with pain, like an animal, and then he began wheezing, and gasping for every breath. I thought he would have broken at least one leg, if not both, and badly, too. The boy was lying at a strange angle in a pool of blood, and I was shouting to some girls, "Get Mr Birch," but instead of getting him they took one look at the boy and burst into hysterics of tears.

'In the midst of all this pandemonium I noticed Joanna. She was ethereally calm, Patrick, she was only six years old and just looked on as a mute observer. By this time most of the other children had hidden themselves in far-flung corners of the playground, crying on each other's shoulders, but Joanna walked up to us and smiled at me, and then took the boy's hand. As her teacher, I thought, I should be protecting her from this trauma, but it was she who seemed to be protecting us.

'"You get Mr Birch," she said, but in fact Vanessa, a teacher we had here for a couple of years, had already called up the mothers of both boys involved. The first mother to arrive was the perpetrator's, and I left Joanna and the injured boy together so that I could talk to her, and tell her what happened.

'She said something completely inappropriate like, "This had better be serious, not just some playground nonsense," and

I assured her that we wouldn't be calling her at work if it were nothing. But when I looked round the boy had gone, and Joanna with him, and they were standing under a tree talking and smiling as though nothing had happened at all. They looked just like a couple of little children without a care in the world. And the pool of blood had gone. That blood had been there, I swear it. I was kneeling by it, I saw it, and I saw the state of his knees. I called him. "John," yes, that was his name, "Come over here and tell Mrs So-and-So what happened." And the boy said it was nothing, and it was his fault anyway, he shouldn't have been throwing stones.

'Joanna was watching him, smiling. There seemed to be some agreement between them; yet equally she seemed at a distance, as if she was a spectator of the whole event, and had nothing to do with it. The picture of innocence, in fact. What is a rational person to think? Did I imagine the whole thing? Was I mad? Or did I just witness a miracle performed by a child? Here was this woman, ranting at me for wasting her time. Should I have argued with her? Even if I'd wanted to, I couldn't. I was speechless.

'It's always annoyed me that the others didn't really bother to look, or that I didn't really bother myself. I'm sure Mr Birch has always considered me over-anxious ever since. But I've no fellow witnesses, and then you begin to doubt yourself, don't you?'

'Did you tell anyone at the time?'

'I tried to tell Vanessa. She was young, open-minded, and I thought I could find an ally in her. But it's quite hard to ask a colleague, "Do you believe this girl in our school is capable of performing a miracle?" I found myself saying I was sorry for causing such a fuss, but from where I was standing the injuries looked as though they might be bad, worse than they were. Vanessa was very nice about it, and for a moment I really tried to tell her, I said something like, "I know those injuries were bad." But lines like that aren't written in the script we adults use with each other. Vanessa was never anything but straightforward and kind. She told me to go home and make myself a nice hot cup of tea. But I didn't. I went to a priest.'

'And what did he say?' I asked her.

'By that stage, of course, I was over-emotional about it. The frustration of Vanessa's reaction made me sound quite mad. It was so embarrassing. Priests don't dismiss you out of hand, they calm you down. By the time I left him I was as suspicious of my story as he was. And the years went by . . . and a couple of years ago I found this church in Sheringham. I'm so sorry about Barry's behaviour. It made me wonder whether that's the church I should be going to.'

'Why do you go there?'

'I admire his energy. You know what you're in for. And the priests in North Norfolk are usually so staid. But we do need some more men in the congregation, you know.'

I shook my head and Jocelyn smiled.

'I'm not surprised,' she said.

'Why do you go to church at all, Jocelyn?'

'Because I believe in God. Because I'm a Christian.'

'But why specifically a Christian?'

'Perhaps you aren't.'

'Which of us needs to apologise to the other?' I asked her. It was an open question. I didn't know.

'Do you read the Bible?' I saw Jocelyn edging towards her 'Thou shalt not covet,' stance and I didn't like it.

'No, I don't,' I said.

'You should,' said Jocelyn, in a hectoring voice that made me want to go home.

'Give me one and I'll look at it tonight, then, I promise.'

She did, and almost immediately I escaped.

I've always been wary of an attitude among avid Bible readers which assumes that one fair glance from an unprejudiced reader at the Holy Word of God will make him succumb. As an under-graduate I'd always been pestered by the God Squadders – perhaps they considered me fair game, I had a sort of searching-for-the-meaning-of-life look about me. But there is a contented-ness among that set which, far from attracting me, repelled me. It seemed to me that they had prematurely become complete, that there was no room even for debate. They knew something you didn't. They had this magic thing called faith, and you didn't.

So I'm afraid when I sat at my kitchen table with the Revised English Bible in front of me I didn't have the open-mindedness that Jocelyn might have expected of me. I felt that I had before me a book called 'What God Might Have Said Had He Got a Voice: a History'. And this book reminded me not of my own experience with Joanna but of mad bearded men shouting on soapboxes outside supermarkets, telling us we were damned and were on our way to hell.

Then suddenly it reminded me of my mother, and the small black leather Bible she kept on her bedside table. Here she was, creeping upon me unawares. The last time I'd seen my parents was on Boxing Day, almost a year before. I'd written to them in the spring, and had wanted to write to them from Norfolk, but could not have borne, on the other hand, to have received a letter back from them. I saw my mother's heavy hand moving across the page: 'How could you do this to us? How could you do this to your wife and son?' In the end, I hadn't even sent them my address. It suddenly seemed a harsh and undeserving rejection.

So I felt the flimsy paper of the book and thought of her. And I thought of myself by her side in church, and of course, memory doesn't do anyone any favours. I saw her trying to concentrate and holding her head high to hear the sermon, occasionally nodding in silent applause. I saw her dark brown hair clipped tight in tortoiseshell combs, and I felt her squeezing my fingers during moments of enthusiasm. It was absurd, I suddenly loved her so much that I found myself close to tears. I loved her for trying to get me to know God. She would have been my age, she would have been thirty-three, and I was her only son, I belonged to her. Of all the people in the world, she would want to know about Joanna. One day I will write, I determined.

I opened the book up randomly and found myself in the midst of a long family tree; then I began on the first page of Genesis:

> 'In the beginning when God created the heavens and the earth, the earth was a formless void and darkness covered the face of the deep, while a wind from God swept over the face of the waters. Then God said, "Let there be light," and there was light. And God saw the light was good; and God separated the light from the darkness. God called the light Day, and the Darkness he called Night. And there was evening and there was morning, the first day.'

I had no problems with that at all; I thought it was a magnificent beginning. Never had the history of the universe and the role of human beings within it been more succinctly or beautifully put; and I could tell Jocelyn that and our friendship would be sealed. In fact, it was such a relief to me that those first verses were so unproblematical, so brilliant and divinely inspired, that I immediately shut the book up and decided to call it a day. I opened my windows and sang out to the starry heavens, 'Let there be light,' and if I'd had a bottle of champagne I would have opened it. As it was I had a glass of Pernod.

I skirted round that Bible for a couple of hours, because I didn't want to read about the vengeful God who told the priests to put to death men who collected firewood on the Sabbath. I didn't want to be reminded of those astute Jewish lawyers who most likely compiled this document. I wanted to think of God as a wind over the face of the earth. I didn't want Him telling me what kind of locust I could eat in times of famine.

But I took the Bible to bed with me and I opened it again. This time it fell open on St Paul's letter to the Romans. Once more I brought to it all the suppositions of our age, that St Paul taught us to separate mind from body, that St Paul taught us guilt and sexual hang-ups. I settled back against the pillows and attempted to read as though it were all new to me. I was a novice; Paul was a man of God. I would listen to what he had to tell me. So I read:

'For we know that the law is spiritual; but I am of the flesh, sold into slavery under sin.' (I sighed.) 'For I know nothing good dwells within me, that is, in my flesh.' (I sighed some more.) 'I can will what I want, but I cannot do it. For I do not do the good I want, but the evil I do not want is what I do. Now if I do what I do not want, it is no longer I that do it, but sin that dwells within me.'

What is it that drives us to do the very opposite of what we know is right? I leapt out of bed, flung an overcoat over my pyjamas, and walked up the road to a phone box to ring Marion. I would ignore the countless times she'd told me not to phone her at home, and tell her that the weekend she mentioned was fine with me. But as I was fumbling through my diary for her number, relishing such a delightful piece of wickedness, I suddenly remembered that I'd never taken it down.

How delicate is the balance between good and evil. Instead of Marion, it was Jocelyn I rang.

'What are we going to do with Joanna?' I asked her.

Jocelyn said, 'Well, what are we supposed to do? Who would believe us? This is something for us to treasure, alone.'

'You're wrong, Jocelyn. We must do something. I'm going to take her to see the Bishop of Norwich.'

The audience with the Bishop was to be at two o'clock on the following Saturday afternoon. I told the Bishop's secretary that I needed to see His Grace urgently, and I told Joanna and her parents that it would be an enjoyable and educational trip to take a tour round Norwich Cathedral. It was a relief to break our silence with such an innocuous and schoolmasterish suggestion; it wasn't a question of inviting Joanna, rather of telling her what I proposed we should do.

We left at eleven in the morning. We sat so stiffly in the car together, Joanna resolutely preferring the view from her left-hand window to the one in front of her, me quite incapable of beginning a conversation which did not mention the weather. An observer would have imagined we were both there very much against our wills. But the truth was the very opposite: Joanna had never seen a cathedral before, and was so nervous and excited that she couldn't speak, and didn't want to be caught out as the tongue-tied child she was. As for myself, I felt I was about to meet a spiritual king at last, to whom I could confide all, and who would trust my version of events and know exactly how to react to them.

As we came into view of the spire for the first time I was aware of Joanna sitting up straight, her eyes transfixed by what she saw, and she whispered, 'Did they build this?' The dear girl's mouth hung open, and she followed that spire with her fiery eyes even as I parked the car and we made our way towards it on foot. As we entered the nave, the colours streaming down from the west window above us, Joanna seemed younger even than her years; her body appeared weightless as though she were dancing; her face lost any wisp of self-consciousness. We looked up together at the soaring height of this place, and we drank in the whiteness, the columns and the arches, the vaulted roof studded with silver bosses. I noticed that the fragile girl began shaking, and I stood behind her and put my hands on her shoulders.

She walked slowly up the nave and I followed her, and the deeper we entered the further back in time we seemed to go. I know that Joanna and I were both conscious of it: it was as though even at that moment the monks were chanting the office in the misericords, the high altar was ablaze with candles, and the old abbot sat on his throne, presiding over all. Joanna knelt for a few moments, and she began swaying and I fancied her eyes were rolling backwards and she was on the verge of entering a trance: I remembered too late that this was the scene of the dreadful visions of Julian of Norwich, in which she endured the passion of Christ, and I was anxious in case Joanna would follow suit. So I took her by the hand and made her get up, and said to her quite firmly, 'Let me show you the chapels, Joanna.'

I was thankful that she didn't object, and when I took her to the ambulatory I was relieved to find that her mood was quite different. She surveyed the pictures and engravings and hidden niches with the joy of a granddaughter visiting her beloved grandfather's old house. The whiteness of the nave had given way to a shadowy haven behind the choir, lit only by a hundred candles placed there by those who'd made petitions for their loved ones; and by these Joanna suddenly stopped. She began to read the petitions that had been left there by worried relatives and friends: John Doyle, the father of four young girls, who'd recently been diagnosed with cancer; a daughter, Carrie, eighteen years old, in a coma after a road accident; a baby who'd been born with a hole in his heart. Joanna began mumbling, and moved her hand to and fro over the candles, and I knew in my heart that a hundred miracles would come to pass that day.

Joanna retained a certain lightness of spirit when I took her to the Bauchon Lady Chapel; and as she saw and recognised each image, that lightness became ever more akin to joy. She rejoiced in the window there; not with the sense of awe which I had noticed when she looked up at the great west window in the nave, but rather with the familiarity of a girl enjoying a photograph album, and pointing out her various aunts and uncles. 'Look at Herbert,' she said, and laughed, referring to the first Bishop of Norwich; and then she mentioned by name other leading members of the order of St Benedict, and said how much she liked them all, as though they were all very much alive. 'But my favourite, of course, is Julian,' she smiled. And there indeed, was Julian at prayer.

'Tell me,' I said, 'Julian. Did you know, do you know . . .' But Joanna wasn't listening to me, she was now utterly absorbed by a painting behind the altar. It depicted the Adoration of the Magi, three foreign kings presenting their gifts to the baby Jesus. I could see that it filled her to the brim, and tears began streaming down her face, and she said, 'It's so wonderful. You see, they knew, didn't they? Those kings knew they were paying homage to the Son of God.'

Then Joanna turned away from the Magi and saw for the first time a painting of the baby Jesus being carried on a white blanket by an old, bearded man.

'This is Simeon,' she exclaimed, 'he's presenting Jesus in the Temple. See how filled he is with the Holy Spirit, see how he witnesses the revelation of Christ. "Now lettest Thou Thy servant depart in peace, according to Thy word. Now I am ready to welcome death," he says.'

I'm afraid I have to confess here that in the midst of her ecstatic praise of everything she saw I was feeling ever more excluded and dismayed. The closer she seemed to breaking into song, the more she irritated me. These phrases she bandied about like all Christians, all this Holy Spirit lark, froze me up, they were words I couldn't understand or connect to. The God I knew didn't need this great panoply of attendants. I don't know quite what I was expecting of her. In fact, so keen was I to see the Bishop that I hadn't really considered this little tour of ours as being more than an excuse and a distraction. And I'm afraid, ungodly as it might seem, her insider-pleasure grated on me. It was time to show her a picture of the Crucifixion.

I thought that any would do. But the one I found was rather conveniently in the chapel next door, St Luke's Chapel. Behind the altar was a medieval reredos made up of five wooden panels: in the first Christ was being scourged, in the second, he was carrying his cross. The third and central panel was the finest: Christ was being crucified, and John the Baptist was comforting Mary in the foreground, while supercilious Roman soldiers looked on. In the fourth, Christ was raised from the dead, and the final panel showed his ascension to heaven. 'What do you think, Joanna?' I said to her pompously. What exactly was I expecting from her? A thankfully sobered spirit? An exposition on the virtues of medieval painting?

Her grief was so great – or at least, at that time I took it for grief – that I may as well have shown a child a picture of her dead father or, worse, a picture of her father being tortured. Joanna began sobbing so convulsively that her knees gave way and she sank to the ground, and I couldn't see for the life of me how I could comfort her: already tourists were popping their heads in to see what the commotion was about, and I had to shrug my shoulders apologetically.

'Joanna, please,' I began. 'This all happened a very long time ago, and anyway, it had such a happy ending. Look at this, Joanna, he's waving from the tomb, he's alive. Look, he came back to life.'

But Joanna sobbed all the more, and at last a guide, paternal and sensible and with all those other qualities of the good guide, came up and asked us if anything was the matter. I laughed and blushed and explained that some of these paintings were quite overwhelming for a child. I patted Joanna on the back and showed how hopeless it was to attempt to comfort her; and the guide, I think, who had initially been rather proud that his Cathedral could elicit such a response in anyone, became rather more alarmed, and asked me if I was her father.

'Actually, I'm her teacher,' I said.

'Would she like a glass of water? Perhaps if . . . I think our other visitors . . . she's crying quite loudly. We could sit in the verger's office a while and make a cup of tea.' The guide bent his head and smiled at Joanna, and asked her if she'd like an ice cream.

'I'm so sorry,' blubbed Joanna, 'I'll be all right in a minute.'

So the guide and I were quite patient, and told each other what a magnificent cathedral it was while we waited for Joanna to be herself again, or should I say, forget herself. And finally she did.

We said goodbye to our new friend, who insisted we come and find him should we have any questions, and sat down in the monks' cloister outside. The fresh air was a relief to both of us, and we sat on the stone seat looking out on to the grassy court-yard. It was now half past one, a mere half hour before our audi-ence with the bishop, and still I hadn't confessed to Joanna the real purpose of our visit. Her eyes were red with crying, and I suggested we had a sandwich in a little coffee shop I'd noticed, but she said she wasn't hungry.

'Your parents seemed quite happy I should take you here,' I said to her, breaking an uneasy silence.

'My mother thinks you're a very important person,' said Joanna, almost accusingly.

'Yes, she did say that, didn't she,' I laughed, as though I'd only just remembered it. 'So how is your mother? How is her fortune-telling? Is she getting a few clients?'

'She hasn't tried.'

'Do you think she has a gift?'

'Why don't you ask me about Jesus?'

'I don't want to upset you. Let's face it, Joanna, you've just been rather emotional, to say the least.'

'Ask me,' she insisted.

So I went right for the centre of things, at point-blank range. 'Was Jesus the Son of God?' I demanded.

'Mary was a virgin. The conception of Jesus was a miracle.'

'And was God his father?'

'Not in the same way as you're a father.'

And thus Joanna took a swipe at me, which I suppose I deserved. All I knew was that I'd never told her about Joe.

'How did you know?' How weak and pathetic I sounded, like a guilty schoolboy.

'Tell me about your son.'

'How did you know, Joanna? Do you read minds, then, too?'

'No, I don't read minds. It was you who put the thought into my head, I promise.'

'What is the difference between an angel and a demon? Perhaps you're a demon.'

'I'm neither, Mr German.'

'You don't have to call me "Mr German". Why are you suddenly so irritating?'

'I'm sorry, Mr German.'

I thought, why am I talking to her like this? What a morose pair we made. At five to two I told Joanna we had an appointment with the Bishop, and she did not demur. At this stage I was no longer tweaking my lame excuses, which in my head had always begun, 'By some extraordinary piece of good luck, the Bishop happens to be here . . .' In fact, I managed to make it sound as if we were visiting the dentist, so that any objection on her part would have seemed churlish and unreasonable.

We left the cloisters and walked across the close in silence. It was strange to leave the magic of that place behind, and rejoin the world again outside the west gate, as we made our way to the Bishop's house.

'It's forbidden to cross the Bishop's gardens,' the gatekeeper had told us. My temper was as unholy as the Bussy's Ford Garage that we walked by, and the Dunn's Taxi Company. The air was thick and claustrophobic, and I looked at Joanna askance, and wondered who it was I was taking to see the Bishop. A fine actress? An expert gamester? A witch? Or simply her mother's daughter? And the Bishop wasn't even expecting her. All he knew was the URGENT written by my name in the appointment book.

The Bishop's house was a mock-Georgian affair built in ugly brick, though a former Bishop, a Percy Mark Herbert, had been quite happy to have his name engraved on a foundation stone in 1958. I rang the bell and it made a tinny sound, not quite serious, and a young man with a floppy fringe and glasses opened the door.

'Patrick German?' was the only greeting he gave us, and he barely registered Joanna at all. Immediately opposite us in an office was a lady at a word processor. She didn't even look up. Our escort, who I decided was probably a theology student doing a Saturday job, brusquely shut the office door in case, so it seemed to me, we might catch sight of something deadly secret. He knocked at the Bishop's door on the right with all the firm authority which one would hope for in an aspiring cleric, and thus we met our man.

I understood at once that we hadn't called at a particularly propitious moment. The Bishop was sitting at his desk, feverishly writing something – perhaps a sermon for the following day – and he didn't even bother to turn round to acknowledge us, but rather lifted his pen-wielding hand for just a second to make plain that he was in mid-flow and should not be interrupted.

Joanna and I sat on rather stiff upholstered chairs while we waited for him to finish. I didn't dare catch her eye for fear her expression might pose questions I couldn't answer. I noticed a modern prie-dieu by the window, which startled me, not only because someone, somewhere, was still eking out a living by making such objects (and it was well made, in white ash), but also because it was quite evident that the Bishop knelt down at this strange piece of furniture in order to pray. I thought of him looking out at his garden while he did so, or reading from the Bible, perhaps. I imagined his purple back hunched over it, which wasn't too difficult, as that was the view he was still offering us even then.

'I'm so sorry to have kept you,' beamed the Bishop, suddenly swinging round to join us, 'but I did want to be able to give you my full attention.' He briefly glanced at a typed sheet on his desk. 'Mr German. And your daughter?' He stood up and offered me his hand, which I stood up to receive. 'How can I be of service?'

The Bishop resumed his seat and surveyed us professionally, if benignly. He was about sixty, with thinning grey hair and a craggy face. He was looking at us over half-moon glasses, which I've always found rather unnerving.

'It's always good,' I began, 'to see that a man can still be inspired.'

'I'm sorry?' said the Bishop.

'You seem so inspired.'

'I don't quite catch you.'

'When you write. You know, your pen was just running off the page.'

'Oh yes. Yes, I do write quite quickly I suppose.'

'Was that a sermon you were writing?'

'Well, actually, yes, as it so happens.'

'It must be a good one.'

'I'm sorry?'

'A good sermon.'

'Well, of course I hope it won't send them all to sleep.' The Bishop laughed a well-worn laugh. 'Now why are you here, Mr German? And your daughter, what's your name?'

'She's not my daughter.'

'Joanna,' said Joanna.

'She's my pupil,' I explained.

'And is there a query you have? Is there something you'd like to ask me? The Bible is often a puzzling book, and I should know,' and the Bishop smiled a well-worn smile.

'It's rather difficult to explain,' I began. 'Perhaps I should have come alone.'

'Perhaps *I* should have come alone,' said Joanna.

'Do you have something you'd like to tell me, Joanna?'

'Yes,' she said, 'there's something I'd like to tell you very much. Perhaps we could take a walk in the garden.'

'Well, if that's all right with you,' said the Bishop, looking at me and raising his eyebrows, 'I don't see why not. Do you like gardens, Joanna?'

'I do, very much,' she said, and she stood up and gave the Bishop her arm.

'We won't be long,' the Bishop told me. 'You know, I could do with a post-prandial walk. Good for the digestion.'

The Bishop gave me a friendly wink and the *Daily Telegraph*. 'So where do you come from, Joanna?' were the last words I heard before they left the house, and I wondered, 'Where indeed?'

From his study I watched the great purple form of the Bishop unlock the garden gate. Joanna ducked under his arm and went

133

ahead. Then from another window I caught sight of them again, as they paused a while by a Christmas rose or some other winter flower. Already the sun was beginning to set, and I looked away feeling I was intruding, and tried to concentrate on the paper he'd given me, and summon up some appropriate reaction to the debacle of the American General Election and the floods swamping Britain. When I looked again I couldn't see them, and after a few minutes that seemed hours I went outside to find them, though I didn't know what excuse I'd give for my fervent curiosity. The garden gate was locked, however, and I felt momentarily jealous and angry that they should have excluded me like this. Then a moment later I saw them through the wire netting bolted up against the window of the ruined Priory. They were kneeling side by side among some lichen-covered stones; perhaps the place is still consecrated, I thought. The Bishop was bowed down, his hands in the traditional attitude of prayer, while Joanna seemed intent on the racing clouds above her, and the cupped palms of her hands were raised upwards, like a supplicant's. She was praying, holding a single musical note, but I couldn't catch her words, and even if I had I would have felt as if I were eavesdropping. She was praying for the Bishop, and the Bishop alone.

Suddenly the Bishop fell down on to the grass, and I heard the man's voice shout out, deep and hoarse, but I couldn't tell whether in joy or in pain.

I was embarrassed and turned away. I tried to get back into the house but the latch had locked it. Then behind me I heard the garden gate open; and I heard them walking towards me over the gravel. I looked round, blushing, fumbling.

'This girl,' the Bishop told me, his face hollowed out by emotion, 'has been sent by God.'

# 9

IT IS A VERY PECULIAR EXPERIENCE to teach a class in which one of the pupils has been sent by God. Particularly one who, to judge from a level of sullenness quite unprecedented, was not a little unhappy.

There were three days left until the end of term and the Christmas holidays. No one was concentrating. The children for some reason spent their lessons eating crisps, and they all insisted quite adamantly that they could bring in party food all week. I played hangman with them; Freckola Nicola brought in her karaoke set and they all sang to Boyzone tunes. I had no spirit either to raise the tenor of things or resist them and insist they got on with some geography. During the greater part of their rendition of 'No matter where you follow, no matter where you lead,' I sat behind my desk in a sort of stupor. Meanwhile, Joanna drifted on the edge of the action. She had never been one to draw attention to herself.

Of course, I was always looking for opportunities to confront Joanna, but even in the car as we drove back from Norwich together I never found a way of breaking the silence. 'So then, what's it like up there?' was the first question that wanted to break out of my mundane head. But though I was certain of the question, I was uncertain of the tone in which it should be asked. How I longed for some kind of spontaneity I could trust in. Instead, I confess, I felt a peevish jealousy of the Bishop, and I didn't doubt they had had a very jolly multi-referential chat about the Bible. But my questions were the questions of a child, and I'm ashamed now that I was ashamed then to ask them. Manly pride is not a virtue.

And these questions kept on multiplying. Tell me, Joanna, do you know God? Does He speak English? Or in heaven do you forget about language altogether and communicate telepathically? Can you see God? What's heaven like, anyway? Is it just a whole load of dead good people saying 'Hi' when they see someone they recognise? And above all, why, Joanna, did He send you here? If God sent you, he did so for a purpose. You have a mission on earth, Joanna. Can you tell me, if you know it, what it is? But I asked her nothing. She must have thought, sometimes, I was the worst disciple she could have chosen.

In fact, how to address Joanna at all was becoming a real problem. Should I genuflect a little when handing her back a piece of work? Should I ask her to make a presentation to the class? It was so difficult to pretend that none of this had ever happened. We neither of us could behave naturally anymore, and when we each of us made some attempt to do so, it seemed artificial. I was gloomy indeed when Jocelyn came to find me at my desk in break.

'Oh,' she said.

I apologised for the empty crisp packets and half-eaten chocolate biscuits.

'Don't worry about that,' she said, 'I want to know about Joanna. I gather it wasn't a success.'

'Who told you?'

'No one told me. But look at you.'

'I'm sorry?'

'You don't exactly look like you've had good news.'

'No, it was good, it was very good!' I tried to sound pleased. 'It was too good.'

'What did he say? Did he believe you?'

'Joanna told him herself.'

'What did she tell him?'

'I wasn't there.'

'But you must know what she said. Didn't the Bishop tell you?'

'The Bishop told me Joanna had been sent by God.' My voice was very flat.

'Oh my God,' said Jocelyn. 'Oh praise be! Oh praise be! I just knew it! In my bones I knew!' And dear Jocelyn was so over-whelmed by the good news that she positively skipped out of the classroom to join the children in the playground – no, my leaden heart couldn't hold her back – and from the window I watched her teaching them how to do a Scottish reel.

After break the din got even worse, but I was hardly aware of it. I could see Joanna through the corner of my eye, as though my sight were the only sense left to me. Her face so pale this morning, though red about the eyes, her hair held back even more tightly away from her face, that I wondered it didn't hurt her. She was sitting on a desk in the midst of this furore, as though this was where she might be more unobtrusively alone. Joanna, sent by God, dangling her feet and hanging her head. How can I sing when you don't, Joanna? What are you doing here?

I looked down at my mended hand and tried to find the place where the wound had been. There was now not even a mark: I regretted that I hadn't taken more notice of it, that I hadn't caught the final moment, when the final damaged cells had been shed and I had become perfectly whole again. I should have had a cross tatooed at the very place, to remind me.

Perhaps God had sent us Joanna to reduce NHS waiting lists. She could run a miracle surgery. We could put her in charge of the Accident and Emergency Department of Norwich General Hospital – wouldn't that be the equivalent of Jesus setting up a clinic at a well-known stable in Bethlehem? 'Let me give you a new hip,' she would say, 'let me sew up that wound. Let me give you ears to hear with and eyes to see with.' Then all the cured would go home and go to church and spread the word. I laughed and thought of Barry Chuck. No one would believe them. God, this little mission You've devised is a waste of time. Look at this girl. She's not up to it, God.

'Are you blind, are you deaf?' Mr Birch was addressing me. I thought he might have just addressed the class. It was their noise, after all. But it worked. Within a moment they were all as quiet as lambs.

'It's Christmas,' I explained, with a distinct lack of joy.

'What's all this mess, it's disgusting. Ralph, what are you eating?'

'It's a Rocky, sir. With caramel, look.' The class tittered.

'Who told you that you could bring in food?' thundered our headmaster.

'He did, sir,' said Ralph, betraying me.

'I didn't.'

'You did, sir,' said the class in unison.

'I meant on Wednesday. I meant on the last day.'

'You didn't complain, sir. We even offered you some. You didn't say to stop eating. We'd have stopped if you told us to, sir.'

Birch looked at me. 'Did you?'

'Did I what?'

'Have you tried to maintain any discipline this morning whatsoever?'

'No, sir,' I said, restored immediately to my inner child. 'Not very much, sir.'

The class laughed, and I laughed with them. Ah, irreverence is so sweet. Mr Birch was understandably furious, and demanded I see him after school.

Mr Birch had the headmasterly knack of turning anyone he spoke to into a child of ten. Thank God they've done away with corporal punishment, I thought, as I went into his office. I was surprised to find him still quivering with anger.

'So how have you found your first term, Mr German?'

'Good. Good.' I nodded, demurely.

'No problems?'

I made a grand theatrical attempt at looking pensive, my chin lifting, my eyes slitting. 'No, no problems,' I said.

'No problems with discipline?'

'No, no. In fact I would say that every member of my class without exception has excellent manners. Joanna, in particular, is an angel.'

'I remember you being rather taken with her a while ago.'

'I'm very much taken with her, yes, sir.'

'You don't call me "sir".'

'I'll make a deal with you. You don't call me Mr German, and I won't call you "sir".

'You know I have to write a report of your progress here for the governors of the school. You have only just qualified. You are in your probationary year.'

'I hope you manage to write a fair report.'

'You're not happy here, are you?'

'Happiness, happiness,' I sighed. What a great actor I might have been. '"For all the happiness mankind can gain/Is not in pleasure but in rest from pain."'

'Have you considered counselling?' asked Mr Birch, diplomatically.

'Why should I need counselling when there is an angel in my midst?'

'Oh, for God's sake. You have a problem. Confront it!'

'I don't have a problem. I have an anti-problem. I'm going to be saved.'

'Mr German, I'm going to give you a telephone number. Marjorie Phipps. She's the on-site counsellor at Cromer comprehensive. If you don't see her by the end of this week I'll have to take it that you're not committed to teaching, if you get my drift.'

'Perfectly, sir.' I smiled, and the stage direction said, 'unfath-omably'.

Somehow I managed to slither blindly on until the end of term, avoiding Mr Birch's anger, Marion's desire ('Friday night,' she kept whispering) and Jocelyn's incessant hymn-humming. Marion told me she was convinced that Jocelyn had got herself a man, but I knew better. On Wednesday, the last day of term, I got the class to sing a few carols. I wrote out 'Away in a manger, no crib for a bed' on the blackboard, and the class sang so loudly that Mr Birch came in and thrust a note into my hand. 'M. Phipps. Thursday 5 pm. Cromer. See her or you're out.' As for Joanna, she couldn't take it, she just ran away. Later, I looked for her in the cloakroom, but she wasn't there. I told the class she wasn't feeling well and I'd sent her home. I thought of her praying. I thought, 'She'll be all right.'

I rather welcomed that five o'clock appointment on the following day. It was a good excuse to get up from the kitchen table, where I'd been sitting in a catatonic state since the postman delivered a letter from my mother, asking me to spend Christmas with them. Oh, it was short, and friendly, and to the point, her only accusation being that she'd got my address from Margaret. No mention of Kitty or Joe. Just sending me 'so much love'. That was all.

Now, Marjorie Phipps didn't love me, nor I her. Not that she said anything in this vein, but it was obvious she had Christmas shopping on her mind. She was doing me a favour. It was the holidays. She was doing Mr Birch a favour. She was there in that claustrophobic over-heated room on sufferance. And I was there as a distraction, I was there for fun.

She smiled, but her eyes weren't in it, and I thought, how much nicer it would be to be with Marion at this moment, who really would smile, and would be hinting with every muscle of her body at the pleasures to come. But I didn't even fancy

Marjorie. Though I was working at it. I kept not so much undressing her as redressing her. I put her in silk and chiffon, I put her in a Wonderbra, I put her in black cashmere. For the woman was in a grey two-piece suit, relieved only by a little salmon scarf at her neck. And though she might have been pretty once, or pretty for someone else, she wasn't pretty for me, and quite frankly she didn't like me, it was quite clear.

'I hope,' said Miss Phipps, 'that you want to be here.'

'Oh yes,' I said, enthusiastically, 'I certainly do. I couldn't think of a place in England where I would rather be. Today. At five o'clock.'

'So why are you here? I don't normally take referrals from other people.'

I wanted to tell her that her hair didn't quite suit her. I wanted to tell her that it was too long, and the curls didn't flatter her face, and made her look tired. Or perhaps she was tired.

'Why am I here? Isn't that a rather large existential question to kick off with? Couldn't you start with my favourite flavour ice-cream?'

'Why are you here, Patrick? You don't mind if I call you Patrick?'

'Seeing as we are on the verge of becoming so close, not at all.'

Ms Phipps sighed and looked as if she were considering getting up to leave.

'Why am I here? I tell you, I haven't a clue. Do other people know? It's a very strange, unknowable world. Do people really know what they're doing living in it? Ms Phipps, I don't have the first idea, you've hit the nail absolutely and squarely on the head. I don't know.'

'I believe you're married.'

'Yes, and I made my vows before God.'

'And are you happily married?'

'Hey, wasn't God called Counsellor? What's that bit from *The Messiah*, you know it – I can't sing very well, but I'll open my mouth and I shall try, Ms Phipps.

'"For unto us a child is born, unto us a son is given: And the Government shall be upon his shoulder: And his name shall be called Wonderful, Counsellor, the mighty God . . ."'

'I sang that at school once. I was a tenor, I was a rather good tenor. Have you ever sung in a choir? Have you ever known what it's like to be part of something bigger than yourself?'

'Are you happily married, Patrick?'

'You know I'm not. I'm separated.'

'Are you happily separated then?'

'Oh no. I would say that I'm more happily married than happily separated.'

'At last, we're getting somewhere.'

'What does the word Counsellor mean? Does it mean you're supposed to give me counsel?'

'You can go home, you know. I'm not keeping you here against your will.'

'It's absolutely my will to be here. You might not know it, but you've already clarified a couple of issues that were lurking insolubly in the brain. Can you sing, Ms Phipps?'

'I don't think that's relevant.'

'I would say it's profoundly relevant.'

'Patrick, I don't know you, and you won't let me know you. Why are you so terrified of being known?'

'Did you know that I already know infinitely more about you than you know about me? You keep looking at your watch. You're desperate to go.'

'You're right. I think you're wasting my time.'

'But my time is yours, Ms Phipps. We should make a pact, to give each other this hour, in good faith.'

'I'm told you're under stress at the moment. I would have liked it if you had been able to tell me that yourself.'

'But I'm not under stress. Look at me. Look how floppy my arms are, look how my head is all floppy too. There's not an ounce of tension about me. But I must tell you something incredibly exciting. Did you know that there's a God? It's quite an extraordinary thing. I never would have guessed.'

'You shouldn't be here at all. You should be in a church.'

'Oh no,' I said, quite insistent, 'I can't pray, you see, I've tried it and I can't get into the swing. You can't think what a bad effect this is having on me. There's even an angel in my class, a dear thing, a sweet sensitive creature who keeps crying, or I think she does. Her eyes are always red nowadays. And you'd think it possible, wouldn't you, with an angel sitting in front of you all day, and a God sitting above you, to make some decent attempt at a prayer? Why can't I, Ms Phipps? What's my problem?'

'I don't think you should be in teaching. In my professional opinion, you are under stress.'

'But I've got rather good at teaching.'

'You are aware that your job is on the line?'

'Then it shouldn't be. Just because this week the children seem to have become rather ebullient. Mr Birch over-reacted. Have you seen him recently? I noticed he was looking very stiff-necked yesterday. It's he who should be here, not me. But if I were you I wouldn't want to be instrumental in either of us losing our jobs on account of a little stress. It's part and parcel of the job, wouldn't you think? Particularly at Christmas.'

Ms Phipps looked at me and then at her watch. She obviously felt relieved at a possible cue to let her go.

'You need to take care of yourself. I do think you need help, but I'm obviously not the right person to help you.'

'I'm sorry,' I said to her seriously, 'I was hoping you could.'

She flinched at my earnestness, but was happy to shrug off the whole interview. 'You're right,' she said, 'Christmas is a difficult time.'

Last Christmas, I'd been with Kitty and Joe, my boy Joe. Not that I in any way wished to repeat that little coterie. In fact, if anything, I was rather jollier now without them. That was the state of things then, and this is the state of things now. There seems no point in confusing them. But I confess, memory, memory . . . if not one's own then other people's, forces one to return to what has been, to look deep down into the spilt milk as though great mysteries lay therein. There was no mystery here. There was never a day when I stopped loving my wife. If we had ever trotted off together to a Relate counsellor, I would have told her I was married to a dream, that I didn't deserve her, that I didn't have the energy within me to keep hold of her, or of my life as it was, or of my son. I had lost my will. I had become a passenger.

I keep my big blue suitcase under my bed. You see, even my suitcase conspires against me, and insists on history, on continuity. Perhaps it'll come with me, on Christmas morning, and the year will suddenly collapse like a concertina, and Kitty and Joe will greet me as though we'd only missed each other since breakfast.

It's Friday, the 21st of December, two thousand years after the birth of Jesus Christ. I'm lying on my bed as tensed up as a mummy. I'm uncertain how to release myself, how to begin flowing again. It's cold, and I'm shivering, but I can't even relax my limbs sufficiently to get myself under the blankets. I have images of Kitty, and Joanna, even Ms Phipps, quite naked now, but I can't shift myself. Then I remember Marion, I remember her scent as she whispered 'Friday night,' I remember desire. Now Marion loves me. Though what that has to do with it I'm not sure.

Why is sin so delicious? Why are the lips of an adulterer so sweet? Marion took one look at my pitiful face on her doorstep and pitied me, invited me in, hinted that she'd prefer to spend

144

the weekend at my house, but I could only murmur, walking cliché that I was, 'I want you now.'

'I've been so starved of you,' whispered Marion.

'Thank you,' I said.

'Did you miss me?'

'Oh yes,' I said.

'You've not been looking yourself lately. You seem so wan, so distracted. Is anything wrong?'

'Let's talk later, Marion.'

'You know, I didn't think you'd come. Sometimes I don't feel you responding to me. Sometimes I think you're avoiding me.'

I tried kissing her to stop her from talking, but failed.

'I know you don't love me. I don't expect you to love me.'

I kissed her some more.

'You're so tense, Patrick! I'm going to give you a very deep massage.'

She made me lie on the grubby carpet of her sitting-room floor. It wasn't right, we had both decided, to defile the marital bed, and though Marion had sweetly offered towels for me to lie on, I said that sounded rather clinical. So I lay there with my shirt off and my trousers loose, the carpet faintly itchy with dog-hair, a view under her sofa of a half-inch layer of dust and a few stray Lego pieces, with Marion concocting little remedies for my obvious malaise. 'Ah,' she said, 'we'll soon get you right, my darling. I shall burn some lemon balm and some sage. We'll soon get you right.'

I'm aware that some women complain we treat them as objects. But grammatically speaking, they always are objects. 'I desire you' has a subject and an object. 'I want to fuck you' has a subject and an object. I grabbed at one of her bottles and found some oil of rose, which I uncorked and began liberally pouring over her breasts and stomach. 'No,' she exclaimed, 'No, please.' She laughed, and told me that it was £14 a bottle and was really for faces, and I said something corny like, 'You're worth it,' with such a rare display of style that she actually believed me and lay back for me, giving me all, becoming absolutely the object of a man's dreams. I possessed Marion till about half past eleven. Then we sat on the sofa together and Marion smoked her first cigarette in ten days.

Now I have to confess that by this stage of the proceedings I was rather tired, and we hadn't quite hammered out where we were going to sleep. The marital bed was naturally forbidden – even we sinners had our scruples; and the sofa-bed in the boxroom was covered in books. The sitting-room, had for me, at least, lost its romantic tinge, and the last thing I wanted to do was drive Marion to my little bastion of purity in Beeston. Then there was this business of de-objectifying Marion, of letting all her annoying idiosyncrasies emerge again to reunite her with personhood.

'What a lovely smell,' I said.

'I know. Actually it's my recipe,' purred Marion. 'Lemon and sage together are something rather special, I think. Would you like some coffee? Or whisky?'

'Some coffee would be great,' I said.

'Would instant do?' asked Marion.

'Oh yes.'

'We haven't really eaten. Can I get you a cheese sandwich?'

'No thanks.'

'Well I'll make one for me and you can have a bite of mine.'

'Okay,' I said.

No sooner had she left the room than I fell fast asleep on the sofa, or at least, that's the plan I hit upon. She would find me, take pity on me, and let me be, or perhaps even cover me with a blanket, while she went upstairs alone. But when she came back she sat next to me and began whimpering, 'Please don't be asleep. Patrick, wake up, it's not fair, don't sleep yet, I'll make the bed up for us in the box room, or we can sleep together in one of the twins' beds. The sheets are quite clean. Come upstairs with me. Let me take you upstairs, my darling.'

When I half-opened my eyes I was appalled to find she had prepared a little tray of goodies, even to the extent of cutting up celery and carrot sticks and serving them with a fancy dish of mayonnaise. And worse, she had reapplied her lipstick, which from my state of semi-consciousness seemed as bright as a hundred-watt bulb.

My half-opened eyes were greeted with such effusions of joy that she told me she was going to put on some music.

'It's not as if we have to get up early tomorrow,' she said, rifling through her CDs to find something 'mellow'. 'The weekend is all our own. Perhaps we shall go for a walk by the sea. Perhaps we should even sleep on the beach tomorrow. I haven't done that for years, Patrick.'

I was pretending to be asleep again. What else can one do *in extremis*?

'Oh Patrick, you really are tired,' she conceded, and I was pushed up the stairs like an octogenarian, and put to bed. Marion and I in a single bed, Action Men all over the duvet, her alien body pawing me: it was a sort of hell-zone. To make matters worse, there was a night light on the bedside table, and Marion insisted she couldn't find the switch. I mumbled, 'Aren't your children a bit old to have a nightlight? Pinocchio with a glowing nose, godammit? Aren't they about twelve?'

'They're only ten,' said Marion brightly. 'Pinocchio's a sort of childhood security blanket for them. I'm afraid he's always switched on.'

'Can't you switch him off at the wall?'

'I'll try,' she said, shuffling and shoving. 'I'm afraid you'll have to get out of bed. The bed's blocking it.'

'Forget it,' I said.

'You're angry, aren't you?' she said, 'But don't blame me.

147

You're the one who needs to get out of bed, and look at you, you're like an old sack of potatoes. It's not even midnight. Do I bore you that much?'

Of course I ignored her, and affected a slight snore. She sighed and turned her back to me; and half-way through the night I slunk away into the blissful solitude of the bed next to it.

At breakfast the following morning Marion told me that she thought my problem was 'us'. She said that she loved me all the more for my deep-seated morality, my feeling that 'committing adultery' (and she whispered the offending words) proved so problematical. Well, it was for her too, she said. This was her first affair. This was the first time she'd been in love since she was a teenager, she'd never thought her heart was still capable of it.

'Don't you mean soul?' I asked her.

'Oh Patrick, you're so spiritual. I don't know what happens during marriage. Why do we become so routine with each other? Sometimes I wonder whether I ever really loved Dominic in the first place, though that's a terrible thing to say. Of course I did. Well, I do. It would be terrible to split up. And the children.'

It was only nine o'clock. Already I felt a great weariness setting in, but I was too lethargic to escape. The only thing I could think of doing was slipping off Marion's dressing-gown, and that killed a couple of hours at least. Then Marion had her second cigarette in ten days.

Finally I understood what I had to do.

'Marion, I can't endure this, I'm so sorry. We're both married. It's not right. We also teach in the same school. It's not even professional.'

'What's professionalism got to do with it?' she blubbed, 'You've never been professional. That's why I love you.'

'Perhaps I'm just making excuses. But it's not right, is it? You're about to spend Christmas with your family, with the parents of your husband. We must stop this, Marion.'

I let Marion cry on to my shoulder, and I patted her back. 'I'm so sorry,' I murmured.

Then I left her and went back to my cottage. There was driving rain at the window, and I hoped she'd think it wasn't walking weather anyway. We wouldn't have had much fun. But I knew, of course I knew (in my heart, in my soul, who cares?) that she'd be crying, and I did briefly wonder if things might have been different.

They say that sleep is necessary for the brain to restore itself, in which case I dreaded to think how many hours short I was of such nirvana. I was like a radio so sensitive to every frequency that I couldn't be tuned, I couldn't stay with any one of them. I couldn't hear the jumble in my own head, the competing messages. I hid in my bed and closed my eyes and concentrated on the rain. When I drifted into sleep I dreamed that my Joe was crawling up the aisle of Beeston church and talking quite happily to the spirit of a dead girl wearing pale pink shoes and ribbons in her hair, and they were saying to each other, 'Of course, he can't pray, can he? Such a shame.' My Joe, sitting like a little Buddha on the marble gravestone in the floor.

By the time the night came I had done with sleeping. Suddenly my bedroom turned from a haven to a prison. At two in the morning I was drinking black tea in the kitchen; at three I was standing shivering on my doorstep, pleading with the wind to blow some sense into me; at four I opened the Bible and read a few psalms; but by five my longing for God was as acute as ever. At six I decided to try singing the psalms, 'As a deer longs for flowing streams, so my soul thirsts for you, O God,' but I didn't know a tune, and I shrunk back at the sound of my own voice, grating and ugly. By seven I was back in my bed, counting shadows. Then at eight o'clock, on Christmas Eve morning, there was a knock at the door.

It was Joanna with her mother.

Joanna's mother had a new coiffure and had dressed herself

in a brown tweed suit like a county lady. She smiled and looked like a gypsy again, her blackening teeth betraying her, her smile too broad.

'I hope we haven't woken you, but it's Sunday, and we wanted to catch you before church.'

Joanna stood calm and impenetrable at her side.

'We wanted to show you this letter. It makes a mother so proud. May we come in?'

It crossed my mind that I was thankful I had slept, or not slept, in my clothes; and I tucked my shirt in and tried to look like Mr German, the man in whom she had shown such confidence.

'Of course you must come in,' I said. 'Come and have some tea. Joanna, do you drink tea?' She declined most gracefully and said she would like a glass of water, and I thought, typical that an angel should prefer water, and then I considered that I'd never actually seen her eat. It somehow seemed incongruous that she would ever even open a packet of prawn cocktail crisps, and I asked her if she'd already had breakfast.

'I'm not hungry,' she said, and I thought, I knew it, she doesn't eat.

'There's chocolate in the cupboard,' I said, in a tone to test all children. But Joanna looked at me with such non-comprehension of my little game with her that I had to look away. I told them to sit down in the sitting-room while I boiled the kettle in the delightful privacy of the kitchen. 'We've some very exciting news for you,' called Mrs Wells from next door, while I was waiting for her tea-bag to take full effect.

'One moment,' I called back, wondering whether the mysterious buoyancy of the tea-bag had anything to do with the company I was keeping.

I came into the sitting-room to find Mrs Wells stationed like a queen on the only armchair.

'Your tea, Mrs Wells,' I said. 'Your water, Joanna.' Joanna was perched on the edge of the sofa, and I was obliged, therefore, to sit next to her. I watched her sip, and I wanted to tell her, 'Go on, if you're thirsty, gulp it down.'

'You're not having one yourself, then?'

'I've just had my breakfast cuppa,' I lied. ('Breakfast cuppa'? Who was I kidding?)

'I think we should get straight to the point, don't you think, Joanna? We, or I should say, Joanna, got a letter from the Bishop yesterday, inviting her to give a talk on Christmas Day. He's asked my Joanna to sit in the Bishop's Chair in Norwich Cathedral itself. And she's only ten, Mr German. You must be ever such a good teacher. She said she managed to have a chat with him the other day. I'm so excited. She'll do it so well, I know. I'm only sorry you can't come to see her yourself.'

'But . . . probably . . .'

'Joanna says you're spending Christmas with your family, and that's as it should be.'

I looked at Joanna and, to do her credit, she blushed.

'I haven't made any fixed plans,' I said.

'Well, fancy that, Joanna, Mr German might come with us.'

'I don't think Joanna wants me to come.'

'But of course she does!'

'Mother, would it be possible to say something to Mr German in private?'

Mrs Wells looked faintly surprised, but agreed to sit in the car. No sooner had she gone than Joanna burst into tears and said, 'I'm so sorry, I've treated you so badly. Sometimes I wonder how I'm going to go through with this, and when I worry too much I always find myself doing the wrong things, and saying the wrong things. I'm so sorry to be a burden to you! I never meant to be!'

'Joanna, why don't I come with you tomorrow? You don't have to give this sermon, you know.'

'Everything important in your life, Mr German, you do by

yourself. Neither you nor I will ever escape that fact. Don't come to the cathedral tomorrow, I beg you. I assure you, this sermon is only the beginning. What frightens me so is the end. Go to your family, Mr German. Go to your son.'

'I promise,' I said, and kissed her forehead. But it's strange how nausea can swamp the most obvious truth.

# 10

IN THE END I WAS QUITE HAPPY to have nothing to do with
Joanna's appearance in Norwich Cathedral on Christmas
Day. I was relieved rather than hurt (but a little hurt, surely)
that she pushed me away from her. Even if she managed utterly
to charm the congregation, even if she managed to surpass the
expectations of the Bishop in the clarity of her sermon, who
would I be, I asked myself, sitting discreetly at the back of the
Cathedral, what role would I have, would I even feel a sense of
pride? But she wasn't my daughter, and she wasn't even my
protégée. Joanna was right to exclude me from the beginning. It
was better this way.

On Christmas morning I did as Joanna had demanded, and
drove to London to see my family. She had also mentioned my
son, but I had brushed the suggestion aside almost immediately.
There is stuff in this life that a pure young angel of ten would
not wish to taint herself with; it would be, quite simply, beyond
her comprehension that I couldn't just knock on Kitty's door
and wish my wife and son a happy Christmas. I laughed to
myself at the very idea, at Joanna's sweet naivety.

My parents had moved to a cul de sac in Cheam some ten
years previously, so the '70s house had never been home to me.
Its one saving grace, and the reason my mother had been so
insistent they should buy it, was a gnarled apple tree in the
garden, perhaps two hundred years old; for my mother had in
her possession an old map of Surrey, drawn in the days when
Cheam was a mere country village, and she liked to meditate on

the fellows of this old tree, long since gone. She would make the point quite often that the cul de sac wasn't a cul de sac at all, but an orchard, and she was the guardian of its last tree.

I began my journey at about five in the morning, wending my way through the lanes of Norfolk in the pitch black. That Christmas day of the year 2000 there was a light drizzle at five, turning to a heavy drizzle by six, when the motorway drained away the last mournful thought from my head and sent me headlong into oblivion. I was so still, so deeply tired, trying hard to locate some kind of rhythm in the traffic noise. I never noticed the dawn that morning; I never noticed the lights at the windows nor the empty streets. When I pulled up outside my parents' house, I folded my arms on the steering wheel and laid my head there. My mother found me. She knocked at the car window.

'Patrick, Patrick?'

I got out of the car and smiled at her. 'An early start,' I explained.

My mother was so visibly happy to see me that I hugged her. 'I never thought you'd come,' she said, 'I honestly didn't,' and she began weeping almost immediately, and calling me 'darling' like she used to when I was a child. 'I've been praying that you'd come. You look so thin, Patrick. I'm so sorry.'

I was too far deep inside myself to cry; and when I saw my father's face at the window, so cold, so indifferent, I retracted still further, and shed my mother's arms.

My father barely said a word for an hour, my mother barely paused. She made me coffee and toast, and filled me in with a whole year's gossip: who had died, who had married, who had had a child, names blotted from my memory. I watched my mother's mouth and eager eyes, and I said, 'Eight pounds two ounces? Really?' when she told me the birth weight of a baby born to the boy who shared a desk with me when we were six.

'And I saw Stephen's mum only yesterday,' she said, 'those twins are growing so. She showed me photos of them, such dear little girls. Stephen's mum's cooking the Christmas dinner this year, they're going to eat at five not to spoil the girls' routine, but they're sleeping the night through now. I thought perhaps after church you might like to pop in and see them all. They'd be so happy to see you, Patrick. You haven't seen Stephen for so long. He's got such a good job now. I don't know if you knew he switched companies. You always were such good friends.'

'Mum,' I said, taken aback at how forced and unnatural that little word sounded,' I've come to see you. And Dad.'

Dad grunted from an armchair which had its back to us. Mum said, 'Of course you have, dear. More coffee?'

I said yes please and Dad said, 'You drink too much coffee.'

He didn't even turn round to make that favourite observation of his. Back in our old house, a mere two streets and twenty worlds away from this, which smelt of cats and damp and Domestos, he'd come home from work with flushed cheeks and bike clips on his trousers, to find me hunched over the stove with a mug cupped in my hands. I looked at the back of the chair and considered the bald crown of this man's grey head and I wondered what I was doing there. My father had left me long ago. I last met his eye when I was eight, perhaps. I remembered my face pressed against the cold sitting-room window, as I watched my dad set off on his bike in the early morning. He had a broad smile on his face and was waving to me, he was waving goodbye. Who'd stopped waving first, I wondered.

Mum came back with a blue parcel in one hand and a cup of coffee in the other.

'I never wished you Happy Christmas,' she said, 'I never even wished you Happy Christmas.'

'Well, wish him Happy Christmas godammit,' said my father. My dear mother froze for a moment before attempting to break into a smile. She obeyed. 'Happy Christmas, dear. The time, where has it gone?'

I thought perhaps she was making some deeply telepathic communication with her son, and was disappointed when she suggested we should be getting ready for the service, which would begin at half past ten. But I couldn't bear it. Behind every name she rattled off was a pair of eyes who would watch me and assess me and criticise me and blame me.

'Oh they'll all be so happy to see you, dear,' she insisted.

'I'm sorry, I can't do it,' I said, 'I'm too tired. I need to rest a while.'

'But it's Christmas, Patrick. Surely on Christmas Day . . .'

'There is a God, you know. You always knew that, didn't you?' I think my tone was lackadaisical, as if it barely mattered.

'Please come with me,' she pleaded anxiously. She tried to understand the bottom of what I was saying, but I was too tired to let her.

'He thinks only of himself,' said my father. 'Come on, Jane.'

Then they left me, and I heard, 'You won't go, will you? Kitty and Joe are coming for tea,' and the door shut behind them.

I can hardly comment on my internal state at that moment. If a camera had been strategically located in some corner of that room, it might have recorded me standing up, bowing, as though to a large assembled audience, and reciting the following in the manner of a nursery rhyme:

> 'Kitty and Joe are coming,
> How jolly how jolly how jolly how jolly,
> But is there honey still for tea?'

Where was I? Who was I? Did my mother know, perhaps? Was she explaining things in the church even now? How I'd switched jobs, and was teaching in a school in North Norfolk, and such a shame that Kitty couldn't follow straightaway.

'Oh, but he still has time to visit his mum and dad when it matters.' Or are the tones more muted? Is pity what she's seeking on the network? Perhaps I've been 'sorting myself out', perhaps I've needed 'a break from London'. What stories is she giving them? And happy family that we are, we're to have a Christmas tea together, and there's the daughter-in-law, what a kind girl, so patient, and there's the grandson, apple of her eye, of course, and we'll all open our presents together round the plastic Christmas tree as though this 'upset' had never happened. Perhaps I'll say to Kitty, 'How nice your hair looks, what a pretty frock,' and I'll say, 'Brum brum,' to my son, and my mother will have her camera and go 'snap snap' and let our great grandchildren think how jolly how jolly how jolly.

Then to my delight it occurred to me that I had a fever. I felt my forehead and it was distinctly hot. How very excellent it is to be ill! What a long time it had been since I was ill, and now I could feel sweat breaking out all over my body. How fortuitous! I shall go to bed, the photo-session will have to be at my bedside, and I won't take pills, I shall just get hotter and hotter, and even Kitty will pity me. They'll bring her up to the darkened room and make her whisper, and I'll whisper back to her and say, 'I love you, Kitty, what have I done?'

I went upstairs to find a bed. There were two spare rooms, one small and empty with only a single bed in it; the other with a double bed with floral curtains and a view over the old apple tree. A vase of crocuses stood on the bedside table; doubtless this was where my mother had intended me to sleep. But how much more Kitty would feel for me should she find me in the single bed, how much more appropriate for the ensuing photo-shoot, the bare walls, the beige blind which had been inherited with the house, which my mother had never bothered to prettify. So I took my shoes off and got into bed. My darling mother! How cold and dry her hands were when she found mine and kissed them. 'Oh Patrick,' she murmured, 'you never told us you were ill. Thank God you're here with us, thank God I can look after you. I'll get a cold cloth for your forehead. You dear boy, you poor dear boy.'

When she came back her eyes were filled were tears, and she made me aware of how dry my own were.

'Why did you get into this bed, you silly boy? You've never slept in this bed, and the springs are so . . . springy.'

'It's all right for me,' I whispered, 'thank you.'

My mother flitted about me finding motherly ways of looking after me: opening the window to let in the air, closing it again when she decided it was too cold. Then she sat down and sighed.

'I never told you, did I, your father and I finally did it. We always said we'd do it when your father retired. We went on a safari, Patrick. We went to Kenya on a tour, and slept in tents, and we had such adventures. Have you ever seen a giraffe really close up? The gamekeeper was ever such a nice fellow. It was always so hot though, so humid . . . Wait, I'm going to get you your Christmas present.'

A moment later she was back again and thrusting the silvery blue parcel into my hand.

Does she not realise quite how ill I am? I wondered, and pushed it back at her.

'My poor darling. Here, let me open it for you.'

My mother had given me a photograph of her and my father standing in front of an elephant.

'Well, of course, the frame's the real present, but I had to find a photo to put inside, and I thought you probably don't have a picture of us, I thought, you know . . . you're so far away nowadays. Perhaps we could come and see you in Norfolk, Patrick. We wouldn't be in your way, we'd stay in a hotel. Oh but a year is much too long.'

Then my mother began weeping again, and my filial hand

sought hers and comforted her. 'I didn't even buy a turkey,' she blubbed. 'Oh I would have, Patrick, but Graham said, "What's the point? He won't bother to turn up. We'd only be eating cold turkey for a fortnight."'

So I held her hand and let her cry. 'Graham said, "Don't interfere, don't interfere." He kept saying you had your own life to lead, but we're part of your life, aren't we? You belong with us, don't you? You never thought for a moment that we'd forgotten you?'

I shook my head and squeezed her fingers.

'Oh I'm so selfish, I'm such a selfish woman,' my mother muttered to herself. 'My poor ill boy, here I am nattering away when I should be letting you have some sleep. I'm going to bake Kitty and Joe a cake. Oh dear, oh dear. I'll wake you when they come, darling.'

My mother got up and instinctively put her hands to her hair to rearrange it, as though hair-management and life-management were inextricably bound. With some difficulty she managed to disengage the beige blind from its catch, and bemoaned the dust which spluttered into the air on its release. Then she kissed me on my forehead and left me to sleep.

Well, sleep is for the pure in heart, sleep is for angels.

Kitty and Joe are coming for tea, let's bake them a cake and mark it with 'B'. How jolly how jolly how jolly how jolly.

And then suddenly, a great gush coming from nowhere, how wonderful, how utterly, joyously, unquestionably wonderful, dizzy-makingly wonderful: Kitty and Joe here in the room with me, Joe a little anxious perhaps, Kitty sitting on the end of this bed because there's no chair in the room, what bliss that there's no chair, that she can't escape, that I can stretch over and reach her hand; and perhaps Joe will be on her knee and look down on me, invalid that I am; do one-year-olds know compassion? And I'll say to him, 'Joe, the last time we met I was looking down on you, and how well you are now, Joe, what a fine son you are.'

But the fever took hold. Wasn't that the plan? I felt myself sinking into incoherence and I thought, 'I'll be able to pull myself together when they come,' so I laid my head heavy on the pillow, and let rival dreams joust for the occupation of it. I waited for the reprieve that my Kitty would bring me. The grandfather clock struck four and deep in sleep my stomach stirred in anticipation; it struck five and the house was still; then at six I saw a woman in the doorway and my heart leapt.

'They never came,' said my mother.

My head lolled back on to the damp pillow, and I lay on my right, on my left, on my back, with my knees up to my chest, with my body straight as a rod. I tried to make my head a blank, but then I saw that it wasn't a blank at all but a huge screen, and a broad ray of white light was shining at it, so that every tiny moth in its path was magnified. Thus began the infestation of the night.

I was aware of my parents arguing downstairs; that clock went on striking, now seven, now eight. Why didn't my mother come to say goodnight, to offer me supper, to comfort me? It was her voice I heard, not my father's – what was she saying to him? Then I heard a baby crying, and I thought, 'They came after all, they'll be here in a minute.' I was aware of the excitement building up in me, my mouth dry, my head alert. But the baby went on crying, and I thought, why aren't you soothing him, why aren't you feeding him, what is it he wants? I called out to Kitty, I called out to my mother. I said, 'Come here, I'll cheer him up, it's me he wants.' The crying got louder, and they couldn't hear me, and I saw that the problem was bats, that bats were flying everywhere about Joe's face, and Joe was just lying in the pram outside in the dark, on Christmas night, kicking his blankets off, and I shouted, 'Can't you get rid of the bats?'

I dragged myself to the window to scare them off myself; I was so angry with them all, I was so angry with their negligence. I pulled up the blind and looked out, but the pram had gone, they must have taken it inside at last. Perhaps they'll come up to see me now, or they might think I'm sleeping. Perhaps I should call down from the landing and tell them I'm awake. But when I opened the door the house was dark and still, and the voices had gone, and my throbbing head didn't let me understand.

There was no hour of the night when I didn't hear the chimes of the clock, and count them one by one. I counted two, three and four o'clock, hoping beyond hope that I might have missed an hour, that I might have inadvertently slept; but that in-between place in which I roamed became ever more menacing. My parents weren't arguing with each other, they were arguing with me. Why hadn't I done my homework? Why hadn't I cleared away the breakfast? Why hadn't I tidied my room? My mother was kinder, though, she came with a flannel and mopped my brow, and she said sweetly, 'We don't punish you often, but sometimes it's best that we do.'

'You've been up already, I see,' said my mother, looking towards the early morning sun pouring in through the wide-open window.

'I've brought you some tea. You look so much better, Patrick. How did you sleep?'

'Quite patchy,' I said.

'You were asleep last night when I brought you a little supper. You were sleeping like a baby.'

I sat up and took the mug from her. 'Thanks,' I said.

'Do you feel like getting up for breakfast? Or would you like it on a tray?'

'I'll come down.'

'Eggs and bacon? Something tasty?'

'Just toast. Thanks.'

'Take your time, don't hurry.'

'I'll be down in twenty minutes,' I said.

My mother cooked bacon anyway. 'I thought perhaps the smell would waken your hunger,' she said. 'You never ate a morsel yesterday.'

My father ejaculated a 'humph' from behind a newspaper; perhaps he meant, 'Good morning.'

'Is it working?' asked my mother.

'Working?'

'The smell. Is it making you feel hungry?'

'Don't you work at Gresham Primary School?' asked my father suddenly.

'That's right,' I said, surprised that he should know.

'Have you registered a girl called Joanna Wells?'

'I have indeed. I teach her.' I sounded as nonchalant as I could.

'Well, apparently she's been sent by God. That is, according to the Bishop of Norwich. He even gave her his Bishop's Chair.' My father laughed.

'I'm not sure what I think of that,' said my mother, anxiously, spatula in hand. 'Now, do you want bacon?'

'Give me that,' I said to my father, trying to snatch the newspaper from his hand. He pushed me away, as though I was nine years old.

'You always were a rude boy, wait your turn,' he said.

My mother put a plate of bacon in front of me; I didn't touch it. We sat there, frozen in time, waiting for my father to finish reading.

'You're in luck,' he said. 'Norwich Radio recorded the little mite's sermon, and it's being broadcast at five this afternoon on Radio 4.'

Even my father listened to her. I could tell this was a real sacrifice on his part: he wanted to tune in to the Boxing Day football scores. We three sat around the kitchen table with cups of tea and an old-fashioned Roberts radio in the middle of it. The

Bishop introduced her; he sounded both earnest and gruff. Joanna had drawn out the hope in him, he said, he left her now to draw out the hope in us.

My mother flinched. 'There's something not right,' she said. 'Ssh, mother.'

When I heard Joanna's voice on the radio, ringing out true and clear, I marvelled at her. I'd never heard her like this. Her Christmas sermon, 2000. I'm quoting the greater part of it directly from the transcript (*Seventeen Sermons*, page 14):

*I am grateful to the Bishop for inviting me to address you. I'm also grateful you should come. Why should you come, after all? Who of you believes the Christmas story, that God touched Man on earth by becoming Man himself? On that day, heaven and earth became as one, God became part of the stuff of this world, not to worship from afar, but to love and to hold.*

*I'm here because that is what we're celebrating today, that is why we've gathered together in this cathedral. I'm here because you've forgotten. But I've not come to blame you, I've not even come to teach you. I've come to remind you of what in your hearts you already know.*

*We live, whether we acknowledge it or not, in the ground of God. Listen first to your own heart, not to the loud opinions of others. Know this, that you have a will, and that will is given by God, it is beyond nature, it is the first cause, it is the source of creation, it is the maker of miracles, even the laws of the universe are in thrall to it. And this power is within all of you.*

*Throughout the history of Man there have been visionaries, there have been men who in some way have apprehended the Divine. But two thousand years ago Jesus was born, and he was proclaimed the Son of God. So why was He the Son? Ask me the question of all ques-*

*tions, why was Jesus the Son? Because he was the first of all God's creation to know God's love, to know it as warmly as a child knows it, in the arms of his father.*

*In the beginning was the Word, and the Word was with God, and the Word was God. The Word is also within you. There is a truth we can all find, which is the truth for all men. I tell you this, we are all of us visionaries. We have our minds, and we have our hearts. We have the power to understand, and the power to love. We have the power to know God. And I tell you this: we shall rejoice.*

My father, who'd been sighing and silently scoffing throughout, took the radio and immediately started retuning it to find football results.

'I'll only rejoice if West Ham have clinched it,' he said.

I looked at my mother while he held his ear to the tuning dial as though he were breaking into a safe. 'Well, what do you think?' I asked her. 'Do you think she was any good?

'Why does she say "visionary"? Why doesn't she say "prophet"?'

She got up from the table and went to the stove to put on the kettle, as though Joanna had been talking about nothing more important than gardening. I followed her there. 'Mother! Mother!' I said, 'Look at me!'

Reluctantly, she did.

'I should have told you this long ago,' I said to her. 'The moment I met Joanna I thought of you, Mother, because you of all people would want to know about her! How can I tell you this? She's the real thing! She's the one! How can I persuade you? Joanna can do miracles! Look, look at this!'

I showed my mother a perfect, scarless patch of skin on my right hand. 'I snagged my hand on some barbed wire while out walking with her, and a fountain of blood spurted out, it just wouldn't stop! Joanna, this girl you've just heard on the radio, took my hand like this, and placed her fingers over the wound. The blood stopped! It just stopped! And the wound closed and dried out all in a few seconds. Now, you believe in miracles, don't you, Mother?'

'Praise the Lord,' murmured my mother, taking hold of my healed hand, tears pouring down her cheeks.

My father turned up the radio. *Newcastle 4, Tottenham Hotspur 2.*

'Praise the Lord,' she said again; but this time, there was a sing-song note I detected, which irritated me to the quick.

'Oh Mother,' I said, 'you don't have to sound like some sort of stupid evangelist. What's "praise" got to do with it? And why, "the Lord"? Why can't you say, "Thank you, God"? Or why do we have to say anything at all? If God knows everything, He'll know if we feel grateful or not.'

*Wigan 2, Millwall 1.*

'Why are you suddenly so angry with me? Rejoice, Patrick, and if you can't, then let me!'

'Praise the Lord, Praise the Lord! How am I doing, Mother, how am I doing?'

'Why are you mocking me?' she cried.

*Arsenal 3, Forest Rangers, nil.*

'Because you're not speaking from the heart, you're making some sort of knee-jerk reaction. Why do you say it? You've always said it!'

'It's like saying "ouch". It just comes out, Patrick,' said my mother apologetically. 'What should I say?'

'Say "great", say "whoopee"!'

*Chelsea 1, West Ham, nil.*

'But I want to say something so much more than that.'

'Then say, "Whoopee a million times, thank you, God!"'

My mother said, 'Whoopee a million times, thank you, God.'

Suddenly my father switched off the radio and looked at me with an expression of absolute coldness.

'It's not her style. Don't fill this house with more crap than you have to,' he said.

Even if my father hadn't given me my exit cue I would have left. I had to return to Norfolk. I had to talk to Joanna. I hugged my tearful mother goodbye, and vaguely looked around for my father who had retreated somewhere in the house. My mother thrust some cheese sandwiches into my hand, and I set out on my journey.

I hadn't shaved for a couple of days, and when I caught sight of myself in my car mirror I decided I should stop off at Beeston to tidy myself up before descending on the Wells household. But in the event I was too impatient. I arrived in the middle of a family meal.

I was greeted at the door by Mrs Wells and the smell of old grease. She took a moment to recognise me, such was my gaunt, wild, stubbly appearance, but when she saw it was me, she put her great fat arms about my neck and kissed me.

'Did you hear what a wonder my Joanna was yesterday? Speaking to that enormous crowd in the cathedral? Come in, Mr Jermond, I knew you'd bring our family luck, didn't I tell you that you would?'

'It's nothing to do with me,' I said.

'Come and have something to eat with us,' she said, taking me firmly by the arm.

'No, no, I'm so sorry. I've come at a bad time.'

'You've come at a good time, come in.'

As we walked through the kitchen she lifted two remaining fish fingers from a frying pan of black oil and put them on to a slice of white bread that rested on her hand. 'My oldest son's staying over at his girlfriend's tonight. Here, you can have his portion. I'll get you a plate.'

There was no question of my refusing it and she took me through into the dingy room where we had sat before. The family was too large to sit round a table, and each lumpen child held a plate on its knee. There were two sofas with four bodies sitting in a row on each of them; and eight pairs of eyes looked up from their plates to peruse the intruder. One of those pairs of eyes belonged to Joanna. As soon as she saw me she stood up, aghast. Her half-eaten fish-finger sandwich fell to the floor, and two cats appeared from nowhere to devour it.

'I suppose you two will have a lot to talk about,' said Mrs Wells. 'You know, Mr Jermond, the Bishop's invited our Joanna back to give another talk next Sunday. She did ever so well, I'm so sorry you couldn't be there.'

'His name's Mr German, mother.'

'Why didn't you tell me? Perhaps Mr German could give you a little help, sometimes, if this turns into a regular thing. Talking of which you might be able to advise us over a rather delicate matter. We've only got one old car, you see, and petrol being four pounds a gallon and that, we were just wondering if the cathedral would be paying . . .'

'I could take her there, if you like.'

Joanna shook her head vehemently.

'That's not actually my drift. You see, we were wondering, or Fred was wondering, whether such a talent as our girl's should go unpaid.'

'Mother, please,' pleaded Joanna. 'Of course I'm not doing it for money.'

'Why not?' said a bloated specimen from the sofa. 'Don't think only of yourself, madam. I haven't had a new pair of trainers in a year.'

Joanna promptly left the scene in tears and I heard her running away upstairs.

'There she goes again,' said another sibling, laughing.

'Kitty, kitty, kitty, kitty,' squeaked a third.

'Perhaps you should go up after her,' said Mrs Wells, kindly.

'I'm not sure she wants to see me.'

'Of course she wants to see you. She owes this all to you. You know what I heard a man muttering behind me yesterday? "That girl's going to be a famous preacher one day." But do preachers get famous? I'm not sure I've heard of any. I don't think I could name you even one.'

'I don't think this is about fame, Mrs Wells.'

'That's just where you're wrong. You mark my words.' Then Mrs Wells gave me one of her funny looks, as though she knew exactly what was going on. We looked at each other for some moments and I could only break the deadlock by suggesting that I went upstairs to see what Joanna was up to.

I found her lying under an old woollen blanket on the bottom bunk. Four children shared this room, and there was a smell of urine and old socks. I immediately went over to the window to open it, but Joanna pleaded, 'No, don't, my mother gets so angry if we let the heat out.'

'I need some fresh air,' I said. 'Can't we go into the garden?'

'Okay,' she said, sombrely, and she found an old jumper under the bed.

'Is that where you keep your clothes?'

'Yes,' she said, without a trace of self-pity in her tone.

'So who do you share your room with?'

'Tom, who's fourteen, and the twins.'

'How old are they?'

'Sixteen. John and Michael. Michael wets the bed. That's why it stinks in here.'

'Doesn't your mother clean the sheets?'

'Sometimes. But we don't have a washing machine. She has to take them to the launderette in Cromer, and that's shut, it being Christmas and all that.'

'How do you manage?'

'You mean how does my mum manage?'

'No, I mean how do you manage, sharing a room with three brothers?'

'I can pray,' said Joanna, smiling at last.

'Please tell me how you pray, Joanna, you've never told me.'

'You've never asked me.'

'Do you say the Lord's Prayer?'

'Not exactly. I don't say it.'

'Then do you think it?'

'I imagine it.'

'How do you imagine it? How would you teach someone to imagine it, someone like me?'

'First of all, you have to know the structure of things. The way things are.'

'How do you know that?'

'I know it because I've been there.'

'Where is this place?'

'This place is heaven.'

'Where is heaven, Joanna?'

'Heaven is beyond time, with God.'

'So God really did send you?'

'He did.'

'Why did he send you?'

'He wanted to say . . . there's been a misunderstanding. He created you, he created me. He created this universe and everything within it. But He doesn't exist within time, like a great angry judge rewarding the good and sending the wicked off to hell. He can't even stop an earthquake.'

'That's his message, is it?'

I heard myself sounding like a clerk on the telephone. Surely if there were to be a direct message from God it would be emblazoned in gold over the sky to the sound of trumpets; and here we were, in this squalid little room smelling of pee.

'You see, God created time. There *was* a beginning, and there *will be* an end; though even to use our human tenses like that is

169

misleading. There is a beginning, and there is an end, and God has the measure of it all. There are some who have glimpsed this structure, they have been with God for the twinkling of an eye and seen us through his own eyes, all of time as an eternal present. Sometimes people have dreams about something which hasn't even happened, but then does happen. Sometimes people have a sense of fate, like they were walking through a life that had somehow already been cut out for them, though it was they themselves that did the cutting.'

'I don't understand,' I said, pathetically.

'God is pure being, living in the eternal present. But we never rest, we never have peace; we move from the past to the future on the crest of a wave. And on our journey the past is already history. All we can do is grieve for it. Our present never stands still, the present moment is a mythical moment. Our future is our only reality. Hope is man's fuel. And the destination of our journey is always God.'

'I wish that were true, Joanna.'

'It is even now. People might think it's a new house they want, or more money, or a better job, and they always imagine that at the end of their wanting there'll be a stillness, a sense of fulfillment, of being met. But one desire replaces another desire, only God can break the cycle of longing, because only God is the true object of that longing.'

'I don't understand why God would have bothered to create beings that were separate from him and would spend their lives needing to be re-united with him. He would have prevented a lot of anguish if he hadn't bothered. Or if he needed someone to love, why couldn't he have made do with a few angels?'

'Where there is Love, there is Other. Where there is Other, there is pain. Where there is pain, there is meaning. God is the Word. We are God's creation. We are necessarily separate from Him. We are a work of art, and as in all great works of art we have our own dynamic, caused not by the artist who set it in motion but coming from itself. God can watch us, admire us, love us, listen to us, but he can only listen. He has chosen to let his creation be. He yearns for us as much as we do Him.'

'But he can evidently send angels.'

'He can, Mr German, he does all the time. But their only power is love. They couldn't even stop a small river from flooding its banks. Unless . . .'

'Unless?'

'If an angel saw a child drowning, and loved the child . . .'

'Yes?'

'Miracles happen,' said Joanna, watching me for my reaction.

'Why did you always insist you weren't an angel? Didn't you lie to me?'

'If only I were an angel, but I'm not. Look at me. Surely you recognise flesh and blood when you meet it? I am mortal. I shall die.'

I took the thin arms which she had offered me as evidence of her humanity and said, 'Of course you're an angel, Joanna.'

'Don't you think I would just fly from here if I could? Just bless this house and fill them all with the spirit they so lack if I could? I was born in this forsaken place. This is my home, Mr German.'

'Then who are you?'

Joanna was uneasy for a moment; and she stood up, and she sat down again, and she played with the ends of her hair. Then she looked at me, point blank, and said quietly,

'I'm Jesus.'

'Oh shit,' I said.

I was sitting in a room with Jesus, Boxing Day 2000. Jesus and I. But no sooner had she made this announcement than she made me promise that I wouldn't tell anyone. She told me, quite straightforwardly, that Jesus' soul had made several attempts to embody itself in the intervening two thousand years. About sixty years after Jesus' death, his first death, he entered the body of a boy from Antioch, but the boy died of dysentery at the age of three. There were other attempts too: but the families into which Jesus was born again were often hostile, and the siblings in particular were jealous and suspicious of any peculiar powers manifested in their young brothers, and discredited them or even, in some instances, killed them. Joanna told me that once Jesus' soul had entered the body of a nineteenth-century Frenchman, and had spent most of his life incarcerated in a madhouse, unable as he was to convince the sceptics around him. So this time round she was going to be cautious. It suited her to be just a girl, sent by God. It suited her to forget about her ability to perform miracles – an ability which belonged to each and every one of us, if we should so choose to channel it. She had another mission. She wasn't a visionary, needing to persuade us most eloquently of some revelation. She wasn't an angel, come to fill us with the Holy Spirit. She'd come, she said, to redeem us, and bring us back to God.

# 11

AT EIGHT O'CLOCK in the morning on the 3rd of January 2001, the first day of the spring term, Mr Birch walked into my classroom looking objectionably pleased with himself.

'Patrick,' he said, 'we have visitors! Let me introduce you to them. They're from *The Times*!'

I tried explaining that I was busy with my new timetable, but he'd have none of it. He clasped me by the elbow and more or less dragged me into his office.

'This is Sally Griffin, who'll be writing a feature on the young angel in our midst,' expounded Mr Birch. Sally was slim and pretty, and wore a tight-fitting suit and stiletto heels.

'You're Joanna's form teacher, I take it,' she purred, and she held out her hand to me. I took it and held it for a moment longer than was polite (more for Mr Birch's pleasure than for hers or mine) and said, 'Patrick German. Delighted to meet you.'

'And this is Sam, the photographer,' interrupted Mr Birch. I didn't like Sam. He had a little blond pony-tail and acne on his forehead. He looked at me and got straight to the point.

'What time does Joanna normally roll in?'

'Roll in?' I queried.

'Pitch up,' he explained. 'It's important I know the approximate time she gets here. I need to take light readings.'

'You intend to catch her unawares?' I asked him.

'You get a natural pose that way,' said Sam professionally. 'Children can be quite self-conscious.'

'I think you should ask her first.'

Mr Birch shot me a furious look, as though I were guilty of obstruction.

'I'm not going to steal her soul, you know,' laughed Sam. For some reason he was beginning to remind me of an ox. I considered telling him he should try breathing through his mouth: his snorting unnerved me.

'Coffee anyone?' suggested Mr Birch, trying to jolly along our little party. Sam looked anxiously at his watch.

'Don't worry,' I said, 'your angel doesn't roll up until a quarter to nine.' Everyone visibly relaxed.

'Does anyone object to powdered milk?' asked Mr Birch.

'I'll have my coffee black,' said Sally, of the pretty calves.

'I must say, I apologise for the chill in here. But a hot drink will soon warm us up!' And Mr Birch, praise the Lord, left us in peace, while he set about boiling a kettle next door.

'So, then,' said Miss Griffin, 'let's sit down, shall we? Would you mind, Patrick, if I turned on my tape-recorder?'

'Do as you please,' I said. I brought in a couple more chairs, and we sat round Mr Birch's coffee table. There were copies of *Model Railway News* lying unashamedly in a pile in the middle of it.

'I'll just check the batteries are working. Hello, hello, are you working, batteries?'

I waited in anticipation.

'Hello, hello, are you working batteries?' said the tape-recorder. Ms Griffin clapped her hands in glee and laid it on the table. 'So,' she reiterated. 'You're Joanna's teacher, are you?'

'I think it's truer to say that she's mine,' I said.

'You're rather a wit,' said Sally, 'I'll quote you on that, if you don't mind.' And she wrote something in her shorthand pad.

'Now, did you manage to get to the cathedral last Sunday?'

'I did,' I said.

'And so did I!' said Mr Birch, gliding into the room with a tray and covering his railway magazines with it. 'Help yourselves to sugar!' he announced. 'Now I was there and I thought Joanna was terrific!'

'She most certainly was,' beamed Sally. 'Now somewhere or other I've brought a transcript. Were any of you in Norwich to hear Joanna's Christmas sermon?'

No one had been. Ms Griffin produced a few sheets of duplicated paper from her briefcase and put them on her knee. 'A shame,' she said. 'Never mind. So then. She chose to speak about "suffering" for her second sermon. Not much rejoicing there. What a theme for a ten-year-old girl to choose!'

'You mean "angel",' said Sam helpfully, fiddling with the shutters on his camera.

'Perhaps, indeed, "angel".' Ms Griffin paused momentously before each word. 'Is there a good divinity department here?'

'We don't have a divinity department,' I said.

'But we do have assembly,' suggested Mr Birch. 'We always have a Bible reading and a hymn, and I always try to make a few suggestions as to how to lead a good life.'

'Yes,' I agreed. 'But no one sings. No one listens.'

'I always say, Patrick, it doesn't matter how much noise we make. What matters is to make the Christian message accessible.'

'Will there be assembly today, Mr Birch?'

'Usually just on a Monday and a Friday, but I could muster . . . if you would like to see . . .'

'Don't bother,' said Ms Griffin. 'Does Joanna come from a religious family? In fact it would be extremely helpful to have Joanna's address; I want to speak to her parents.'

'You can't,' I said.

Mr Birch glared at me. 'I don't see the harm in it,' he said. 'Though I honestly don't know how much help they'd be.'

'I want to know the kind of background Joanna comes from,' pursued Sally. 'Are they enjoying Joanna's spell in the national headlines?'

'I think hugely, as any parent would. In fact, I had a few words with them after the service.' And Mr Birch proceeded to give Ms Griffin a very full account of them.

Oh yes, I'd seen the three of them chatting animatedly: Mrs Wells covered in make-up, purple lips and rouge up to her ears; her husband pristine in a new suit; Mr Birch leaning over them magisterially; and all of them seemingly thrilled to be in the company of the other. And then I saw the star of the show herself, Joanna, who became a child again the moment she stopped addressing us, and no one knew quite whether they should be offering her a glass of orange squash or entreating her to bless them, and as a consequence they all but ignored her. I watched her standing alone in the Jesus Chapel, transfixed by the Adoration of the Magi.

'So do you think they'd give me an interview?' Ms Griffin pointed her stockinged knees in Mr Birch's direction, and cocked her head on one side. I wanted to tell her that it didn't suit her.

'The secret is,' grinned that pitiful man, rubbing his fingers together, 'they're strapped for cash. They told me so. They were wondering how they could claim expenses . . . a large family and all that.'

'I don't think a fee should be a problem. But of course, if you wish to withhold their address perhaps I could meet them, or Mrs Wells at any rate, when she delivers or picks up Joanna from school.'

'Joanna walks, I'm afraid. But I see no harm in giving you her address. After all, it's all spreading the word, isn't it?'

'Indeed it is.'

'I'm off,' said Sam, suddenly. 'She might be early. Anyway, I've got to read the light.'

'That sounds like a religious experience in itself,' I said.

'Do you know what she looks like?' asked Ms Griffin.

'I'll point her out to you,' said Mr Birch, escorting him out into the playground.

No sooner were we alone together than Sally pulled her skirt down over her knees and assumed a deadly seriousness.

'So what do you think of all this?'

'All this? Is there something to think?'

'Who is Joanna?'

'I don't understand your drift.'

'Is she a good pupil?'

'Yes, she's clever, a good poet.'

'Where do you think she got her ideas from?'

'It's not just the over-twenties who have a monopoly on thinking.'

'But it's not what she says that is so exceptional. Her parents could have instructed her; even the Bishop. What is so strange about her . . . what is so alarming . . . is the sense she has of her own authority.'

'She's been given God's authority.'

'Well, yes, but, "God"!' She sounded like she'd swallowed something whole.

'You don't believe in God, I take it?'

'I suppose I don't. Or at least, in my own life I haven't seen much evidence. A failed marriage . . . you know the stuff, you know the catalogue of modern woes.'

Then Ms Griffin's knees made a sudden comeback: Mr Birch had reappeared, and brought Jocelyn with him.

'Jocelyn, this is Sally from *The Times.*'

'God exists, Ms Griffin,' I said.

'That sounds rather heavy, Patrick,' laughed Mr Birch, uneasily.

'It's a fairly heavy statement.'

'I don't think Ms Griffin is here to discuss God, but Joanna.

Now, if you'll excuse me, she'll be here in a few minutes,' and he left us again, to resume his strategic position in the playground.

Good old Jocelyn. I knew she's leap to my defence. She gave Ms Griffin the full throttle of the schoolmistress's glare. 'God and Joanna are inseparable. You can't write about the one without the other.'

'Did you ever teach her?' That skirt spoke volumes. It even covered her pretty calves this time.

'I did,' said Jocelyn with pride.

'And? Was she exceptional then? How long ago did you teach her?'

'I taught her when she was five and six.'

'Yes?'

'She performed miracles even then.'

We all looked at Jocelyn. She could have been an angel herself, that morning. She was radiant.

'What do you mean, "miracles"?'

'Ask Patrick.'

'No,' I said.

'Did she perform a miracle on you?' Sally Griffin was suddenly alert.

'No,' I said. 'Come on, let's talk about her sermon.'

'She did, didn't she?'

'It's not fair that you should ask me.'

'Why shouldn't the world know? Why do you want to keep it to yourself?' Ms Griffin smiled.

'It's not what Joanna's about. I beg you not to mention it.'

'I don't understand your problem,' said Ms Griffin.

I watched Jocelyn look guilty, confused, defiant. 'Honestly, Patrick,' she said. 'I think people should know.'

'It's not right, Jocelyn,' I pleaded with her. 'Not yet.'

'Both of you have obviously been influences in her life,' baited Ms Griffin.

178

'You've got it in one,' I said, 'you've found her guides and inspiration, and you can sleep easy in your bed. All is explained.'

Then Marion came in and told Ms Griffin in flat, angry tones that Joanna had come; the photo had been caught 'spot on' and her colleague was eager for her to join him outside. Ms Griffin smiled at me sheepishly and went out; Marion sat down in her chair and spat in her coffee. 'The press should be barred from this kind of exploitation,' she said. 'How could you lot even bring yourselves to speak to her?'

'It's not every day we have a girl like Joanna in our midst,' said Jocelyn, defensively.

'Is she so special, Patrick? I almost came round to ask.'

'I suppose she is,' I said. I asked her if she'd had a good Christmas.

'No,' was her reply.

Jocelyn was visibly fretting at this reminder of a secret history. 'I must be getting on,' she said, coldly. 'The bell's going in ten minutes, you two. You might have things to see to.' She shuffled away and left us to it.

Marion couldn't even look at me. 'God, I hate this,' she said. 'You'd think *The Times* was slightly above this crap, wouldn't you? How can you stand by and watch?'

'I don't know what I'm supposed to do. I don't know whether to protect her or ring up the *Mirror* and ask what's keeping them.'

'For God's sake, Patrick, she's a girl of ten.'

'You don't know her.'

'How well do you? I'm sure she's clever, perhaps she's very clever, but so? Let me tell you something, if she was a warty old woman the newspapers wouldn't even be giving her advertising space. But how these young things capture the public imagination. So sweet, so pure, so, dare I say it, angelic.'

'Did you ever read her sermon on suffering?'

'What did it say? "Don't worry, life's hard, but God loves you"? Or did it say, "We need a little more suffering because we've discovered a ratio between unhappy people and people who spend awfully long hours in church"?'

'Here it is,' I said, picking up Ms Griffin's newspaper. 'Read it, Marion, then tell me what you think.'

'I'm not going to read this. There's nothing I don't know about it. I'm not going to kowtow to a ten-year-old.'

'Then I'm going to read it to you.'

Marion stood up as if to go, but I said to her, 'Please stay. Please listen. She was amazing, Marion. The cathedral was almost full, it didn't faze her at all.'

'Then she must be an angel,' scoffed Marion; but at least she sat down again to listen.

*Imagine a world without suffering. There's a clear stream running at the end of every garden; there's a vegetable patch where the earth is so rich that any seed that's planted there grows into great fat marrows and cabbages, carrots and beetroots, all yours for the picking. Your house is large and airy, your children always well-behaved, your jobs are always satisfying, your wives and husbands forever young and good-looking. Everyone has a swimming-pool, and friends come to sip wine with you, and soak up the sun. No one mourns, because death doesn't happen here; and no one is born who is not fit and healthy and excels in all he does. But nor does anyone lose in this world: people run for the pleasure of running; people swim for the pleasure of swimming. No one is jealous, no one wishes they were married to a friend's wife, no one wishes they were richer, because they already have everything money could buy.*

'So this is Joanna's idea of heaven, is it?' derided Marion.
'Oh no, Marion. This is what she says: '*So what.*'

'I bet the audience liked that.'
'The congregation is what's it's called.'
'Read on then.'

*Where is there room for compassion in such a world?
Where is there room for love? And above all, where is
meaning? Is this what life is all about, is this the prize, a
light and easy pleasure for ever? No one would bother to
learn, because everything that can be learned in books
would be known already; no one would even say 'sorry',
because nothing would ever be done that could cause
offence, the limit of genuine human contact would be in
the saying of 'please' and 'thank you', and this would be
a custom rather than a feeling born in the heart. Nor
would there be any room for stories in such a world: there
would be no villains and princesses, because everyone
would be a princess; there would be no just cause to fight
for, because there would be no grievances. And what kind
of love would we all feel in such a world? It would be a
what-shall-we-play next? kind a love, where everyone is a
winner, and no one knows loss. It would be a shallow
love. It would be a meaningless love.*

*For there to be meaning there have to be opposites:
there is no pleasure without pain; there is no good
without bad. Perfection has no dialogue with perfection.
If we were perfect, God would have nothing to say to us.
If God was imperfect, we would have nothing to say to
him. But the lines of communication are open, and the
language is love.*

The bell went, and Marion stood up to go. 'All I can say is I
wish sometimes God would swap places. It's tough always being
on the imperfect end. I want to spend at least five years in a
bath scented with lavender oil.'

'I think He tried once,' I said.

'What do you mean?'

'He sent Jesus.'

'Oh for God's sake, Patrick, has she really got to you?'

'Don't worry, Marion. He failed. First time round He failed.'

One of the advantages of having a God-sent pupil in our school was that we no longer had to spend a freezing break watching the kids skipping and playing hopscotch. Joanna's very presence ensured that not a rude word was said: evidently the parents had so filled their offspring with angel stories that the poor mites rather had the wind taken out of their sails. So we staff sat warm and snug inside with cups of tea, sorting and sifting the hundreds of letters that were either addressed to Joanna, requesting a prayer or a blessing, or to Mr Birch, asking his permission for yet another interview. We had spoken with Joanna, explaining that we were in her hands: we could either fend off the intrusion, or at least some of it, or arrange times for the various journalists to come and speak to her. She told us that it was probably best she spoke with them all, though she said so in a tone which suggested she would sooner speak with none of them. The photograph in *The Times* proved to be an enormous hit; in fact even now it's the one that's reproduced most often, the one we've come to know and love. Of course, it's not the posed profile that was chosen a couple of years ago to decorate the euro; but as a picture of the ordinary schoolgirl arriving at the gate, as a picture of one of us, there's been none to match it.

Every afternoon when Joanna went home we gave her her letters. We would offer to drive her: Mr Birch, too keenly; Jocelyn, too religiously; Marion, too protectively; myself, too desperately. So quite wisely, she preferred to carry her correspondence in a rucksack, and she went home on her old route, and I imagined her singing and swaying under a tree, and I thought, 'At least someone somewhere is feeding you, Joanna.'

Then one day in late January I noticed a very curious thing. I was in the staff-room at break, warming my hands on the radiator by the window. It was a particularly cold day; I saw children with blue lips, rigid with cold, and I rather felt I should be out there to jolly them along, but was unable to resist the comfort of my legs being up against the hot metal. I saw Joanna, standing as still as a temple, watching some girls skipping; I saw one half of a game of football, and Ralph scoring a goal.

Then I noticed Susan, poor dumpy Susan whom I'd previously assigned to a sausage factory. She was kneeling at the side of a boy in the form below her. She had her eyes shut, and seemed to be concentrating very hard. The boy was lying, clutching his elbow, evidently in some pain; but Susan seemed calm, and took the boy's hand in her own, and held it firmly. Then she began to move her other hand an inch or two over the elbow itself, in a very precise way, beginning at the outside and working towards the middle. I called Marion over from where she was marking books, and I asked her what she thought Susan was doing. Both of us knew, of course. Susan was healing him. Joanna must have taught her how to heal.

But the moment the boy felt the pain leave him, far from thanking his healer, he looked terrified, and kept touching the place on his elbow where the wound had been. Meanwhile Susan had run over to Joanna, and was talking animatedly to her.

'So what do you think of that, then?' I asked Marion. 'Who taught Susan to do that?'

'If I were Matthew I'd prefer a bloody elbow and a good night's sleep. He'll think Susan's a witch.'

'Go on, Marion, admit it. Susan healed him.'

'I don't know what to think.'

'And look, Joanna's come to cheer Matthew up, and she's succeeding.'

'I never saw the wound. Which means there might never have been one.'

'Marion, you saw it. As clearly as I did.'

'I didn't, not for sure. I couldn't swear in a court of law that I saw it. The fact that people are so enchanted by the super-natural, so long for it to be true, doesn't make it true.'

'Meanwhile, you, Marion, I take it, believe in the healing properties of lavender oil.

'No, I don't. It just smells nice.'

'Personally, I don't like the smell.'

'Then you're wrong, Patrick. Everyone likes the smell.'

'Experiences aren't right or wrong. Experiences aren't subject to verification. You believe someone because you trust them. If someone tells you he's in pain you believe him because you trust him. Likewise if you have . . . if you have . . . if you have another kind of experience . . .'

'Ah, so there's the crux. A great bolt of lightning has struck you, right in the middle of your soul.'

'Actually, it did, once, but I've rather been ignoring it. No one seemed to want to know. No one trusted me.'

'Then you should have gone to a priest.'

'I did, I went to two, but they didn't trust me either.'

'So what makes you think I'd trust you? Incidentally, I don't.'

'If you don't trust me, what about those hundreds of thou-sands of people throughout the whole of history who've had extraordinary experiences . . . Do you believe none of them? Okay, people who think they've had dinner with fifteen angels have probably made a mistake, but what about those people who feel somehow God touches them when they hear a piece of music?'

Marion shrugged. 'It's a manner of speech.'

'No, Marion,' I said, 'it's not.'

Then suddenly there were tears in Marion's eyes and she said, 'I hate myself for still loving you.'

'I simply hate myself,' I said, and held her hand.

On the blustery evening of Sunday the 4th of February there was a knock at my door. I was, in fulfilment of my New Year's resolution, attempting to read the Bible. My armchair was drawn up closely to a fire spitting listlessly in the grate; the book of Job was open on my knee.

It was our vicar. I was, in fact, pleased to see him, which surprised me as our last meeting had been such an embarrassment. It might just have been that I was in the mood for company, but I also noticed that he'd lost his air of being closer to God than I was. He suddenly looked vulnerable, and I liked him for it.

'Roger,' I said, I hoped warmly.

'I'm so sorry to drop round so late, I would've rung . . .'

'But I don't have a phone. I know, I should get one.'

'It's impressive nowadays to manage without. Sometimes I wish I could.'

'Come in,' I said. 'I can't say, "Come in and get warm" because I fear you won't. I'm down to the bottom of a bag of coal. But let's have some whisky.'

He accepted; and I noticed how, by the light of that puny fire, he looked rather pale, ill even. He was wearing the same hand-knitted jumper he had worn on that first night we met, that crazed night up in the church, and I thought of all the love that his mother or his wife had knitted into it.

'I saw you in the cathedral this morning,' began Roger.

'Oh yes,' I said, 'I was there.'

'Of course, I've often seen you. It's rude of me not to have said hello.'

I shrugged. 'You're a busy man.'

'You teach Joanna, don't you?'

'I do.'

'That day you dropped round, I suppose you wanted to talk about her. I'm sorry. I must have seemed quite insensitive.' The poor man seemed rather too apologetic.

'Joanna is not everyday news, Roger,' I said. 'I can hardly hold it against you that you weren't looking for it.'

I'd given Roger my armchair, while I sat on a low stool beside him. Our desire to be near the few burning coals had inadvertently brought us very close together. We sat hunched over our whisky in the low light; then Roger sighed and I asked him, 'What do you think of Joanna?'

'I think she's wonderful,' he replied. But he spoke so flatly, so sadly, even, that I asked him what his reservations were.

'Reservations? I don't have any. The first time I saw her, on New Year's Eve, all I could do was praise God for sending her to us. I felt this was history in the making. I had postponed my own services till the evening, but during evensong . . .' Roger paused.

'Yes?'

'I thought, "Who am I?" As I preached that night, when I should have been so inspired, I could only think, "Who are you, God? Does Joanna know you, or do I know you?"'

'Perhaps you both know him,' I suggested.

'Yes, perhaps everyone knows him. Perhaps there are as many gods as there are people. Yet we all believe in the one God, Patrick, that's what joins us up together, that's what the Church is. We are the preservation of orthodoxy. We are the body of Christ. We say the Creed together, and if we are good Christians, we believe it with all our hearts!'

'Do you?' I asked him.

'Sometimes I don't know what I believe. It's just alarming, can't you see, when a ten-year-old girl comes along to question you. Who is this Joanna that she can do this to me? Why should I trust her?'

'Roger,' I pleaded with some passion, 'If you do nothing else with your life, trust her! Listen to me! I'm telling you this because you're a vicar, because you'll know what to do. This girl, this extraordinary girl, is . . . Jesus.'

I paused before I said that word, wondering how best to say it. That pause might have scuppered my case, because the effect of it was that Roger began looking at me hard, and I could see him wondering whether I was either mad or a co-conspirator. But rather than accuse me of either he began rolling a small piece of paper between his finger and thumb.

'I shouldn't have told you, should I?'

Roger flicked the paper pellet into the remains of the fire. We both watched it light up for an instant before dying.

'No, I wish you hadn't,' he said. 'I don't believe it.'

'Perhaps I shouldn't tell you this either,' I said. 'Look at my hand. See there? I snagged an artery on some barbed wire. That's what I wanted to tell you that day. Joanna put her hand on it and stopped the bleeding, just like that.'

Roger took my hand but barely glanced at it. What was there to see, anyway?

'I'm sorry,' he said, 'you asked me if I believed in miracles, I remember. The answer is, I don't really. My faith doesn't stretch that far. Can you understand that? I'm being honest with you. Joanna is inspired, she's a fine preacher, she's a prophet, even. Some of us are closer to God than others. But I can't come the whole way with you on this.'

'Don't fret on that score,' I sighed, 'I've not gone very far down the way myself. Look at me. I teach the girl. I can testify . . . I can testify . . . I would defend Joanna in every corner of this earth. But what is faith, Roger? What is faith?'

By the time Roger left, we were, if not exactly friends, at least fellow-travellers.

The invitation for Joanna to be a guest on *The Big Breakfast* took everyone by surprise. Mrs Wells opened the envelope which fell on her doormat and spread the good news. By now Joanna was receiving three or four invitations a day, but they tended to be from religious organisations of one sort or another. When a very excited Mr Birch told me, I threatened to resign if he let her humiliate herself like that. But he told me that Joanna was keen to go ahead (why was Joanna confiding in him and not in me?) and when Roger said, 'I don't see the harm in it, I imagine TV is the evangelist's dream,' I realised the time had come to stand back and let events take their course. I even managed to persuade myself that some good might come of it.

So one afternoon a limousine arrived at the school to take Joanna to a London hotel. Her parents were already sitting in the back of it, and when Mrs Wells saw me, down whirred the electric window, and she called me over to her and said, 'Praise be, Mr Jermond. God is really making things happen.' A clean-shaven Mr Wells leant forward and waved, and a whiff of cheap after-shave escaped into the Norfolk air. 'My name's "German",' I said, weakly, but I had long given up on them. My Joanna cut as tragic a figure as I had ever seen her: a skinny shadow of a girl, still dressed in her school uniform and, despite the size of the car that drove them away, forced (or so I imagined) to sit between her parents.

But Roger and his wife had no misgivings. They were confident that Joanna would be quite wonderful. 'After all,' exclaimed Mrs Halliday, 'She has God's blessing. And incidently, we do hope you'll be watching *The Big Breakfast* with us.' So at 6.30 in the morning on Wednesday 7th February, I stumbled via a few cold puddles to the vicarage, where I was promised a full English breakfast.

Their house immediately reminded me of how pleasant it was to have your toes and fingers warmed right through; and though Roger himself was quiet and anxious, Mrs Halliday bombarded me with questions about Joanna, what she was like to teach, how she'd reacted to her sudden fame, what her parents had thought about it all, where was she staying in London . . . My dear Joanna, sharing a bedroom with her parents, a family room. How could she bear it? What would they ask her to say and do? I imagined that trio getting up at four in the morning, Mrs Wells giving her a dress to wear, Joanna donning it like a sacrificial robe. I imagined them being greeted at the studio, the parents talking too much, Joanna too little.

The kitchen was covered in photographs: the Hallidays had grown-up children and grandchildren and, though I politely asked their names and ages, if you had asked me even a moment later I would have forgotten them. I noticed a half-knitted baby's cardigan and a bag of blue wool on the sofa, a bookshelf of local history, an open book of prayers by Michael Quoist. I envied their ability to belong, to be of this world.

'Do you know what time Joanna's slot is?' asked Roger, turning on the TV.

'I've no idea,' I said, 'but I'd imagine they'd be wanting a fairly large audience – I should think later rather than sooner.'

'One egg or two, Patrick? Bacon? Sausage? Roger, how about you?'

But Roger and I told Mrs Halliday, all pukka and bright in her floral apron, that frankly neither of us had much of an appetite. Perhaps after Joanna had 'done her bit' we would feel more in the mood for a slap-up breakfast.

'Haven't we a bottle of champagne somewhere, Roger?'

'I can't think of champagne now, darling,' said Roger.

But Mrs Halliday insisted that somewhere, but goodness knows where, she put a bottle away for a special occasion, and if ever there was a special occasion it was now, and she set off merrily to find it.

But Roger and I were far from joyous. We sat nervously on the sofa, mugs of Nescafé in our hands, transfixed by *The Big Breakfast*. Roger murmured that perhaps we should pray, and I noticed that from time to time he closed his eyes – whether to escape the full throttle of Denise Van Outen, or for a moment alone with God, I'm not sure. His wife joined us for a few moments, to tell us the champagne was now in the fridge getting cold, but at the sight of Denise lasciviously biting into supermarket sausages, dressed in tight leather trousers and a frothy pink shirt, she tut tutted and left us to it.

'People always think sausages are the sexiest food you can eat but I'm not so sure, Johnny,' purred Denise.

'Myself I prefer chocolate. Melted chocolate. I like eclairs. I like licking the chocolate off the top,' slavered Johnny.

'I like squashing my hands into the middle of a great spongy jammy yummy cake. It's making me quite squirm all over just to think of it,' giggled Denise.

And Roger and I squirmed with her.

'Is there really an audience for this?' asked my innocent companion. 'Has Joanna seen this programme? Is it really appropriate?'

'I'm afraid it's too late now. She might have been better off with *Richard and Judy*.'

'How's that poor girl going to deal with them?'

'She's tougher than you might imagine,' I said, thinking the opposite.

'A few little agony questions for you here, Denise, the wise one. A love problem from Gavin in Eastbourne. He wants to know, "How much do you have to spend on a girl before you can expect her to go to bed with you?"'

'Well, Gav, my advice to you is give up, you're obviously a right bastard.'

'Who thought of inviting her? What is she going to say?' Roger had gone from red to white and was now stable at grey.

'At least Denise didn't say, "Thirty-five pounds should do the trick, Gav." You never know. She might be a real gem underneath. You wait, Joanna will come up trumps. There she is, look.'

But when we saw her neither of us could say a word: we could only watch, aghast, powerless.

'Is she on, is she on?' Our last merry note was Mrs Halliday's, and she came in and sat beside us, ready to enthuse.

'I don't know why they ever invited her. She's a child,' murmured Roger, and indeed, never had it been more apparent that that's exactly what she was. Joanna was standing like a stray waif amongst a jolly crowd which had presumably been invited into the studio to laugh along at all the jokes. They all had their names on their lapels, and were clapping and giggling and eating the last of the sausages with their fingers. Joanna had a badge with her name on it too, and the very thought of her standing there, enduring the patronising hands of whoever attached it to her, made me feel sick. She looked like a young doe, stunned by the motorway traffic speeding past it, non-comprehending of this other world she had stumbled upon.

'This is exploitative rubbish,' exclaimed Mrs Halliday.

'There are poltergeists in Bexhill,' exclaimed Denise. 'Yes, telephones have begun dialling themselves.'

'Strange but true,' added Johnny at her side.

'Mysterious phone calls are being made and we don't know who's making them.'

'Perhaps it's God.'

'And to tell us whether it's God we've got our very own angel on the show.'

'She's a lovely girl, and she's all the way down from Norfolk to tell us all about God. Joanna, you come forward, love. I bet you can tell us a thing or two. Here we are, you sit down between Johnny and me. First of all, we want to know, who's making those phone calls?'

'I don't know,' said Joanna, and the girl was so quiet, so still, that she scarely seemed to be breathing.

'You'll need to speak up, Jo, you don't mind if I call you Jo?'

'She's not interested in some stupid phone calls, Denise. Joanna, you tell us about God, then. You tell us in your own words.'

Joanna looked at them both as though she hadn't even understood the question; and there followed a ghastly silence in which Johnny and Denise looked at each other anxiously, and the audience looked glum.

Denise tried another route: 'Tell us about your school, Jo. What lessons will you miss this morning, then?'

'Come on, Joanna, you show them.' Dear Mrs Halliday, rooting for her with all her might; Roger with his eyes closed, doubtless praying; and myself, exhausted from hoping too much, bent double in defeat.

'She can't win them all,' soothed Mrs Halliday. 'You men need some old-fashioned egg and bacon,' and she was off again, task in hand. But Roger and I couldn't move. We sat there, mesmerised, after Joanna had been sent back into the crowd to find herself 'a big breakfast'; and a fashion designer from Hull found herself in the hot seat, and that sunny trio began singing together: 'Where did you get that hat, where did you get that hat?'

The smell of hot bacon and the first few rays of sunlight were doing their best to rouse us from our miserable state of apathy, but it was in fact the 8.50 slot on *The Big Breakfast* that finally brought Roger to his feet. Hundreds of tea cups in soft-focus passed before our eyes, interspersed with every sacred object you could name: a chalice, a mace, a prayer-book, even a crucifix, and all this to a tune that might have been composed in a school playground: 'More tea, vicar, more tea, vicar, more tea, vicar . . .'

'What, in the name of God, do they think they're doing? Is there no sense of what is decorous?' spat out Roger.

But we went on watching. There was a further audience, this

time, which had been squeezed into a studio decked out to look like a small chapel, and Johnny had dressed himself up as a vicar, and Denise was a nun with buck teeth. It dawned on us that this was a game, the point of which seemed to be guessing, quite arbitrarily, the number of cups of tea the vicar had served to his parishioners the previous afternoon. Viewers at home were invited to ring in and guess. 'Two hundred and ten,' guessed the first. 'Lower, lower, lower,' chanted the little audience in the chapel. 'One hundred and ninety,' guessed the viewer. 'Lower, lower, lower,' chanted the audience.

Roger was pacing the room like a caged animal: 'Good God, this is intolerable, turn this rubbish off, Patrick.'

But suddenly I noticed Joanna in the chapel, and made Roger sit down to see. She had crept in at the back, and it was apparent to both of us that her attitude was quite different. Of course, we only saw glimpses of her; perhaps the cameramen were embarrassed by her presence and kept skirting over her, but it was obvious to both of us that Denise had spotted her and was wondering how best to react. But Joanna refused to be ignored, and she shouted out, 'Higher, higher, higher.'

'Oh look, vicar, we've got a visitor. Let's welcome back Joanna.'

Johnny was too professional to be fazed by the intrusion. 'Welcome back Joanna. What d'you think of our little chapel, Joanna? Is it home from home?'

Denise shot Johnny an embarrassed look and was obviously considering removing her buck teeth. Joanna was now making a path for herself through the crowd, and Denise and Johnny were desperately searching for a strategy to deal with the unexpected denouement. It was the audience that dictated the only course of action Denise the nun and Johnny the vicar could take: they were preternaturally silent. They wanted to hear what Joanna had to say.

Joanna stood before them with utter composure.

'I'm sorry,' she said, 'but God didn't make any phone calls to Bexhill.'

Denise and Johnny laughed with relief.

'So what did he do, Jo?' A man shouted out from the back.

'God created us,' she said, simply.

'Who remembers their Bible then, folks? It was a seven-day job, wasn't it?' Johnny was bringing it all in line.

'You mean six days, you blasphemer,' threatened the nun.

'It wasn't quite like that,' said Joanna, gently, like a patient mother.

'Tell us how it was then, Jo.' That was Denise, resigned at last to listen.

'Go on, Joanna, tell us how it was,' said the man at the back.

And we all waited for her to tell us.

Joanna paused. All fear had been taken from her, and the sudden strength in her was so extraordinary that Roger clutched his wife's hand and whispered, 'Praise be to God.'

We waited, and never has a silence been so palpable, so part of the structure of things. Then finally Joanna began to speak, gently, but with an authority I had never before witnessed, even in her.

'Once we were only in the mind of God,' she said. 'We were just an idea. God is the sum of all the laws of nature, and his will breathed life into them. But he made us in his own image. Our ability to reason has made God's laws intelligible to us; our ability to love reflects God's own ability to love us; and the power we have within in us to create is comparable to the power of God.

'I tell you now, we all have that power to create, not just a piece of music, not just a work of art, which thank God I know you value, but you have the power within you to do something more than that. Like God, you have imagination. Imagination is power. Even at the beginning of the last century Einstein understood the relation between power and matter: how energy creates matter, how matter creates energy, how tightly interwoven are the two. I want to show you this morning exactly how tightly.'

Denise and Johnny were smiling their professional smile; but, by now, each of them had lost control of the situation and they knew it. They made no secret, however, of muttering into their microphones, the net result of which was to inform the viewer (across the bottom of the screen) that the programme schedule had been delayed.

'1 want you to imagine an orange. I want you all to imagine one. I want everyone at home to imagine one. How many people will be watching us, Denise?'

Denise finally removed her buck teeth to explain that she wasn't sure.

'Could it be twenty million?' asked the dear girl.

'Oh no,' exclaimed Denise, 'I don't think as many as that, do you, Johnny? Well, you never know.'

'I need twenty million people.'

'Well, I'm sorry, but people have gone to work by now, or school, there's just not twenty million people around.'

'But you must get them.' Joanna looked directly at the camera and said, 'If there's someone who's asleep in your house, wake them; if you're a schoolteacher, tell the school to watch me; if you're at work, get your colleagues to come. We shall create a moment in history. We shall create a moment for your scientists to ponder over forever.'

Well, she did it. Barely ten minutes elapsed before the countometer which had appeared on the bottom right of our TV screen told us that the magic figure had been reached: over a third of England was with her, with our Joanna, and seven years on anyone could tell you what they were doing when the phone call came, or the banging on the door, or the manager calling them away from their workstations to watch . . .

'I need everyone to think of an orange,' said Joanna. 'A ripe, round orange, to fit here, in the cup of my upturned hands. I shall count to ten, and then you must all imagine it as well as you can, not too big, not too small, an orange unbruised and perfect. Think of its colour, its texture, think of its roundness, think of the place where it was plucked from the tree. Praise be to God, imagine.'

The image was only faint, of course. If we had anticipated something solid, something you could throw into the air, and feel, or even eat, then we might have been disappointed. It was more like the ghost of an orange: or even less than a ghost, because its outline hovered and was uncertain of itself. But anyone who saw it never forgot.

# 12

IN THE HEADY DAYS following Joanna's television appearance, a nation woke up, as it were, from a stupor. If there's a
God out there, then what should we do about it? Evangelical
Christians already knew: they would break out into song at bus
stops, on railway platforms, in supermarket queues. Muslims
and Sikhs likewise became lighter in step. They embraced not
only each other but Christians in public, with the words, 'Many
religions, one God, brother.' Closet Christians came out in
droves, those who'd been to church as children, those who'd
always paused to wonder at Christmas and Easter. Lapsed
Catholics suddenly found themselves knocking at the doors of
seminaries and successful businessmen threw in the towel to
become hermits in the Western Isles.

There were those, however, who claimed that Joanna's
'conjuring trick' was no more than a typical piece of modern
television: getting a child to play along with those special effects
was just one more example of how the media would exploit at
all costs. But if this had been the case, the believers argued, how
was it that both Denise Van Outen and Johnny Vaughan
resigned by the end of that famous week, after two miserable
days trying to emulate that light-hearted banter which had won
both of them such a name for themselves? Why did every single
member of that original studio audience – yes, Lenny Dee,
Sandra Murdoch, Dick Hammond (household names to us now,
and great preachers of our time) – and indeed everyone involved
with the production of that programme, find themselves not

only making confessionals to countless national newspapers and magazines, but actually radically changing the way they lived?

I think the secret to Joanna's success was that her advice on how to get closer to God was not only easy to follow but a pleasure to perform. Gone were the masochistic rituals of the Middle Ages, gone, to a large extent, was guilt, and the counting and measuring of sins. 'Sin,' she told Jenni Murray on *Woman's Hour* (27th January), 'is anything which causes alienation from God; when the conscience becomes so close-packed and dense that the pale blue sky can't be seen beyond it. Conscience only feels like conscience when it's near the surface; fear it when you no longer feel it, when it becomes like scale encasing the soul.' She suggested that we remember or, if our memories were unreliable, then imagine, what it was like before we were enveloped by the stuff of this world: the noise of it, its artificial light, its love of fear; and to find a quiet place where there was nothing to distract us, where we could contemplate and receive and be still. This was a time, she said, when our souls should feel like warm wax, when our will must be utterly surrendered, when we must listen with our whole being to the music of God.

But though religions across the world had understood the importance of this act of submission, and its ability to make you aware even of the contours of your very soul, there was a further way to respond to God which we had all but forgotten. Yes, we were happy to be reminded of God's love for us in prayer, in solitude, in contemplation; but we had forgotten how to show our love for him, by adoring him, literally, bringing our mouths to him, in song and music of every kind. We had forgotten how to rejoice. 'I have come,' said Joanna, 'because the lines of communication between our two worlds have become frayed. Music is the language of God; it is the child of absolute number and pure emotion. But we can not only hear it, we can sing it. So sing now: sing in joy and sing in pain, sing to God.'

But I didn't sing. Rather, I watched Joanna's story unfold at a distance, and my predominant emotion was far from joy. Rather, it was an overwhelming protectiveness for Joanna herself. She insisted on staying on at the school, and I like to think we provided some sort of a refuge for her. I also like to think she sought me out in particular. She no longer seemed as aloof as she did, but saw us, I hope, as a team: Joanna and I taking on the rest of the world.

I would watch her working through simple equations, sucking at the end of her pencil, and wonder, 'What does Joanna really know about absolute number? If she heard a prelude of Bach, would she recognise it? Would she say, "Ah, here is a man who understands mathematics!"' Or then there was a time when I watched her copying down a picture of a Celtic cross, and ambled over to her desk to see what she was making of it. I said to her, 'The others have chosen yellow to colour it, but you have chosen brown. Why is that?' Joanna merely shrugged. '"Why?" is not always the right question,' she said.

But of course that didn't stop me from looking for theological clues in everything she did or said. Even now I thumb through Joanna's exercise books looking for some hidden code among the lists of capital cities or time zones; I look for reasons why she neglected to use a comma in some punctuation exercise. Doubtless one day they will be stored in the manuscript department of the Cambridge University Library, and researchers of the future will approach them in much the same way.

Thankfully Joanna's classmates didn't share my scholastic preoccupations. They weren't even preternaturally good, but displayed the same natural good humour and occasional over-exuberance that they always had done. It was only when I watched them from the classroom window during break that I realised things were quite different now. There was no more football, no more skipping. Rather, the children would gather round her and listen attentively to what she told them. All we teachers instinctively knew that we weren't welcome – their souls were still like warm wax, while mine, even then, was a dry and crusty thing. And though I've never found out the exact content of her playground dispatches (for the children themselves have given me various and often conflicting accounts) seven years on I can confirm that three-quarters of those who heard her became healers in their own right. Ralph, in particular, has not only been the medium of the most spectacular examples of healing (giving sight, in one instance, to an eight-year-old girl who had been blind at birth) but at the tender age of eighteen has set up a school for others to recognise their own gifts.

It sometimes seemed that while others were being reborn I was waiting to be born for the first time. The situation seemed laughable. There I was, so close to her, so believing in her, so trusting that she was the one for whom the world had waited for two thousand years, yet some part of me remained as cold and ungodly as a fish. And finding myself partly in the public eye myself, as her teacher, whom should I confide in, or at least, consult? Both Roger and Jocelyn were like aliens to me now, glowing and happy but in some sense, gone. It seemed so ungrateful to confess to either of them than I was any less joyful than themselves.

It's true, I did seek out a clergyman or two in the first few weeks. Ironically, they were the new celebrities: few papers or magazines didn't carry an interview with one or other of them. But they all seemed lost on their own trajectory, their old version of 'faith' tested too hard, the new, all too powerful but as yet with no history, no fingertip assertions, no natural home. While being interviewed on the radio, they would find themselves literally overcome by the extraordinariness of what they were saying. When asked their opinion on who Joanna actually was, their replies were quite feeble; they floundered, laughed, deflected the question. 'But we know who she is!' said one, quite typically. But no one said it, no one said she was Jesus. I knew, but what good did it do me?

Instead they would urge us to worship the Lord. 'Praise him!' they would exclaim, and many evidently did. But I just thought of my mother and her 'Praise the Lord!'s and shrivelled inside.

Mr Birch, meanwhile, proved himself far more adept at worship than I: not only did he worship Joanna herself (peering odiously through the small window in our classroom door at any odd time of day) but he worshipped a large number of those who came to visit her in the afternoons. Journalists were beginning to come from America now, and almost every country in Europe. Many an editrix held Mr Birch in her talons, the happiest of prey, and demanded to take a look at Joanna's academic work. They asked to see her poetry; Mr Birch would rush to duplicate yet another copy of it. They would ask for an interview with her parents, and Mr Birch would arrange the fee.

I loathed these interviews. Marion, rightly, refused to attend them right from the beginning. Jocelyn and I didn't speak, but somehow felt it our duty to be there. Joanna herself seemed tired and uncomfortable. I would watch Mr Birch lean forward on his chair, his gestures large and ugly, the creases on his too-tight trousers straining, giving for the umpteenth time an account of the assembly at Gresham Primary School, and how, if there was to be a visitation from the divine realm, North Norfolk was as pure and likely a place for it as anywhere in the world. 'God knew what he was doing,' he would grin, 'when he sent Joanna to us.'

Then, one afternoon, while Mr Birch was waving off a large-hipped, ruby-lipped Austrian fraulein at the school gate, and Joanna was putting on her coat ready for her journey home, she said to me, 'Mr German, when people come to meet me I don't want you or Mr Birch to be there. Just Mrs Fairbrother.'

I said, 'You should have mentioned it before, Joanna. Obviously, that's how it's should be.'

'Thank you,' she said. And almost as an afterthought she added, 'I promise you this, sir. One day the grace of God will be with you.' I took her hand without thinking, I felt so grateful to her. I tried to think of something to say. But she just put her finger to her lips, and whispered, 'Ssh, Mr German. Sometimes it's better not to say anything at all.'

Marion and I became friends again or, should I say, friends at last. She was in a worse state than I was. At least I had certainty; while she was doubting her very doubts, and barely knew any more how to make a stand. Her husband Dominic was trying to get her to go to a church in Holt, he'd even enrolled the twins in Sunday school.

'He comes home humming these tunes,' she complained. 'I feel like hitting him.'

'Why don't you?' I laughed, feeling a certain solidarity.

'Because he'd forgive me,' she said seriously. 'And that would be even worse.'

'You should come to Norwich Cathedral with me one Sunday,' I said, never expecting for a moment that she'd take me up on it. 'I'd really appreciate that,' she said, touching my elbow meaningfully.

She might have been distinctly less appreciative had she realised she'd be sharing a car with the Hallidays. So there we were: Roger and his wife emanating joy from the back seat, Marion and I stewing in our own anxiety in the front. Mrs Halliday asked Marion, 'So what's it like being with Joanna every day?' Marion mumbled that it was very inspiring, but Mrs Halliday couldn't hear her above the noise of the motorway. 'What?' she shouted from the back, 'What was that you said?' Marion turned round and shouted back at her, 'Very inspiring!'

This was on 18th February, and was Joanna's ninth sermon. By now it was necessary to arrive two hours before they began, just to be sure of a seat. Televisions had been set up in the close, and a thousand worshippers braved the weather to huddle there in their overcoats. It amused me that one of the first faces I recognised that morning was my counsellor at Cromer, but I was too embarrassed to wave. We saw Jocelyn on the arm of Barry Chuck, no less, and Marion whispered in my ear, 'Bloody hell, she's looking beautiful. I bet they're lovers.' And I whispered back, 'But they might not be. That's the more extraordinary thing.'

Mr Birch had two pews of worshippers rapt in his every word, and though we couldn't hear him we could imagine well enough that he might be giving an account of the fine assemblies held at Gresham Primary School. And all around us, while we were waiting, everyone was talking about Joanna, about how much she had affected their lives, how they were living at a time which would be remembered as holy for ever.

Then all of a sudden there was a hush; the organist began to play a Bach prelude, and the Bishop emerged from the vestry to conduct the service. Joanna herself never appeared until the time came to give her sermon. I imagined her praying, perhaps, or looking through the vestry window at the people gathered in the close and finding the strength within her to address them. Then after the second hymn, and after the lesson had been read, the Bishop sought Joanna and brought her back with him to the main body of the cathedral, looking as small and fragile as a bird.

I could see that Marion was fretting for her. She and I stood there like anxious parents, while her real parents held their heads high and looked as proud as punch. Joanna walked up into the pulpit, and the Bishop followed her, with his large avuncular hand resting on her shoulder while she addressed us. I think on that particular occasion she was less steady than usual, she was certainly shaking at the beginning. Marion whispered to me, 'For God's sake, doesn't that man realise what he's putting her through?' And I whispered back, 'Just you wait, Marion. Listen to her.'

Joanna's ninth sermon is now, of course, one of her most celebrated. In case a reader doesn't have a copy of Joanna's *Seventeen Sermons* at hand, I shall quote from it at length (page 62, illustrated edition):

> *The power to create is within all of us. But not only are we lost in the business of this world, but we find ourselves no longer necessary to it. We no longer weave our cloth: it is woven for us. We no longer dye our cloth in colours we have found in nature: the cloth is dyed for us. We no longer decide how to clothe ourselves: designers tell us the clothes we should wear and how we should wear them. It is not the ascendance of science that has lost us our God: God and science are one. It is the consequence of having our ears deafened and our voices drowned by the machines that govern us. For hundreds of years men have sung over their work, sung as they've gathered in their harvest, sung melodies over their needlework, but now we have factories and tractors and traffic; we close our windows on the world because the world has come to represent noise and disharmony. Once we rose with the first light of day, with birdsong; then we rose to the chimes of a church bell, and now to the electronic drone of an alarm clock. Is it a wonder we have lost God, when our hearts have been so starved of the ways of apprehending him?*
>
> *Science never took God away from you: science revealed God. Would you sooner believe in magic? That the universe sprang into existence because of some*

*cosmic alchemy? That the laws of nature that gave us life itself came into being from nothing? Can you believe that with all your hearts? Can you believe that the spirit of man is nothing more than a cosmic hiccup? Look to science to tell you how: and the more you look, the more you will find the stamp of God; but when you begin to ask why, then, and only then, will you begin to see his face.*

*Science never took God away from you: you pushed him away yourselves. You stole the very days away from him. You made your own light. You made your own time. You merged his seasons into one, and hid in a dark room. But your most grievous sin was to steal the birthright of every child born: to tell him that he couldn't, when he could. You told him that he couldn't paint, that he couldn't sing, that he couldn't tell stories. You told him there were only a few who could, and to shut up and listen, and make them his idols. You extinguished the light within your own children, and pretended it was never there.*

Thus spoke the child of all light.

When she had finished she hung her head, and all three thousand of us were silent for as long as a minute. Because Joanna took us somewhere else, and it was hard to resume the banalities of finding one's place in the service sheet, or the number of the following hymn. It was even hard to find the correct expression when meeting the eye of your neighbour in the pew. I looked at Marion and raised my eyebrows, but Marion was lost in her own thoughts.

At this point in the service the canon would take over; Joanna found it quite beyond her to be present at the eucharist. We watched the Bishop take Joanna by the hand and lead her down the steps of the pulpit. Joanna told me he would take her to an office adjacent to the presbytery, and together they would pray and drink sweet tea together. It was only during the last hymn that they would appear again, with the Bishop making the final blessing. 'May the peace of God, which passeth all under-standing, keep your hearts and minds in the knowledge and the love of God, and of his son Jesus Christ our Lord.'

Then when the organ began to play, I whispered to Marion, 'Listen to that, that's just what Joanna says, there is the heart and the mind, and the one loves and the other knows.'

'I can see you're becoming quite the disciple,' whispered Marion back to me. Then, when I looked hurt, she managed, 'She was very good, Patrick.' But I could sense there had been no ground-breaking conversion experience. Then again, who was I to talk?

At the end of the service we were more or less hemmed in. A good number of the congregation were quietly weeping and had no intention of moving on, and I noticed, to Barry Chuck's credit, that he was one of them. He was still kneeling and his head was bowed down, while Jocelyn was standing at his side with her arms outstretched, as though she were saying, 'Take me up into your arms, Lord.' Roger and his wife had likewise moved to another planet, and there was no point nudging them on to beat the traffic out of Norwich.

I looked out for my counsellor but couldn't spot her, and was suddenly distracted by the strident voice of Mrs Wells. She was giving a graphic account of Joanna's birth, of her reluctance to be born, and how in the end she 'had to have a Caesar, and I'd had eight children before her, and gave birth as easy as peas in a pod.' Then I heard her husband complain, 'It's no good being rich in spirit if you're poor in body. Joanna has to share a bedroom with three of her older brothers. It's not right, in a civilised country.' I watched an eager lady writing out a cheque, while others turned away.

We stayed, that morning, to watch the whole show wind down. We watched the momentarily transported return to the world, their silent awe revert to chatter. We watched the BBC cameramen pack up their cameras, and the sacristans take the silver to the vestry. But it was the demise of Joanna herself which made me feel so sorrowful. If Marion hadn't been with me I would have gone up to her. She resisted so absolutely the gratitude of those who came to thank her that quite soon nobody bothered to do so. When the Bishop eventually had to leave her, to attend to other business, Joanna waited in the shadows of the ambulatory, and submerged herself in a solitude where no one could reach her.

I watched her parents find her and tell her it was time to go. Her mother said, 'Hurry up, Joanna, the car's waiting outside.' I walked up to them, I couldn't help it.

'Joanna, Joanna!' I exclaimed. I don't know quite what it was I wanted to say.

'Wasn't she wonderful today! Everyone was spellbound!'

'Mrs Wells, they were,' I said.

'Same time next week, then!'

Mrs Wells put her arm round Joanna and I saw her flinch.

'Come along then, young girl,' she said, feigning affection.

'The car's waiting!' reiterated Mr Wells, impatiently.

Joanna looked at me sadly and walked away between them.

Every schoolchild, every household has a copy of *Seventeen Sermons*; many have the three-DVD set of them. Unfortunately, Joanna's first three sermons weren't televised, but audiotapes abound, as does the tape of her famous appearance on *Start the Week* with Jeremy Paxman, her only venture into broadcasting after *The Big Breakfast*.

As I write this there's a transcript on my desk, published, as it so happens, by that self-same publisher I deserted all those years ago. There's a close-up of Joanna's face on the front of it. Ah yes, she looks holy here, her hair is tied back more loosely than usual, her eyes are luminous, and I recognise the Romanesque column behind her: she's giving a sermon in Norwich. As I flick through it I realise there are passages I've come to know well. Even the characters who appeared with her are now mainly remembered for their association with her: Robyn Brett, over from America to publicise her new book *Four Essences* about the human spirit; and Tod Chatwin, fresh from giving a lecture at the British Academy on *The Evolution of Sexual Preening*.

I want to quote a section from it, more as an indication of the way in which Joanna managed to hold her own with adults who were all well used to expounding and defending their beliefs in dialogue than to add to the hundreds of commentaries on Joanna's thought which are already available.

Tod Chatwin was invited to speak first: he was, in essence, a propagator of the theories of Richard Dawkins – 'We are survival machines – robot vehicles blindly programmed to preserve the selfish molecules known as genes.' Robyn would have none of it. 'What room have you left for humanity?' she cried out in her South American drawl. 'What room for goodness? For individuality?'

'I haven't ruled anything out,' insisted Tod, unfazed. 'Of course we're good to each other. It's in our interests to be good to each other. And isn't individuality rather attractive? Anything which is attractive is highly to be recommended.'

Robyn found herself unable to be still for the duration of Tod's description of the biology of the peacock. 'No! No! No!' she cried, 'What you say might be true about a peacock, but stop there, please! Let's talk about human beings!' Paxman had no alternative but to let Robyn have her say, there and then. 'Over to you, Robyn,' he said, 'Who are we?' It's at this point my transcript begins:

ROBYN There are four essences located within the human psyche: they are the physical essence, the emotional essence, the mental essence, and the spiritual essence. In order to be fulfilled, these essences have to be in harmony with one another, but this can't happen until the mental and emotional issues are resolved. I'd like to explain to Radio 4 listeners at this juncture that Tod has a handkerchief up to his mouth. I think he's suppressing a laugh. Perhaps he considers he has no emotional issues to resolve.

PAXMAN Robyn, tell us what happens when we resolve our mental and emotional life.

ROBYN Only then do we begin to be in touch with our spiritual essence: the flash of inspiration, the scent of magic, the knowledge of unity, the understanding, somehow, of a greater love than human passion. All four essences: the physical, emotional, mental and spiritual, are linked to the heart. But the spiritual essence is particularly closely linked to the heart.

JOANNA What do you mean by 'the heart'?

ROBYN I would have thought, Joanna, you of all people would know about the human heart.

JOANNA I know what the heart is. But I don't think you know.

ROBYN The heart is what makes us human.

JOANNA And does the heart likewise make a cow a cow and a horse a horse?

ROBYN Then what do you say it is?

JOANNA I say the heart is the soul.

ROBYN Then let's call it the soul. I have no problem with that.

JOANNA But if you say the spiritual essence is closely linked to the heart, you are in fact saying it is closely linked to the soul, though nevertheless different. How is the spirit different from the soul?

ROBYN I actually said, 'spiritual essence'.

JOANNA So how is 'spiritual essence' different from spirit?

ROBYN 'Spiritual essence' is part of a human being.

JOANNA And spirit is not? But 'soul' is a part?

ROBYN If you want me to say there is something metaphysical about human spirituality, I'm afraid I can't do that, Joanna. I was in the US when you did that miracle on TV, and we have that sort of trick done quite well, thank you, every afternoon on five channels. Religion has done more damage to this world than it has good. It's instigated torture, Jo. Did they teach you about the Spanish Inquisition at your school?

JOANNA Religion is the human response to what is holy. It's in its nature to be flawed. But God is like the light within a lantern, and the glass of the lantern is of many colours. Tell me, do you believe human beings have a soul?

ROBYN I believe human beings have a human soul, of human dimensions, and which ceases to exist on the death of the body.

JOANNA So what do you think the soul is made of?

ROBYN It's a feeling. We all have it. And if we didn't have bodies and neurons and stuff we wouldn't feel that feeling.

JOANNA It seems to me you don't believe in the soul at all.

TOD You're on my team, Robyn. We know, you and I, about the full range of emotions we human beings are capable of. You're in a restaurant, you've had a couple of glasses of first-class chablis, and you're gazing into the eyes of a beautiful woman.

ROBYN That is not a spiritual experience.

TOD Okay then, how about gazing in awe at a flock of swooping swallows?

ROBYN What are you trying to say?

TOD I'm saying that I'm as spiritual as you are. I'm saying there's a feeling, and it might just as well have been greed, or contentment, or anxiety, and we stick a label on it. What's more, this spiritual label of yours is in the modern day rather like the label 'powerful'. To some women, in fact to a lot of women, it's rather like an aphrodisiac.

JOANNA He's right. You don't believe in the soul, Robyn. You believe in a word.

ROBYN Spirit doesn't always have to end up at God's feet.

JOANNA Spirit is always at God's feet. The word 'spirit' is a human invention, and is at the mercy of biologists.

TOD You're at my mercy, Robyn.

ROBYN I am not. Biology can't give us the whole story of what it is to be human.

TOD You don't need any explanations from up on high. Evolution is all that we have. What is is what is.

JOANNA Yes, Tod, and what will be will be.

TOD And what has been has been. Human beings developed over millions of years. We are the consequence of million upon million desirable genetic mutations. We are, in the form we take, inevitable.

ROBYN What about the mutation that made man wake up one morning and appreciate the beauty of the cosmos, or dance, or music?

TOD It's not at all difficult to explain man's love of beauty.

Beauty has always been equated with symmetry. The symmetrical face, the symmetrical body, and indeed, the body of a dancer, is a sign of health. Should it be surprising to you that our forebears should wish to mate with healthy specimens of the species?

ROBYN We all know that beauty is skin-deep, Tod.

TOD When I was reading your book last night, Robyn, I gathered that one's physical essence vastly improved its quality if the other essences were well taken care of.

ROBYN Yes, I have a holistic philosophy.

TOD Well, so do I, Robyn. Mind, body and soul are all one, and always have been one.

PAXMAN Are you satisfied, Robyn?

ROBYN Okay then, Tod. Tell us, what do you think life is about?

TOD It's not about anything. Life is DNA. Life is go go go.

ROBYN And that's it? We are born, we live, we die, just so that we can go go go, as you put it so prettily?

TOD Don't think I underestimate the potential of DNA. Its complexity is undeniable.

JOANNA Yet you are missing the point. How did the whole complex universe come into being, with laws which would, inevitably, produce intelligent life? That kind of design doesn't happen by accident. Once life is there, yes, it knows how to develop and replicate itself. But how did everything come into being? The coincidence seems too fantastic. A palace might as soon appear after a sandstorm in the desert: towers, windows, marble floors – and you would say to me, 'All the atoms necessary to build that palace already existed, and they just happened to find themselves in the correct order.' Even over billions and billions of years, coincidences like that just don't happen.

TOD Anything that has happened was bound to happen.

JOANNA That answer is too glib, Tod. You know it is. What is it that you fear about creators? Do you feel about our own earth-bound artists that their creations were bound to be, that there was no energy on their own part that made it happen?

TOD Ah, so now you're turning artists into mystical beings.

JOANNA Not just artists, Tod, but anyone who is aware of their free will. For the body, in which I include the physical brain, serves as a filter and sometimes an obstacle to the soul. Those in the east have learnt to transcend the body, but if the body is healthy there's no advantage in adopting such extreme measures, and in some cases, the body, particularly the brain, is useful to us. But when the filter is blocked, in other words, the body is ill, the soul must either transcend or wait to be released.

TOD (laughing) You mean when you die.

PAXMAN Are you saying there's life after death?

JOANNA Don't look to me to tell you this. Look to your physicists. Energy never becomes nothing, the smallest particle never simply disappears, and nor does the energy generated by the human personality.

TOD Hell, I don't want to be a disembodied Tod Chatwin.

JOANNA Then don't be. Take care while you can.

PAXMAN You're now telling us, Joanna, that the soul is a form of energy?

TOD I'd like to know what form. I'd like to know why we scientists haven't managed to locate it.

JOANNA It's only souls who can seek out souls, Tod. You may as well give a book of logarithms to a dancer as use the tools of analysis to come to know the human spirit.

PAXMAN I'm afraid we've only a few seconds left. Any final word, Joanna?

JOANNA We crave the mind of God, Mr Paxman. Tod, through his science, and Robyn, with her essences – we are all of us craving the mind of God.

PAXMAN On that rather more conciliatory note, thank you very much.

The decision to invite Joanna to address a congregation at Hyde Park on Easter Day was made by the Archbishop of Canterbury, and it was a popular one. For three weeks the press was full of it. There were, of course, diehards of the Church of England who could never defer to a ten-year-old girl; but the Bishop of Norwich, being as he was an exemplar of gravitas, somehow made the advent of Joanna seem almost expected: glorious, yes, but glorious within the realm of belief, rather than beyond it.

During the first two weeks of April, there was also a puzzling correspondence between the Archbishop and the Pope, which historians are still trying to piece together. The Pope asked the Archbishop *di spiegare precisamente cio che e stato rivelato:* the evidence, as he saw it, wasn't yet sufficient. There followed an increasingly impatient request by the Archbishop as to what this evidence might consist of; but there was no resolution and, in his own address on Easter Day, Joanna was never mentioned.

The preparations took a week: enormous screens were put up at almost a hundred locations, along Park Lane and the Serpentine, and well into Kensington Gardens, so that everyone might glimpse Joanna as she addressed us. There were two dozen filming platforms, decorated with the logos of a hundred television companies: from America, Australia, Japan and seemingly every country in Europe had its representative. The media bandied guesses as to how many people would turn up on the day, and all the train and bus companies promised a full and free service into London that morning. Then as soon as the songs had been chosen (and who exactly had chosen them? Was it the Archbishop? Was it Joanna? Was it the Queen? How the chattering went on) every newspaper published song-sheets, with the recommendation they should be learned by heart, and the suggestion that even if people couldn't get to see Joanna in person they might sing along at home.

The Dorchester offered Joanna their Terrace Suite on the ninth floor for the Saturday night, 14th April. The anniversary of this night now registers within me a feeling even more powerful than the day which followed it, because this was the last time I ever spoke to my Joanna. I was aware, as her teacher, that during the month of March Joanna was beginning to withdraw. She had resisted every pressure to leave school, to tour the world with a tutor and preach; she explained, quite simply, that it was unnecessary, in the same way as it was unnecessary for her to perform miracles. She knew her mission, and she would perform that mission for God with all her might.

I was at my cottage in Beeston when Mrs Wells called round and told me about their invitation to stay at the Dorchester; and she told me that Joanna wanted to have supper with me there. I felt touched, more than touched, by Joanna's request. I was also angry with myself for feeling weighed down by it. I didn't want to be important; it frightened me. I knew that Roger wasn't intending to make the trip down to London: they were just going to be 'glued to the TV', and I'd told him I might well be joining them, I hated crowds. But there was a deeper reason I didn't want to go. The whole occasion for me seemed literally unbearable – in some sense it would be too much for me to bear. I had an instinct to hide myself away, till it had become history, till it had become safe.

I arrived at the Dorchester at eight o'clock. I felt absurdly anxious, and even found myself drinking whisky at the bar – flawed as I am, drink has never been a habit of mine – before standing in a lift lined with mirrors, and being forced to look at my reflection. I remembered immediately the poem Joanna had written for me once, about how I couldn't look in mirrors. I wondered if I'd changed.

Mrs Wells met me at the door, though I hardly recognised her. Her hair had been dyed black; and a hairdresser had evidently spent many hours concocting a top-knot made of elaborate and tiny plaits; and her dress was a huge extravagant affair in black organza.

'Come in, Patrick,' she said, 'You don't mind if I call you Patrick? We're like old friends now, after all.' Even her voice was quite different. I asked her what the occasion was.

'The occasion? The occasion? How can you ask such a thing? Dining in the grandest hotel in the whole of London and you can ask what the occasion is? Have you no manners of your own?'

'I'm sorry,' I said, 'I don't really have any smart clothes.'

'At least we're not going to be eating in the public dining-room, I suppose. Come into our private dining-room and I'll fix you a drink. Would you fancy a glass of wine?'

'No, the man would prefer beer, wouldn't you, mate?' Mr Wells was already there, inspecting the bottles on a drinks trolley in the corner. 'There are some funny things here,' he said, tweaking his newly groomed moustache, 'But not to worry, there's Fosters in the fridge.'

'Actually, would it be possible to have a glass of wine?' I ventured.

'I told you he'd like wine, Fred,' piped up Mrs Wells.

'Okay then. Wine. No problem,' said Fred. 'I'll get you some from the fridge because this stuff's a bit warm.'

'The waiter's going to come up in a moment with the food, we could let him serve it,' said Mrs Wells, plumping up the folds of her dress.

'You don't want to wait, do you, Pat? Just hang on two ticks.'

And off Fred went, to begin rummaging around in the fridge.

'Where's Joanna?' I asked her mother, who had now ensconced herself in an armchair and was flicking through a copy of *Tatler*.

'What pretty young things there are about nowadays.'

'Where's Joanna?' I asked again.

Mrs Wells looked momentarily nervous. 'It's all a bit much for her at the moment. She's been a bit quiet. We're just letting her rest a while. She was so happy when she heard you were coming for supper.'

'But aren't you going to wake her?'

'I don't think she's exactly sleeping.'

'What is she doing?'

'She's . . . how do you say it? She's doing what Joanna does. She's . . .'

'Praying.'

'Yes, that's the word. She's praying.'

Joanna suddenly appeared in the doorway like a vision. Her hair was wild and loose, her cheeks were flushed, her eyes were sore from weeping.

'I'm here,' she said. 'Would you mind if I spoke to Mr German alone?'

'Yes of course, my dear. Fred, Fred? Have you got that wine yet for Pat? What are you doing in there? One moment, Patrick, I'll just see what he's up to.'

'It's so hot in here. I need to go out on the terrace.' Joanna was uncharacteristically firm.

'I'm not sure about that,' said her mother. 'Fred, Fred, where have you gone?'

'I need to speak to Mr German. I need to be outside.'

'It's too nippy, young girl, you look feverish already.' Then there was a knock at the door, and Fred appeared from nowhere to answer it. Dinner had arrived.

'Mr German, come on, quickly.' Joanna thrust her slender

warm hand into mine and took me out on to the terrace.

'A coat, a coat,' called Mrs Wells after us.

'Come on,' insisted Joanna.

'Don't worry, I'll look after her,' I called back into the room.

So we stood out there on the terrace, Joanna and I; and she never let go of my hand. I squeezed it, as though I had it within me to comfort her, and I remember thinking, 'This is no angel's hand, this is a mere child's hand, it's so soft, so delicate, so young.'

'You don't have to go through with this, you know,' I said to her.

She was looking out straight ahead, her eye upon the platform they'd erected for her, as though it were a scaffold.

'There's not a soul who would hold it against you if you backed out now, Joanna. Look, you've brought all these people together to celebrate Easter Day. Isn't that enough? The Bishop of Norwich could hold the service, he could say you weren't feeling well or something.'

'That would be a lie,' said Joanna.

'Then tell the truth. Say it's too much for you.'

'If I were alone in this, it would be too much,' she whispered. But I had never seen her look more alone. Her shoulders were hunched forward, her hair was covering her face. I wanted to scoop her up and take her far away. I wanted to be her father and say, 'This has all got out of hand, darling. I think we should go home.'

Then she whispered, so quietly I could scarcely hear her above the traffic, 'It's all right, sir. All will be well. If you close your eyes you can hear a stormy sea, can't you? You might even imagine there were stars.'

Her mother called us inside. Joanna looked at me. 'Please don't stay for dinner, don't let that be your memory of me. Remember the stormy sea, sir, remember that.' Then suddenly she flung her arms about my neck and kissed me. 'May God bless you,' she said.

But that night I didn't so much remember the stormy sea as the stormy visage of Mrs Wells and the fragile glance of her daughter as the door of the Terrace Suite closed in my face. I should be ashamed of myself, Mrs Wells said. I'd had an invitation to have dinner with a girl who was better than a princess, yet I had something better to do, had I? Had I?

I'd made no plans at all. I hadn't even thought about where I'd sleep that night. Sleep seemed too great a luxury, I'd not considered it. I hadn't imagined ever saying goodbye to Joanna, or a time to fill which was not exclusively hers.

The park was kept open that Saturday night, and apart from a radius of some five hundred yards from the Route of Kings and the Parade Ground, there were tents scattered as far as the eye could see. There were bonfires, camp stoves, guitars and singing all through the night. I wanted to shake them, I wanted to wake the children sleeping in their parents' arms, I wanted to interrupt their pretty singing and their bloody descants and say, 'Something's not right here! Do you know at what human cost you're having a pleasant night out? Do you know the suffering you're causing? Look up at that terrace there, that one where the doors are tightly shut! There's a girl in there, do you know that? And she's been crying, and she's probably crying still, and you're the cause of it, all of you!'

By two in the morning I was crying myself, alone there sitting on the banks of the Serpentine. Almost everyone was sleeping by now, and the camp fires were dying down. I tried to pray. I began, 'Dear God, dear God,' but no words were out there with which to continue it. My demands were too great, yet I didn't know what they were.

A fisherman from Northumberland found me. He said I

seemed distressed but I denied it. He crouched down next to me as if I was a lost child, and told me that I could have his tent should I wish it, and he would share one with his brother who'd travelled down with him.

'You've come so far,' I said to him.

'Aye, that I have,' he said.

'Your faith must be very great.'

'Mark ye,' he said, 'the gal is Jesu Christ himself. He's come agin.'

He took me back to his tent and gave me a couple of blankets. I thanked him, and told him he was right about the girl. Then at last, I slept.


In the morning I sat with the fishermen. We drank tea out of tin mugs while dozens of technicians milled around us, connecting cables, testing loudspeakers, adjusting the angles of the television screens. We watched the very altar being carried up on to the platform: it was an old oak trestle table covered with a white linen cloth, and on it was placed a simple wooden cross; and later I saw a woman sewing four pockets on the corners of the cloth, and into each one she slotted a lead weight to prevent it blowing away. We watched chairs and benches being set out for the dignitaries: the Queen had let it be known that she and her family would be spending Easter at Sandringham as usual, and the good wishes and the flowers she had sent in her stead were not enough to satisfy the brothers, who told me quite confidently that she had made a great mistake and would regret it anon.

The service was to begin at noon or, more precisely, at the time when the sun was at its zenith, which happened to be at eleven minutes past. But already by nine it seemed as though the whole of Hyde Park was full – there were, perhaps, already a million people there. At ten the Bishops began to arrive: the official records show that there were twelve from the Church of

England (Coventry, Chichester, Ely, Salisbury, Winchester, Gloucester, Peterborough, Gloucester, York, Durham, Worcester and Norwich). The remaining fourteen, including the Archbishop of Canterbury, made the excuse that they had their own congregations to attend to. There were also a number of Bishops from the Eastern Churches: four Greek Orthodox, two Russian, and an Imam from Turkey. And though no Mullahs were there, either British or from any other country, surveys have suggested that over a thousand Muslims came to hear her, who took seriously the possibility that Joanna might be God's last prophet.

There were no service sheets; instead the service would follow a format which was then exceptional but is now the norm. Joanna would preach at the beginning, and then there would follow about twenty minutes of silent prayer, when we might remember God and his love for us, in the way that Joanna taught us; and finally we would sing together in worship, six songs of praise which everyone had been learning by heart for weeks and, to judge by their rehearsals the previous night, would sing lustily. By midday, so the official estimate goes, there were three million of us standing shoulder to shoulder in the six hundred acres which constitute Hyde Park and Kensington Gardens, three million voices on the cusp of singing out in joy.

Sometimes I would look up to the terrace on the ninth floor of the Dorchester Hotel, but I never saw Joanna there, and the curtains were kept firmly closed. I wondered whether Joanna was praying, or crying, or having a bath, or getting dressed, or perhaps eating toast and marmalade. I didn't know whether in retreating so into her room she was merely following the instructions of her parents or whether she couldn't bear even to glimpse the crowds which were waiting for her.

At ten to twelve the Bishop of Norwich addressed us. I noticed that he himself looked drawn, and that here was probably another of us who had slept very little. He welcomed us, and wished us happy Easter, and said that he had never seen a crowd in all his life one tenth the size of this one, and that that we should be assembled in the name of God was a wondrous thing. But he also reminded us that 'Joanna is a girl, who has her eleventh birthday next month. She is also God's missionary. She expects no adulation in her own right. I trust you will show her respect. But please don't cheer, or shout or rave. She is not a pop star. Make it easy for her to address us here today. As you know, she has been spending the night in the Dorchester across the road, and right now I'm going to fetch her and bring her to you. Praise be to God.'

And it was only then that I began to feel confident that everything would be all right. For if anyone could, this was the man who would look after Joanna. Soon she would be with him, out in the warm, wet air of this spring morning. Here was a man of God, who was large and strong both in body and spirit, and I suddenly knew deep in my bones that Joanna was right, all would be well.

Then the Bishop stepped down from the platform and walked through the crowd making a pathway with his mace as he did so, and demanding that it should be kept four feet across. We only knew he had reached the hotel when those closest to it let out a cheer; I imagined Joanna appearing in the doorway and greeting him, the secret smiles exchanged between them. Then everything was quiet again and we knew that Joanna was on her way. We all craned our necks to catch sight of her, but to no avail, as she was so small – though the top of the Bishop's mace kept us informed of her progress.

At last we watched the Bishop climbing back on to the platform, with Joanna close by him on the inside, as if he were protecting her from us till the very last moment. Then I saw her face just for a second and I thanked God, because she was immaculate, because there were no signs of weeping but only of strength. Her fair hair was tied back severely, as was her habit, and today it revealed a face of such purity, of such beauty, of such serenity, that any qualms I might have had that Joanna might lose her nerve immediately shrunk away. No one was even tempted to cheer her: our sense of awe was too great. We could only wonder.

The Bishop also seemed relieved to see Joanna so well in herself, and we saw them talking to each other, and smiling. I could see the Bishop wondering if he should give a further introduction, but he thought the better of it, and simply helped Joanna on to a small podium which had been positioned in front of the microphone. He seemed uncertain as to whether he should stay on the platform during her sermon: in Norwich he had always stood by her while she spoke, but now it seemed inappropriate, so he stepped down and found a place between the bishops of Coventry and York.

There were three million people there: yet we could feel the spring breeze across our faces and smell the blossom. Joanna was quiet, and still, and didn't speak perhaps for a full minute. Then she began:

*I have been sent by God. I am his messenger. I am the bearer of his love for you. I am also the bearer of truth.*

*I see before me millions of souls who have yearned to make their peace with God. Yet over the years you have fallen away, you resist him in the name of pride. But the gifts he has given you, you have taken: the gift of speech, of using words which are invisible, in which you have invested a certain faith, perhaps too much; the gift of numbers, of imagining numbers higher than you would ever count to; the gift of music, in which you set the different notes together, to make harmony; the gift of vision, with which you create something which has never before existed; but above all God has given you the gift of love. And he gave you these gifts so that you might come to know him.*

*You are God's creation. But it is you, not God, who have the power to make His creation perfect, to make it whole and reveal its holiness.*

*Is the artist forever correcting his work?*

*He fills it with his spirit, but then he stands back.*

*He listens, he watches, he judges.*

*God is patient.*

*But you shake your fists and cry out, 'God, how can you let this evil happen?'*

*Do you imagine that God has wished this evil upon you? Do you imagine that he does not grieve for you? Even God is subject to the laws of his own making. But God preceded his laws. He is above and beyond them. And God is love.*

*God is the light shining on the water. One day you will find his Kingdom, and you will understand.*

Suddenly Joanna stopped, and she began to look about her. All her composure left her, and tears began streaming down her face. Then she said, as though she could barely comprehend it herself, 'The sky is full of angels.'

We all looked up, and we saw blossom being carried on the wind, and I think we all thought, 'She's referring to the blossom.' It never occurred to us for a moment that she would die. When the man's voice shouted out 'Blasphemer,' when we heard the shot, when we saw Joanna fall, we barely reacted, and for my own part I can say it felt as though I had been shot, too, I was winded of any emotion at all. For a full few seconds a terrible silence hung upon us, broken only by the wailing of the very perpetrator of this act, who pushed himself through the crowd with eyes so wild that none dared resist him, but rather made space for him to move on. (His name was Christian Newell, and heaven forgave him).

Then I can neither remember what I thought or how I felt; my first conscious memory is of being restrained by the fisherman who had given me his tent. I told him to lay off me, to let me go to her. I told him that I loved her.

'Aye, that we all do,' said the fisherman.

'You don't understand, I know her,' I pleaded.

'Aye, that we all do,' said the fisherman.

'I'm her teacher!'

'Then do you want to be the cause of more death? Look!'

The crowd was beginning to heave up on to the platform, and the bishops, who had been sitting at the front, were begging for calm, and pleading with the people to stand back; and police appeared from nowhere, shouting instructions and redirecting the rampage. The Bishop of Coventry leapt up on to Joanna's podium and called out, 'Don't stampede! Keep back! There's nothing that can be done! Joanna is dead!'

The word 'dead' cast a spell on us. We were numb and dumb and still again; we were like wax dummies falling into a sea, resisting nothing, seeking oblivion. And the only sobbing which could be heard was not mine, but came out to us half-amplified from the platform itself. The Bishop of Norwich was bent double over her, stroking her hair and cheeks, kissing the girl's forehead. At last he took up Joanna's body and laid it on the altar, so that it seemed like a sacrifice; and several of the bishops came up to join him there. It was the Bishop of Coventry who suggested that we all pray. So we did, we prayed with all our hearts, and many of us began to weep.

And then a very curious thing happened. It wasn't immediately apparent to the congregation, and there are conflicting reports, even now, as to how it came about. At the beginning, I believe, some suspicion fell on the Imam of Turkey, as he was seen hovering near Joanna's head, and muttering incantations – levitation is something that we Westerners are apt to dismiss as trickery. But Joanna's body began to rise up, slowly at first, and the bishops were embarrassed, and hid her from our view, in case she should suddenly fall. We only became aware of what was happening when Joanna's body was about a foot above the altar, and she went on rising higher, two feet, three; and she did not lie on the air stiffly, as one associates with Eastern levitation, but as though she were being carried.

The bishops could say nothing, but stood back to marvel with the rest of us; and we all watched the gentle girl, with her hair hanging behind her, and her blue dress caught on the breeze. 'My God, my God,' cried out the Bishop of Norwich, and he sank to his knees; but in my soul I cried out, 'Joanna.' We all let the tears flow down our cheeks, every one of us, tears which had laid dormant for so many years. Whether the source was grief or joy we didn't know: we were like children who had lost their mothers; but then again, like children who had found them. All our eyes were fixed upon Joanna: higher and higher she rose, until she was no bigger than a bird, until she was one with the sky.

But there was a further miracle, which, if anything, was even greater than the one we had witnessed. It had been happening to us all the while, but only now that we were alone to gaze upon our own hearts did we understand the full extent of our redemption. What strikes me now is that the experience wasn't so much spiritual as physical – it was as though layer upon layer of sediment had been keeping my soul encased, and had kept me from my God, but now they fell away, like sloughed-off skin. But if I found my God, what other things did I find? The agony within me was as bright and fresh and sharp and raw as the joy, and all I knew, while the crowd about me began to sing, was that I must find my Kitty, my wife, my son, my Joe. They sang out, three million people in unison, they sang, 'Praise my soul the King of Heaven,' and all I could think was, Kitty must be singing among them, of course she's here, today of all days. So I struggled through the crowd, and I found some bent double with weeping, and others with their arms reaching up to heaven, rejoicing in the way that Joanna had let us remember.

Suddenly I noticed my parents on one of the screens above me, because the cameramen had now turned their cameras on to the crowd. I thought, 'My mother will know where Kitty is, she'll know if she came,' but for the life of me I couldn't recognise the place where my parents were standing, nor the buildings behind them. As I was searching out landmarks to get my bearings, I looked up at the screen again, only to see them fall into such an embrace, my father kissing my mother with such passion, that I could only look away; and then all I was aware of were couples embracing, and not just couples, but friends, too, and parents lifting up their children to hug them. I moved on through the crowds, and I called out her name, but by now the singing was so loud that anyone who noticed me must have thought I was just singing too.

By three o'clock the crowds began to disperse, which allowed me to move more quickly through them, and those who were left began to sit or kneel, or even sleep. A number of the very young were also beginning to complain that they were hungry and wanted to go home; and it occurred to me that Joe would be hungry too, and that even if Kitty had been there, they'd most likely have left by now.

I found a phone box and rang the number of our flat, but no one answered; so I tried to get through to her mother, but Margaret wasn't at home either. Perhaps Kitty was caught in traffic? Or perhaps she was walking – private cars were banned that day within a two-mile radius of Hyde Park – in which case I would walk too. Suddenly it seemed to me quite obvious that that was exactly where she was, on her journey back to Balham, and if I walked quickly I might even catch up with her. Yes, soon we'd be in each others arms like all those other couples, because we were meant to be, Kitty and I, because she was my very soul. The streets seemed to guide me to her; I could have been blind-folded and known the corners to turn, and by the time I'd arrived and rung the bell it seemed as though a mere second was separating us.

She wasn't there. But I was so certain that she was I decided the bell must be broken, or that the singing in Hyde Park had rendered her temporarily deaf, or perhaps she had fainted, or been carried away in prayer, or perhaps she was fast, fast asleep. So with no hesitation I climbed up on to the window-sill of the ground floor flat and pulled myself up on to the roof of the porch, so I could knock on her window, and it even made me smile to think of her seeing me there, and saying, 'You silly old fool, come in,' and she'd kiss me and say, 'Joe, say hello to your father, he's come back to live with us.'

But when I looked through the window, no, there was no Kitty, and this was no home that I knew. I never lived in this place. The curtains were different, the carpet was a different colour, the furniture modern and ugly. I thought I must have got the wrong house; but then I saw a bill on the floor with Kitty's name on it, and my God my God there was another name beside it, a man's name that I couldn't make out, and then I saw his shoes half-hidden by the sofa, and a leather jacket behind the door, and a packet of cigarettes on the table – Kitty never smoked, Kitty hated smoking – and underneath the cigarettes was a child's book. Kitty, does this man read to our Joe? Does Joe sit on his knee and look at picture books with him? Is this why you never came to see me at Christmas? Is this what you were keeping from me?

It took me six hours to drive back to Norfolk, almost half of that time to get out of London. But I was thinking to myself, 'Let this take a lifetime, why hurry? Where am I going anyway?

Now I know that life is a mere waiting for death, and I know how to wait, I can do it. I don't even have to listen to the radio to distract me, because the truth is nowhere but in my soul, and I can live with that. This life is the punishment which I deserve for my blindness, and, God willing, I shall learn to live it the best I can.'

But if my attitude on that journey amounted to a kind of strength, some kind of understanding of the task I had ahead of me, by the time I reached Beeston I had no more backbone in me than a jellyfish. I could bring myself neither to open the door of that cold cottage, nor visit Roger in my present despair, when I imagined that his own family were in quite a different mood, so in the end I went up to the church as it seemed the only place that might contain me. I let myself in, but when I turned on the light I turned it off almost as soon. I needed the dark as badly as I needed sleep, as badly as I needed all consciousness to be taken from me. Please God, let this be my reprieve, let me sleep here in your sanctuary. So I lay on the stone floor and I tried to pray like Joanna had taught me. I tried to imagine the structure of things, and God himself, Love beyond Time, and I cried out to him and said, 'Dear God, give me strength.'

I prayed, and suddenly the draughts in the church subsided, and immediately above my face I was aware of a certain warmth, and I whispered, 'God, is that you?'

Kitty said, 'Sweetheart, it's me.'

# Epilogue

IT'S SUMMER AS I WRITE THIS. We live in Norfolk, a couple of miles from Sheringham, and when the day is clear we can see the sea from our bedroom window. Joe is eight now, so strange to think of him almost as old as Joanna was then. I'm watching him right now, in fact, from the window of my study, and he's teaching his younger brother Ben to ride a two-wheeler bike. 'Just watch what I do,' he's saying, biking as fast as he can to the end of the garden and back. We have a baby too, Mary, who's out shopping with her mother, and they might go down to the beach if the weather holds out. I told Kitty that I hoped to finish writing at four, and if she wasn't home by then we'd come and find her with a flask of apple juice and doughnuts.

In September Ben will join his brother at Gresham Primary School, where I'm the headmaster, and have been ever since Mr Birch decided to become a missionary in India five years ago (where I believe he's settled in rather well, and even had a book published last year on 'Great Indian Railway Journeys'). Jocelyn is now a curate, though she still lives locally and comes to see us. Marion teaches at a primary school in Cornwall, and the last I heard from her was about three years ago when she sent me a postcard telling me she was pregnant. 'Twins again!' she wrote, 'This time, girls!' But there's no reference at all to the things we went through together. The picture on the front is of Truro Cathedral, but is this because it has come to mean something to her, or because she imagines it might mean something to me?

I've also been studying her use of exclamation marks: there are five in seven lines. So unlike her, I think to myself. Marion never exclaimed about anything, except in indignation. And these particular exclamation marks are too upright, too jolly, too bold. Is she saying, 'This is a wonderful thing!' or is the tone rather more hysterical, 'I can deal with it! I can deal with it!' Whichever, she won't let me ask her. She's left me no address.

Shortly after Joanna left this world her parents came to see me. They were grieving for her in a way that I would have thought them incapable of, and Mrs Wells, in particular, took my hands and kissed them. But they were only human, after all, and over the years few can have been faced with such temptation as they. Their village, not unnaturally, has become a shrine to Joanna; and people travel far and wide to meet them and ask them questions about her childhood: whether they thought she was Jesus, whether she could perform miracles, what she was like to live with. And of course, everyone insists that the house she was brought up in remains exactly as it was when Joanna lived there; and when they see its poverty, they exclaim, and lavish large cheques on Joanna's family . . . oh yes, the Wells are a very rich family indeed.

But something about them reminds me of Sisyphus pushing his rock to the top of the hill. Scores of volunteers have offered to look after the shrine and donate any gifts that are made to charity, but the Wells will have none of it. For how is it possible to turn a blind eye to an income in excess of a thousand pounds a day? They can't leave the house for fear that crooks would cream off their profits, or that a house emptied of Joanna's real-life parents would inspire less generosity than it does. So they live in all their old grime, and their bank accounts are brimming, and when, for a mere fortnight, they took a fancy holiday in the Caribbean a few years back, the reaction of the media was such that they never dared venture abroad again.

But what of England? What has happened to England since Joanna's death? Forgive me for only being able to write about the remarkable changes that have been happening in my own country; if your interest takes you further afield, I suggest you search on the internet.

I think what has astonished everyone who writes and thinks about such matters is the speed at which our culture changed tack. It used to be the decade that carried with it a certain identity: the '40s, '50s, '60s, all of which evoke a different mood. But by the autumn of 2001 there were few institutions in which Joanna's influence could not be profoundly felt. Twenty-eight per cent of all schools incorporated a half-hour period after lunch when the desks were moved to the side and rest mats were laid out on the floor. The lights were turned out, however gloomy the weather, and the children were told to lie still and close their eyes and envisage God's love for them in the way that Joanna had instructed. Sometimes, too, a child or a teacher would play a succession of single notes on a musical instrument; and each note was allowed was allowed to vibrate until its natural close, and in this way the children were taught how to listen.

More surprising even than this was the effect on the adult workplace. Initially, about ten per cent of all companies provided a quiet room for their employees to retreat to at various times of day; but when researchers confirmed that the wellbeing of the workforce improved so dramatically that production actually increased, in our present day a contemplation room is considered as necessary as a cafeteria.

But alongside the new appreciation of silence came an understanding of the importance of music. Notice boards in newsagents – if ever these have served to illustrate the spiritual condition of a people – began to proliferate with requests for singing teachers, musical instruments, song-sheets. Songwriters no longer wrote their songs for pop stars but for the people, and pop stars suddenly found that the songs which sold were no longer those with the snazziest, sexiest video footage, or the cleverest special effects, but simply the ones with the best tunes, which could be sung by any old Tom, Dick or Harry. In fact, that very same Tom, Dick or Harry found that songwriting itself wasn't as difficult as they had once supposed, and they began humming little ditties and musical phrases that seemed to come from nowhere.

Dusty, rusty instruments were brought down from the attic and everyone who could began to play again. That was seven years ago: only three years later a survey found that two-thirds of Europeans were learning an instrument, and one-third of young people aged eighteen to thirty carried a harmonica with them in their pockets.

Another interesting musical development has been the increase in the popularity of the harp, particularly among older players and academics. The fact that traditional church icono-graphy portrays angels plucking their harps is a slight embar-rassment to them; their inspiration, they maintain, are modern-day radio astronomers who, in 2002, succeeded in tuning in to the sound of the big bang, and distinguished three separate musical notes. Latter-day string theorists, or those physicists proposing the now generally accepted model of the universe as being composed of an infinite number of resonating strings of particles, have redescribed the universe as 'one huge symphony', and the human being's ability to tune into it as 'miraculous'. As I write, physicists are taking their theories even further, managing to locate melodies in the far-flung corners of our galaxy.

And then there was the day in the autumn of 2004, I remember, when the tabloid newspapers were enchanted. Four hundred insurance brokers of Lloyds of London stopped work one Monday morning to sing in their great hall and from the balconies rising three floors above it. They sang songs from

Bach to the Beatles, culminating in a moving rendition of Bob Dylan's 'Blowin' in the wind', and it serves as some kind of yardstick of our spiritual progress to mention that the vast majority of them sang with their hearts.

In 2005 the national newspapers began to enclose song-sheets of their favourite 'Songs of the Day', so families could sing together over breakfast or any other time of day. Besides the well-known hymns, there were folk songs, songs by Bob Dylan and Andrew Lloyd Webber, arias from operas ('advanced', confessed the newspapers), Bach cantatas. Buses and train carriages of commuters would break into song, as did queues in banks and post offices, and those who found themselves sharing a lift in offices, shops or blocks of flats.

But it would be wrong to paint a picture that was completely rosy. It was the churches that struggled the most. For years the Christian churches had sought unity with each other. One might have imagined that Joanna's coming would have forced them to eschew their differences and unite behind her. But no one could agree on her significance. Who was she? Had she really been sent by God? Then what light does her coming throw on the beliefs of the last two thousand years? Would she have supported the creed? I knew the truth, of course, as did the Bishop of Norwich, and perhaps others did instinctively, as had my Geordie fishermen by the Serpentine, but as each year went by it became harder and harder to reveal it. As a consequence, the number of denominations has more than doubled, as they wrestled to work through Joanna's theology. Whether the revelation of Joanna's true identity will make a difference, I doubt. Human beings have their own opinions about things, God be praised.

Oddly enough, British Muslims found Joanna easier to accept than many Christians. Joanna's philosophy, they argued, had much in common with Islamic philosophy. Our understanding of the nature of God, they suggested, progressed over the centuries. Jesus had been a prophet: he appears in ninety-three verses of the Koran. Mohamed was the prophet who succeeded Jesus, and Joanna was the prophet who succeeded Mohamed. For Joanna never claimed to be the daughter of God; nor did she discuss the Trinity, which is another anxiety for Muslims (though Christian theologians see a marked resemblance of the Johannine description of Man as Mind, Body and Soul, with the Trinity of Father, Son and Holy Ghost). And the final stumbling block for Muslims, namely that the Christian Bible is a hotchpotch of different writers with different interests, themselves translated and re-translated so that much of the original meaning has been lost, has been blown away. Modern technology has seen to it that Joanna's exact words are known now and forever more.

If theologians have been forced into going back to the drawing-board, so have philosophers. After fifty years of being in thrall to the legacy of logical positivism, and the blind alleys which pure reason has taken us down (not to mention the horrors of the twentieth century), the soul has finally been reinstated. This does not mean we have discarded reason and the lessons of the Enlightenment – we love reason, and we must feed our brains well – but rather these last few years have seen a plethora of important academic papers on the human soul: *How the soul apprehends truth; Communication and the soul;* and *How do we know when the soul errs?* For we all know that the soul is no more infallible than the brain, and we try to teach our schoolchildren the difference between superstition and truth.

I'm writing these last few words well after midnight. Kitty's complained that I haven't even come down to supper, but she knows what I'm doing up here, she knows it's important. I've been using as a desk light Joanna's lamp, by which I mean the one she inspired. We have one hanging in the hall, too, which is the more traditional place for it, but Kitty had this one made specially for me as a Christmas present last year. It's made of seven different panes of glass, each of a different colour, and refers to a passage in her thirteenth sermon (13.68). For, depending on the pane you look through, the light has a different colour. So the light is both the same, and different. Let us rejoice in our difference, said Joanna, for colour is beautiful, colour has its own truth.

I have written this book in all honesty, as a testament to Joanna, but also as a testament to myself. When I look back at its beginning, to my life as it was then, and to those dilemmas which puzzled me to the point of self-destruction, I understand what it was I found so difficult. There was a habit we all had in those days of setting ourselves apart, of saying to each other, 'I'm all right, Jack,' when we might have said, from time to time, 'I'm not, really.' We stuffed ourselves so full with the false God of self-esteem – with the sin of 'pride', as it used to be called – that we forgot we're all in this together, that life is hard, and that love is the only thing that can redeem us.

## Merete Morken Andersen OCEANS OF TIME
£8.99    ISBN 1 904559 11 5

A divorced couple confront a family tragedy in the white night of a Norwegian summer. International book of the year (*TLS*), longlisted for The Independent Foreign Fiction Prize 2005 and nominated for the IMPAC Award 2006.

## Michael Arditti GOOD CLEAN FUN
£8.99    ISBN 1 904559 08 5

A dazzling collection of stories provides a witty yet compassionate and uncompromising look at love and loss, desire and defiance, in the 21st century.

## Michael Arditti UNITY
£8.99    ISBN 1 904559 12 3

A film on the relationship between Unity Mitford and Hitler gets under way during the 1970s Red Army Faction terror campaign in Germany in this complex, groundbreaking novel. Shortlisted for the Wingate Prize 2006.

## Booktrust London Short Story Competition
## UNDERWORDS: THE HIDDEN CITY
£9.99    ISBN 1 904559 14 X

Prize-winning new writing on the theme of Hidden London, along with stories from Diran Adebayo, Nicola Barker, Romesh Gunesekera, Sarah Hall, Hanif Kureishi, Andrea Levy, Patrick Neate and Alex Wheatle.

## Hélène du Coudray  ANOTHER COUNTRY
£7.99    ISBN 1 904559 04 2

A prize-winning novel, first published in 1928, about a passionate affair between a British ship's officer and a Russian emigrée governess which promises to end in disaster.

## Lewis DeSoto  A BLADE OF GRASS
£8.99    ISBN 1 904559 07 7

A lyrical and profound novel set in South Africa during the era of apartheid, in which the recently widowed Märit struggles to run her farm with the help of her black maid, Tembi. Longlisted for the Man Booker Prize 2004 and shortlisted for the Ondaatje Prize 2005.

# Also available from
## www.MAIAPRESS.com

### Olivia Fane  THE GLORIOUS FLIGHT OF PERDITA TREE
£8.99    ISBN 1 904559 13 1

Beautiful Perdita Tree is kidnapped in Albania. Freedom is coming to the country where flared trousers landed you in prison, but are the Albanians ready for it or, indeed, Perdita? 'Thoughtful, sorrowful, highly amusing' (*Times*)

### Maggie Hamand, ed.  UNCUT DIAMONDS
£7.99    ISBN 1 904559 03 4

Unusual and challenging, these vibrant, original stories showcase the huge diversity of new writing talent coming out of contemporary London.

### Helen Humphreys  WILD DOGS
£8.99    ISBN 1 904559 15 8

A pack of lost dogs runs wild, and each evening their bereft former owners gather to call them home – a remarkable book about the power of human strength, trust and love.

### Linda Leatherbarrow  ESSENTIAL KIT
£8.99    ISBN 1 904559 10 7

The first collection from a short-story prizewinner – lyrical, uplifting, funny and moving, always pertinent – 'joyously surreal . . . gnomically funny, and touching' (Shena Mackay).

### Sara Maitland  ON BECOMING A FAIRY GODMOTHER
£7.99    ISBN 1 904559 00 X

Fifteen new 'fairy stories' by an acclaimed master of the genre breathe new life into old legends and bring the magic of myth back into modern women's lives.

### Dreda Say Mitchell  RUNNING HOT
£8.99    ISBN 1 904559 09 3

A pacy comic thriller about Schoolboy and his attempts to go straight in a world of crime. An exciting debut, winner of the CWA John Creasey Award 2005.

### Anne Redmon  IN DENIAL
£7.99    ISBN 1 904559 01 8

A chilling novel about the relationship between a prison visitor and a serial offender, which explores challenging themes with subtlety and intelligence.

# Also available from
## www.MAIAPRESS.com

### Henrietta Seredy  LEAVING IMPRINTS
£7.99  ISBN 1 904559 02 6

Beautifully written and startlingly original, this unusual and memorable novel explores a destructive, passionate relationship between two damaged people.

### Diane Schoemperlen  FORMS OF DEVOTION
£9.99  ISBN 1 904559 19 0  Illustrated

Eleven stories with a brilliant interplay between words and images – a creative delight, perfectly formed and rich in wit and irony.

### Emma Tennant  THE HARP LESSON
£8.99  ISBN 1 904559 16 6

With the French Revolution looming, little Pamela Sims is taken from England to live at the French court as the illegitimate daughter of Mme de Genlis. But who is she really? 'Riveting and very readable' (Antonia Fraser)

### Emma Tennant  PEMBERLEY REVISITED
£8.99  ISBN 1 904559 17 4

Elizabeth wins Darcy, and Jane wins Bingley – but do they 'live happily ever after'? Reissue of two bestselling sequels to Jane Austen's *Pride and Prejudice*.

### Norman Thomas  THE THOUSAND-PETALLED DAISY
£7.99  ISBN 1 904559 05 0

Love, jealousy and violence in this coming-of-age tale set in India, written with a distinctive, off-beat humour and a delicate but intensely felt spirituality.

### Karel Van Loon  THE INVISIBLE ONES
£8.99  ISBN 1 904559 18 2

A gripping novel about a refugee in Thailand, in which harrowing accounts of Burmese political prisoners blend with Buddhist myth and memories of a carefree childhood.

### Adam Zameenzad  PEPSI AND MARIA
£8.99  ISBN 1 904559 06 9

A highly original novel about two street children in South America whose zest for life carries them through the brutal realities of their daily existence.